THE
HOUSE
SHARE

BOOKS BY CARLA KOVACH

THE
HOUSE
SHARE

Carla Kovach

bookouture

Published by Bookouture in 2022

An imprint of Storyfire Ltd.
Carmelite House
50 Victoria Embankment
London EC4Y 0DZ

www.bookouture.com

ISBN: 978-1-80314-549-5
eBook ISBN: 978-1-80314-548-8

I dedicate this book to those who are feeling a little lost and lonely after leaving their past behind to start anew. I hope there are sunny skies ahead on the horizon.

PROLOGUE

Twenty Years Ago

Again, I sit in a toilet cubicle crying my eyes out. PE always does this to me. I'm not good at it and the names they call me stick. No, I can't run well and I can't get a ball into a hoop but is that a reason to make my life a misery? Then there's other things like me always being mistaken for less than my fourteen years. I know I'm sinewy and bony and whatever else they like to tease me with. Wiping the last of my tears away with the coarse school toilet roll, I feel my burning face, knowing that it's red and blotchy.

It's no good sitting here all day with the smell of urine turning my stomach. However much I want to, I can't hide in here forever. There are other lessons today and I could do without another detention for being late even though it's not my fault. I have to avoid being in the communal area when they're busy. Pushing the main door open, kids come and go, slamming lockers and gripping books and folders under their arms. The hum of lesson changeover rattles away and the smell of cheese crisps catches in my throat as I inhale.

I scurry along, head bowed and shoulders hunched over as I stare at the floor. The best thing I can do is make myself as small and invisible as possible. Glancing from side to side, I can see that it's safe to open my locker. My fingers shake as I twist the numbers on the combination lock. I yank it but it won't open so I pull and pull. I check the numbers, then I realise that I've turned the second number to nine instead of six. My locker squeaks as I eventually get it open. That's when I see the note that has been pushed through the slats. It contains one word and it's the most hurtful word ever. They have called me *that* name since I began high school and they never let up.

Louise nudges me into a locker. 'Move.' Then she finishes with the name, saying it at the top of her voice so that everyone can hear. I can't even think it in my head. Some things hurt too much. It all started at the well, that's when I first got called that name and it's never ended. I'll never forgive the girl who came up with it.

With one final nudge that knocks my chin into my locker, Louise leaves me and sashays towards Glen, the boy she's been seeing for a couple of weeks. She flicks her long honey waves while applying a coat of pink gluey lip gloss.

She hurt me. We were once close and I don't know what I ever did wrong to change things so suddenly. I used to follow her and her friends to the well in the field, hoping that she'd let me join in. They'd walk through Beoley Woods at night, leaving our Redditch estate behind so that they could make out and smoke. All I wanted was to be a part of that, to be friends with them. That was when they started to do bad things to me and Louise laughed like I was dog crap on her shoe. And it all still goes on now. I can't wait for the summer holidays to start because I need out of this hell. I stay back, hoping that she and Glen are going to turn that corner and leave me alone. *Keep still, keep silent and keep your head down*, that's what I keep telling myself.

It didn't work yesterday. Louise spent half of maths throwing bits of paper at me. The others laughed and joined in. My eyes had filled but I'd held in those tears. There's no way I'd let them see how much hurt they were causing me. That wasn't the worst of it. Not once had I felt them attaching chewing gum into my hair.

'Baldy patch has a red face.' Louise howls with laughter as does Glen and the others. So much for remaining silent, still and keeping my head down. A sea of faces close in on me, blocking the light from the end of the corridor with their open upturned mouths and stares. I place my shaking hand over the patch of removed hair from where I cut the chewing gum out. After washing it with everything I could find, it beat me. All I had left to fix things was my dad's decorating scissors.

I need to get away from them but they've formed a barrier. 'Let me through.' My voice barely carries.

'I don't think so.' Louise kicks me in the shin sending me back into the wall. Behind her, I catch the whispers that seem to be coming from everywhere. 'Who's been crying? We haven't upset you, have we?' Her grin is all I can see.

I shake my head and break eye contact. My heart is gathering momentum, so much so that I see prickles in my vision and I'm gasping for breath. If I can't get away, I'll faint and I can't let them see me like that. With all I have, I crash past her, slamming into the row behind and then the row behind that. A boy I don't know grabs the collar of my blazer and pulls me back, throwing me to the floor. The howls and shrieks spill out, like magma being forced from an erupting volcano. About twenty pairs of eyes stare in my direction. Fingers point and laughter rings through my ears then they all chant that name again. Curling up in a ball, I place my hands over my ears and close my eyes, willing it all to be over. Someone punches my cheek and a wet blob lands on my hand and I recoil, grossed out by the spit. Slowly, I release my fingers from my ears and open one eye.

'Quick, Mr Smith is coming,' one of the kids calls out, and with that the corridor empties leaving me and the gangly teacher, who knows that I'm being bullied but never does a thing. He's no exception. They're all the same.

'You're going to be late for history. Best be on your way.'

I almost stumble as I stand, the kick to my shin stinging like mad.

As I hurry towards the history classroom, they're all there, waiting. My torment never ends. I ignore their sniggers and stare ahead. Control of my emotions is the only thing that will see me through. I can't let them break me.

I take a seat and gaze out of the window at the sandbags lined up against the outbuildings. Rain crashes against the windowpane, and that's when the banging of feet on my chair starts. It never ends. A tear slides down my cheek and all I can do is hope that the lesson will go fast but I know it won't.

Louise makes the sound of a crying baby and points at me and the rest of the bullies roll up paper and throw it at me. I've never felt so alone and I can't go on like this.

ONE

LIBBY

Present Time
Monday, 10 January

Libby broke into a jog as she turned into Grover Street, knowing she was running late on such a big day but that was nothing new. With each footstep, a splash of slush found its way into her boot and her cat, Einstein, meowed like he was about to be bathed. As she stepped, her foot squelched. No wonder she couldn't feel her ice-cold toes any more. The twenty-minute train delay had been the cause of her anguish. She could kick herself for never learning to drive. At thirty-one years of age, she should have her life sorted but Libby operated in a stressed-out bubble and the sheer thought of driving on a busy road filled her with fear. Everything was not going to plan and the van containing all her worldly belongings would arrive soon.

As she approached Canal House, she spotted her new land-lord pulling up the *To Let* sign from the front garden. After a couple of strenuous heaves, it popped out, leaving a hole where it once stood. He threw it to the floor before nudging it against the dwarf wall. As he leaned back, he blew an icy mist into his hands and rubbed them together. Libby stopped and undid the top button of her red winter coat, boiling hot from the many layers she was wearing. As she steadied Einstein in his basket, she coughed to get her landlord's attention. The man turned and smiled. She removed her woollen hat, ruffled her fingers through her flattened blonde hat-hair and took a step closer to him.

'Mr Simmons? Nice to meet you again.' She held her hand out.

'Oh, call me Tim, please. Everyone else around here does. It's great to finally have you move in, Miss Worthington,' he replied as he shook her hand.

There was something about the way he said her name that made her pause as she took it in. 'Libby, definitely call me Libby.'

'Lovely name.' He smiled widely exposing a set of perfectly white teeth. Unsure of how to take his compliment, she looked down and bit her bottom lip. Awkward was her middle name. Or maybe she didn't quite know where to look. She had liked him when he'd shown her around the flat two weeks earlier. With his tall, stocky build, he reminded her of a rugby player. She guessed that he was probably around her age, if not a few years older. His short back and sides brown hair complimented his hazel eyes, the ones that were still looking in her direction. He broke their eye contact first, embarrassed by her embarrassment and Libby thought the slight nervous tic was rather sweet.

Handsome as he was, Libby could not get involved with anyone right now. She'd left Gary in the night and now there was no going back. There was no way she'd screw up this new beginning, she couldn't afford to. Her paltry savings pot that she'd kept hidden from Gary had just about paid for the deposit on this tiny rental. That was her escape fund. She swallowed as she thought about him arriving home off shift and seeing what she'd left for him. She'd seen him angry on too many occasions. Gasping to catch a breath, she shook her head. He didn't know where she lived. She was safe.

'Libby, are you okay?'

She nodded and bit her bottom lip. Right now, she was fine but give it ten minutes, an hour, maybe even a couple of hours, a tirade of trouble was coming her way.

'Anyway, I should show you around the communal area and your flat. I've had it professionally cleaned, the carpets have been steamed; the windows are sparkling, so it's nice and fresh for you. Here, let me take your cat.'

Libby passed him the basket containing her chubby, ginger, feline companion. There was no way she could have left him behind. Although Einstein always seemed light when he slept on her lap, she realised he was quite a lump after carrying him for twenty minutes from the train station. Tim held the cat up to his face and he purred. 'I love cats. What do you call him or her?'

'Einstein.'

'That's so cute.' Tim let out a snigger.

She nodded. 'It's because he looks so clever and his hair sticks up. I was going to call him Ginger but I think he likes Einstein.' She laughed and continued making small talk. Tim crunched on some ice-covered grass before stepping onto the pavement and unlocking the front door.

The view of the house was exactly as she remembered. Double-fronted, traditional red-brick with a solidness about the yellow door and outdoor porch area. The individual postboxes were fixed to the right of the front door and above it the sign told her that she was about to enter Canal House. It excited her that she'd found somewhere in Birmingham City Centre. She could walk to work and she was close to the fashionable canal area. The Brindleyplace eateries were some of the best and she couldn't wait to embrace her new life. Libby looked up at her new flat window, upstairs and to the right. Blocking the view of her living room were the old-fashioned net curtains that were there when she viewed the property. They weren't exactly contemporary, but she reminded herself that the rent was cheap.

As they stepped into the hallway, their footsteps echoed on the diamond-patterned tiles. Traditional Victorian cornice ran around the edges of the ceiling and the high picture rail was in keeping, as was the oxblood paint on the walls.

'I'll show you the communal lounge area first. It's not much but you can see the backyard from it. It's nicer in the summer. May I leave Einstein here for a moment?' He pointed to the cat basket.

'Of course. He'll be fine in his basket.' A front door led to flats on either side of the grand staircase. She hoped her neighbours were friendly, she could use some new friends as most of her social circle had been more Gary's friends.

'Follow me.' He brushed the damp droplets off his coat and led the way, past the stairs, along a dark corridor. As they passed a trigger point, a light came on, leading the way. 'Here's the lounge. As you can see there's a well-stocked bookcase, a TV and a couple of sofas. In the summer, the patio doors can be opened and I put some garden furniture out.'

'Wow, I didn't realise I'd have access to the garden.'

'That would be my failing. I forgot to show you this room when you came to view the property. The flats are cosy. It's nice to have somewhere a bit more spacious to sit sometimes, which is why I did this room up last year. Right, let's get you into your flat.'

She could already picture herself sipping wine with the other residents while the sun beat down on them. 'What are the neighbours like?' she asked as she followed him. He picked the cat up and started climbing the stairs.

'Never have any trouble with them. Two women live in Flat A, Michaela and Kirsty. You'll probably meet them shortly, they're always coming and going and they're really friendly. Flat B is occupied by a man who's been here years. Hardly ever see him though as he's always away on business. He shouldn't give you any bother. You've probably got the quietest flat living above him. I live in Flat C, so I'm your closest neighbour. My mother used to manage this house and live here but since she deteriorated, I've moved in to look after the place. It wasn't a part of life's plan but we can't plan for everything.'

'Sorry to hear about your mother.' They approached the top of the stairs. Tim handed Einstein back to Libby.

'She lives somewhere where she's looked after, day and night. I see her a lot, which is good.' As he reached into his coat pocket, the bunch of keys jangled. 'The silver key is for the main door downstairs, the gold key is for your flat door and the one with the red rubber top is for the patio doors in the communal room. I'll just show you in, then you can get settled and warmed up.' Tim opened the door and led her into her new flat. She inhaled furniture polish mixed with bleach. 'Let me show you the kitchen first.'

The winter sun shone through the kitchen window, reflecting off the stainless-steel draining board. With only three wooden-fronted cupboards and a small fridge freezer, she was pleased that she'd packed in a minimalist way. The room was so tiny, she couldn't lie down on what was left of the floor space.

'It's fully functional which is all I need.' Libby stepped out of the tiny space and back into the living room.

'I've left the table and two chairs against the back wall and I know the living room furniture isn't up to much but if you get your own, I'm happy to remove it. It'll give you something to use for now or you can keep it here. Up to you entirely.'

'I'm grateful that it is furnished.' The beige carpet looked almost sad. Libby knew she'd need a rug to cheer it up a bit. As she'd come away from her relationship with nothing to her name, she'd have to endure the lumpy blue two-seater sofa, the mismatched chair and the magnolia walls. This flat was a far cry from Gary's flat with its en suite bedroom, all the mod cons and an intercom system.

'On to the bathroom. Luckily, you have a bath as well as the shower above it. Again, it has everything you'll need.' The walls were completely tiled in white, which Libby was thankful for. 'You have a large airing cupboard, though. It's big enough to have a party in.' He laughed to himself. 'Oh, in the communal lounge, there's a tiny room at the one end with a washer-dryer in it. I forgot to show it to you but you can head down and have a look when you've settled in. You're welcome to use it whenever you like.' Libby remembered him mentioning that when she viewed the place. 'Lastly, the bedroom. It was a struggle but I got a double bed in there for you but I had to get rid of one of the wardrobes. The mattress is new, so new it still has the polythene on it.'

'Thank you for everything.'

Tim had gone above and beyond. When she said that she had no furniture, he'd insisted that he get her some. It might all be a bit worn and chipped but it meant everything. He'd helped her in so many ways already.

'You're more than welcome. I like everyone here to be happy so if you have any problems at all, just knock, okay?'

Libby nodded and smiled. Einstein began scratching and meowing from the dark hallway. Libby left the bedroom and crouched down. 'You can't come out yet, mister.' She lifted his basket and took him into their new living room where it was lighter. The cat scratched and turned. Ignoring his whining, Libby went back into the bedroom and gazed out of the window at the backyard. The grey slabbed space was dusted with untouched snow. She peered at the flat roof extension that ran across nearly all the communal space, stopping at her bedroom, then she opened the sash window and looked down. Einstein could easily come and go. He liked being inside but he wasn't a house cat. He'd go insane if she kept him in all the time. It wasn't like when they were at Gary's with their downstairs apartment and cat flap leading out to the garden. She shook away the dark thoughts that were creeping in. Gary's shouting had sent poor Einstein darting out of that cat flap, scared.

'Is it still okay to leave this open so that my cat can come and go when I'm in?'

'Of course it is. It's your home and it's his home too. I want you both to love it here. I did check with the others, no one is allergic to cats so he's free to roam around the house too. Is everything alright with the place?'

'Yes, it's great. I know we'll settle in fine.' She looked up at Tim and he looked down. Their conversation was running dry. 'Are you from round here?'

'Yes, lived round this way most of my life,' he replied with a slight smile. 'Where are you from?'

'Redditch, originally,' Libby replied.

'Ah, Redditch! Been there shopping once or twice. Is that where you lived before here?'

'No, I've just moved from Five Ways. I've lived and worked in Birmingham for four years now.'

'Yes, I remember, didn't you state on your application that you work on the main street coming up from New Street Station?' He stroked the stubble on his chin.

'Yes, Top Staff Recruitment. I fix people up with jobs. Now I live here I can walk to work instead of taking the bus.' Libby felt her phone vibrate. It had to be Gary. A sick feeling whirled in her stomach. Knowing that Gary wasn't going to sit back and do nothing didn't make her feel any better.

Tim was oblivious to her anxiety. 'I walk down there most days, we've probably met a few times already without knowing it.' He could tell her mind was elsewhere. 'Anyway, I'll leave you to settle in, work to do and all that.' He walked towards the door. 'Bin day is Wednesday. Your bin is next to the front door but sometimes the bin people leave them down the side of the house after emptying them. I know you ladies don't like to drag your bins all the way round so you can leave it there.' Libby smiled at his thoughtfulness. 'Oh, and your heating switch and thermostat are both in the bathroom cupboard. I put it on for an hour this morning to warm the place up a bit. You may want to switch it on again, we're heading for a bit of a freeze this week. Right, I'll catch you later.'

As soon as he left, she pulled her phone from her pocket and wiped the tear from her cheek as she read the message. It was one word but it stung like a nettle. The harassment had started.

TWO

LIBBY

She stared at the message.

Bitch!

Einstein's whining filled the room and if she didn't let him out soon, he'd scratch his way out. 'Okay, I'm going to let you out.' She bent down and undid the buckle on the basket. The cat squeezed out before Libby had fully opened the door, then he rubbed the side of his body against her leg. As he purred, he started rubbing his head against her other leg so she picked him up and hugged him closely. He'd never let Gary pick him up like this, he knew that Gary was bad for her.

She hoped the van would hurry with her belongings and, more importantly, Einstein's litter tray and food. 'Sorry, Einstein.' She grappled with the hungry cat and placed him head first back into the basket. 'I can't have you escaping while we're emptying the van.' The cat pushed backwards to avoid being locked back in. Libby nudged him in and slammed the door shut before he could escape. Once again, the cat whined.

She walked through to the bedroom and leaned on the edge

of the plastic-covered mattress before falling onto the bed and lying back. Thoughts of her new future swirled around in her head. She looked at the message again and sniffed. The sleeve of her coat had ridden up. She stared at the cut on her arm. Her face flushed as she pulled the sleeve back down and pondered how things might pan out. Would Gary find out where she lived and drag her back to his place? She'd never had to cope alone before and he knew it. She'd either depended on her big sister, Olly, or Gary. It was time to finally grow up and look after herself. With a pounding heart, the warmth spread across her neck and chest as anxiety prickled. The plastic mattress covering crackled in her ear. She turned her head to escape the noise. Bang, bang – the pounding continued. She jerked up and gasped for air. *Breathe*, she thought, as she tuned into her cat's whines.

Someone rang the doorbell. She went to reach next to the door for the intercom button before remembering that her new flat wasn't equipped with one. She ran down to the main door. The 'man with the van' she'd hired was standing next to his mate, carrying a couple of boxes.

'Shall we bring 'em straight up?' The thin man, wearing the all-in-one overall, had a dense Birmingham accent. He stepped over the threshold.

'Yes, please, follow me. It's just upstairs.' Libby led the way.

'They all seem to be upstairs lately. Be glad to retire,' said his mate who was much older. 'Doing my bleeding back in.'

'Can I help?' Libby held her hands out to take the box off him.

'No you can't. You're the customer,' replied the man in the overall. 'He's always moaning. Come on, Dad, just get on with it.'

'No rest for the wicked.' The older man shook his head as he passed her.

Fifteen minutes later they'd stacked Libby's boxes in the

living room. As she said goodbye she tipped the men. Soon they were gone. She spotted the box marked Einstein. Considering she'd been up most of the night packing, she was pleased with how organised her belongings looked. Yawning, she opened the box and pulled out the cat litter, tray and cat food. She unbuckled Einstein's basket and he wandered around the flat exploring his new environment.

'We're going to be very happy here, Puss,' she said as she lifted him up and cuddled him. As she opened the sachet of cat food and poured it out, Einstein jumped out of her arms and whined as he wrapped himself around her legs. She rubbed her eyes. All she wanted to do was sit down and rest. She left Einstein to eat as she lay on the sofa.

She closed her eyes and listened to the sounds of the area. Cars passed by, a child shouted, then a knock at the door made her flinch. She opened her eyes and stood. As she opened the door, her phone beeped in the living room.

'I'm popping out to the shops. Can I get you anything? Do you need milk or bread?' Tim started wrapping his striped scarf around his neck.

'No, I'm fine thanks, got to pop out myself in a bit. Thanks for offering though.'

Tim nodded, and then continued down the stairs. He looked back at her and smiled as he reached the midway point.

As she closed the door she thought about her sister, Olly. She'd call her later and thank her for helping her find the flat. There was no point calling yet as Olly would be having a lie-in. She always worked late. Libby walked back to the living room and started to unpack her clothes and bedding. Her phone beeped again. There were two more messages and a missed call, all from Gary. Her heart pounded as she opened her inbox.

I'm sorry. What more do you want? You don't have to be such a cow about things, it wasn't all my fault. Look in the mirror, that's who you need to blame. And you took my cat! Just get home, now. G

His cat, that's what he thought. Libby had bought Einstein, Libby loved him and Libby looked after him. Gary had never lifted a finger for the cat since they got him as a kitten. Now he wanted him.

As for his flat being her home, that was a lie. Home was meant to be a place of safety. The last thing she'd felt was safe while living there. She flinched as she pulled her top up to examine the green and yellow bruising that still painted her side.

She deleted that text and the last two calling her a bitch. How many more would he send? Which bit of 'it's over' didn't he get? She never wanted to see Gary again. Her leaving was his fault. It was only a shame that she hadn't left him earlier. Another message.

You can't ignore me forever. We have to talk. You know I love you. I shouldn't have called you a bitch. Come on babe, I'm desperate for your call. I'll make it up to you, I promise. I can't live without you. :(G

The difficult thing was she could remember all the good times, but she also knew they were all a big lie that had driven her mad; she'd even doubted her own sanity when he'd spun lie after lie. He'd taken her to places she didn't want to revisit, ever.

Once again, on Olly's advice, she deleted the text. Olly never liked him. She could see the real him he'd so cleverly hidden from Libby, but then again, her sister was far wiser than Libby had ever been. Gary was history. For the life of her, Libby couldn't work out why Gary had been so cruel. She'd blamed herself for working long hours. He hated the times she'd visited her sister. His constant calling had made Olly suspicious of her relationship but she'd always defended Gary. Never again. At home, he always had her full attention to the point that she'd even sacrificed spending time with her own friends who she'd since lost touch with. All she knew was that it was over. She wished Gary would accept her decision and move on.

As she held her phone she was tempted to call him and explain why she'd left. He hadn't expected her to leave so suddenly. She pictured him reading the note she'd left when he'd arrived home that morning after working the night shift at the hotel. In the letter, she'd laid out all the evidence of his deception, the list of his lies and then there was the heartfelt closing paragraph about how she couldn't live in fear any longer. Maybe it was the wrong way to go about it, maybe she should've spoken to him properly but she knew she couldn't. If she did, she'd still be there now soaking up his apologies and affection. Her only option had been to escape without him knowing.

Today was the start of a new chapter. She'd been scared and excited for it to happen, and now it had happened. Her phone beeped again.

I bet your bitch sister put you up to it?

Deleted. It was now gone into the cyber-bin like the others. No one but Gary made her want to leave. Now that her belongings had arrived and Tim had left her alone in the flat, she finally let the tears fall. She never expected to feel this hollow and the longing for Gary hadn't just disappeared, it was something she'd have to work on. It was hard. So hard.

She selected Olly's number in her phone and pressed dial. She'd wake her up, but Libby needed her sister. She didn't have the strength to go through this alone.

THREE

LIBBY

Friday, 4 February

A few weeks had passed since the move. Libby smiled as she took in the new striped rug, the modern Paris prints and the scatter cushions. Her flat now resembled a home and Einstein was using the window to go outside. The new lamp gave the room a cosy feel at night that brought warmth to her solitary life.

She hoped the past few weeks would have given her some distance from Gary, but they hadn't. The texts never ended. One minute he'd say how much he loved her and couldn't bear to let her go, the next, anger spilled out in every word. She blushed with embarrassment at the huge bunch of flowers that he'd sent to her workplace yesterday. The pink and white roses now sat in a vase on her windowsill. She inhaled the rose perfume and forced herself to remember how toxic their relationship had been and that he couldn't accept that she'd left him.

Logging on to Facebook for the first time in a fortnight, Libby clicked on her notifications. Her stomach fluttered as she remembered all the 'sorry' messages that Gary had bombarded her with. She couldn't check Facebook, Instagram or WhatsApp without seeing a fresh message pop-up. She shook her head as she deleted yet another message that she had no intention of replying to.

Libby, I love you. You can't discard me like this. I know I've screwed up in every way possible but I'll do anything. Please give me a chance. I'm sorry. Don't leave me like this. I can't live without you. X

Bashing the keyboard with her hand, she wondered how long this would go on. She hadn't spoken to him since leaving. Maybe she'd gone the wrong way about it all. With closure he might move on. A moment in time passed through her thoughts. Love doesn't leave just because you want it to. She'd given everything to Gary, too much. She stared at her 'in a relationship' status. Taking a deep breath, she changed it to single, something she should've done weeks ago. Had she done enough? She bit her bottom lip. Her sister's words echoed through her thoughts. *Block him.* She held her trembling finger over the unfriend tab. It wasn't enough. He'd see everything she ever shared. She pressed the tab, then she did the same on Instagram. Biting her lip, she wondered if she'd done the right thing.

She jumped as a huge slam filled the building. It was the first time she'd heard Mr Bull in the flat below. All she knew about him was his name because it was stuck to his postbox. She placed her hands flat on the worktop and pushed up to get a better view outside. He was nowhere to be seen. Disappointed, she planted her feet back on the ground. The friendly little houseshare was anything but, that's why she was having a party to get to know everyone better. Gary would have hated a party in their apartment, he was always people averse.

She flinched as Mr Bull's door slammed again, and then silence followed. He hadn't left his flat, that's why she couldn't see him outside. As she listened in silence, a chair scraped followed by another bang. Einstein jumped onto her lap as yet another bang came from beneath, followed by a chair scrape. She pressed Olly's number and she answered immediately. 'Alright, sis.'

'Yes.' Libby paused. 'I did it.'

'Okay, am I meant to guess?'

Libby exhaled. 'I finally blocked Gary so he should get the message soon.' She wasn't going to mention the flowers.

'I'm proud of you. You know it's the right thing to do and if he keeps messaging you, get the police involved. It's harassment.'

'I know, but I did just leave him without—'

'Stop.'

'Stop what?' Libby knew that Olly was right but she was also harsh, maybe too harsh.

'He cheated on you and I could see how controlling he was even though you pretended he wasn't. He wouldn't leave you in peace for more than five minutes. When you stayed with me, your phone would go all night. He's not right, seriously, and he was never around. You need to get him out of your head.'

Olly was right. She needed to forget him. She only wished her heart would allow her to. At times, he was the most loving man in the world and she still craved that part of him. The last few weeks had been lonely. 'Okay.' She stared at the roses.

'Promise me you won't answer him, meet him or call him? He's bad for you and I'm sick of seeing my little sister hurt. How's work? Is that tosser still bothering you?'

'Trevor?'

'Unless there's another tosser that you haven't told me about.'

'A little. It's all part of the job. We get people like that sometimes. It'll all be fine. I can handle him.'

'Right, I have to leave for work. I can't wait to see you and your new flat tomorrow.'

'Don't get too excited.'

'Well I am. Catch you then.' Olly ended the call with a couple of air kisses. She checked her phone, expecting a tirade of angry messages from Gary but there weren't any – yet.

The knock at the door made her jolt up. Einstein ran into the corner of the room. As she opened the door, she was surprised to see Tim holding a plate covered in cling film. His lumberjack shirt, slightly opened at the top drew her eye in. She smoothed the kinks out of her hair. 'Sorry, I'm a right mess.' She brushed the cat hairs off her black leggings.

'Don't apologise at all. I just thought I'd see how you were doing as we haven't had the chance to speak much. I hope you're settling in fine.' He pushed his black-rimmed glasses further up his nose. She'd never seen him wearing them before but she liked them. They suited him. 'I might be wrong here, but you've seemed a bit stressed lately so I've made you dinner. I'm working on my cooking skills and wanted to test them out on someone.' He held out the plate of food. They'd hardly spoken and he'd noticed how stressed she was. She'd done more overtime than ever, constantly worried about Gary and she hadn't been eating properly. Even the leggings she was wearing were sagging all over the place. Maybe he'd noticed how much weight she'd lost when they'd met in the hallway.

'Thank you. I don't know what to say.'

'You don't have to say anything, I hope you enjoy it.' He paused, Libby looked at the food. 'It's chicken wrapped in bacon with new potatoes, and a cauliflower gratin. It might not seem too adventurous but until a month ago all I could do was make an omelette.'

Libby paused, trying to find the right words. 'I haven't told you I'm vegetarian. I don't eat chicken but that gratin looks the business.'

'Damn, I'm so sorry. I didn't realise. It's okay, I'll test it on one of my mates next time I see them.'

'Look, come in. I'd love to eat the potatoes, and the gratin looks tasty. Maybe I could just leave the chicken. Would you like a coffee?'

Tim smiled and followed her in. She took the food and led him to the kitchen.

'So, how are you settling in?' Tim stood by the door as she put the kettle on.

'Okay. You're right about this flat being a quiet one. I never get disturbed at all and I've met Michaela and Kirsty, they're lovely. I haven't met Mr Bull yet. I heard him earlier.'

'Yeah, that guy seems to vanish into the night. I never see him but then again, I don't need to. He always pays his rent so we're good.'

'I suppose he's the perfect tenant.' She popped the dinner into the microwave and set the timer.

'You're all perfect tenants. I'm blessed in that way. My mum would be happy with the way I've been managing things. She was so much better at it than me but I'm getting better.'

Libby opened the coffee jar. 'How do you take your coffee?'

'Lots of milk, two sugars, please.' She'd probably made a mistake, inviting her shy landlord in. She passed the mug of coffee to Tim and the microwave pinged. Einstein darted into the kitchen and rubbed his body against her legs.

'That smells divine. It's like the air is thick with butter and cheese. Would you like the chicken? Seems a shame to waste it?' She arched her eyebrows and smiled.

'I'm fine. I've eaten. You could give it to Einstein,' Tim replied.

'He's already smelled it and assumed he's getting some.' Libby chopped the chicken and bacon, then dropped it into Einstein's bowl. The cat spat the hot food out, then seconds later he swallowed it down in big chunks.

'Come through.' Libby nudged past Tim and led him to the living room. Warmth radiated from his body. They both smiled at each other awkwardly before sitting on the small sofa as she'd left piles of her work on the chair. Libby shuffled closer to the arm leaving a gap between them, not wanting to make him uncomfortable but she was still close enough to smell his musky aftershave.

'You've made the flat homely. I like your prints. Paris is one of my favourite places. There's nothing better than an evening walk along the Seine.'

'I hope to go one day.' She bit into a potato as her cheeks flushed. She cleared her throat. 'I got them in town the other week. It really does feel like home, now. I love it here.'

'Glad to hear it.' A bus rumbled past, then all she heard was Tim breathing. She laughed and then he did, breaking the silence.

'This is a top gratin. Do you cook like this every day since you've taken it up?'

'No, just sometimes. Well, when I get time really. Do you cook?'

'No, I'm pretty useless. Packet ramen and boxed lasagne. I'm always run off my feet but who knows, maybe I'll give it a go one day. Do you have any other work or do you just manage this property?' He'd mentioned that the property had been his mother's business and she wondered what else Tim got up to. *Was she checking him out?* She coughed away the last bit of potato that she nearly choked on.

'I'm an accountant, I work from home. I also manage a few other properties in our family portfolio.'

'Wow, so you're super busy.'

'Yep. I used to work for an accountancy firm until my mother got taken ill, but I gave that up to look after her and the business. It's all down to me to keep it going. It's her retirement and our inheritance so I have to take care of it all,' he replied.

'Our? Do you have siblings?'

He smiled and placed his hand on the arm of the chair, creating a bit more distance between them. 'Yes, my sister is lovely. She works in London but she calls a lot.'

'I'm so sorry, I'm being really nosy asking you all these questions.'

'Sorry, what for? We're friends now. You've eaten my food so that's as good as signing a contract.' He let out a laugh.

Libby smiled back, glad that she was getting to know him better. She was really warming to Tim. He was kind, slightly shy and welcoming in every way. 'We so are friends. With food like this, we have to be. How is your mum?' As a friend, she should ask him questions like that now.

'She's got late-stage Parkinson's. It's been a sad journey watching this once independent woman deteriorate the way she has.'

'I'm sorry she's so poorly. It must be hard for you and your sister seeing her like that.'

'She can't always remember us. It's upsetting, not being remembered. Anyway, less of me and my problems. I can't dwell on it as there's nothing I can do. How's the world of recruitment lately?' He leaned back on the sofa, his legs stretched out. Libby jumped over them, taking the plate out to wash.

'Manic. In fact, I have a load to do tonight as you can see.' She went back in with the clean plate and passed it to him. 'In fact, I really have to get on with it.'

'I know how you feel. I've got tons on the go so I should get back.' He stood and walked towards the door.

'Well, thank you so much for the food. It was really kind of you.'

'And thanks for the coffee. Can I just ask you something?'

'Of course.' She was right, he liked her. It was obvious.

'Would you like to go out for dinner sometime, maybe in the week?'

She thought of Gary and the relationship she'd just got out of. It was okay to admire this good-looking guy from afar but a relationship or even a date was a long way off. There was no point in confusing her feelings at the moment. It wouldn't be fair to Tim. Besides, he was her landlord. If she messed things up with him, she'd have to move and she didn't want that. 'I can't, I'm sorry. I'm really busy with work. Thanks for asking.'

'That's okay. I totally understand. I accept your invite by the way, for your party tomorrow. See you then.'

'Cool, see you tomorrow.' She did the right thing. Jumping into anything right now wasn't on her agenda.

Grabbing her tablet, Libby scrolled through Facebook knowing that she had unfinished business. She clicked into her privacy settings and began looking for the button that allowed only friends to see her profile. She knew she'd left herself open for too long and she didn't want any of Gary's friends spying on her. As she scrolled and searched, her phone lit up. She placed the tablet beside her and her stomach dropped as she saw the message pop up.

I need to see you now. You have to see me. How can you do this to me L?

Her phone vibrated and buzzed. Tears welled in her eyes. He couldn't accept they were over and it was eating up her insides. Churning and gnawing from her throat to her stomach.

Was she being unfair? Tears meandered down her cheeks. Was she upset because of Gary's texts or because of the feelings she still harboured for him?

I know you've got someone else. I bet you're with him now.

Had he found her? Was he outside right now and had he seen Tim through her lit-up window? Gary didn't even have her address but she wouldn't be surprised if he'd followed her home from work one day. It wouldn't be the first time he'd embarrassingly turned up at a café or restaurant while she was entertaining a client. She ran over to the window and stared up and down the path at the many people walking around. A group of women passed all dressed up for a night out and a couple of men were hurrying for a bus. She glanced into the darkness and spotted the tail end of a yellow worker's jacket trailing in the cool breeze as the person disappeared around a corner. Swallowing, she hoped it wasn't who she thought it might be. No, that was a ridiculous thought. She clicked on Gary's messages and deleted them.

FOUR

LIBBY

Saturday, 5 February

Libby placed the buffet food down on the table. Michaela and Kirsty from downstairs had accepted her house-warming invitation, and now that Tim had, her mini house-warming would go off well. It would be cramped but fun. She'd also invited Mr Bull. He hadn't replied but that didn't surprise her. She grabbed her phone and scrolled through Facebook. One of her old school friends, Ellen, had tagged her in a post to show her the furry addition to her family. She clicked like on the cockapoo.

Libby danced towards the window before jumping up and down, excited that Olly was here. Her lovely sister wobbled on her heels as she struggled to wheel her case along the bumpy pavement.

'Olly.' Libby lifted up the sash window, then waved and shouted. She ran down the stairs and out of the main door. Flinging her arms around her sister, she said, 'I've missed you so much, you look really well.' Olly let go of her case handle and hugged her back.

'It's been too long, sis. Have you lost a shedload of weight? I do worry about you.' She stepped back to assess Libby. 'Never mind, let's get this party started.'

Libby grabbed Olly's case and they both walked towards Canal House. Wearing a beanie hat and a black leather biker jacket, Olly looked too fashionable to be warm as she tottered beside her in spike-heeled boots. Her dyed-black poker-straight hair was almost frozen to her cheeks. 'How's Scott?'

'He's okay. So this is what the place looks like in real life.' Olly looked up.

'What it lacks in luxury, it makes up in friendliness. It's cosy here and they didn't object to me bringing Einstein. No one else would have us and everywhere is so expensive.'

As they entered Olly removed her hat and followed Libby who bounced her case up every step. 'Here, let me take your coat and then I'd best get sorted. Everyone else will be here in a few minutes. Make yourself at home.'

'I like what you've done with the place. Nice pic and is that a new rug?'

'Yes. It's my impeccable interior design skills that did it. You know what good taste I have.' Libby giggled.

'Of course it is, sis. Who else is coming?'

'For definite, the two girls who flatshare downstairs and the landlord, Tim. He's a nice guy.'

'Oh, nice like "hot", is he?'

Libby looked to the side and pressed her lips together. 'He's a nice person.'

'Nice as in an okay nice, or sexy nice?' Olly grinned as she pulled a face.

'Oh shut up and open the crisps.' Libby threw the family-sized bag at her sister. There was a tap at the door. 'Come in, it's open.'

'Ah, Michaela, Kirsty, this is my lovely big sister, Olly.'

Michaela shook Olly's hand. 'Nice to meet you. Call me Micky.' Kirsty stayed behind Michaela and gave a little wave. Michaela ran her hands through her bright red hair, fluffing it up a little.

Kirsty beamed a wide smile from her red lips. 'It's great to meet you, hun.' Her large black top floated over her apple-shaped figure.

'Ah, you're from Wales? I love that accent so much.' Olly tilted her head, not needing a confirmation.

'The accent gave me away. I'm originally from Cardiff.'

'I live in Tenby now. It's a long way from Cardiff though.'

'I wonder if Mr Bull will come. Does anyone know his first name by the way?' Libby wondered if the girls had met him.

'Never met the guy,' Michaela replied. Kirsty shrugged her shoulders.

Libby walked over to the speaker and blasted the volume up, then she poured the wine into glasses.

Tim still hadn't turned up. Maybe she'd offended him when she turned his dinner invite down. He seemed too pleasant to take offence and when he left her, he seemed fine.

As she swigged her wine, she reread the message that Gary had sent earlier, begging her to call him. She knew one thing, she couldn't tell Olly how persistent he was being.

She had her sister staying and her friends over, yet she still felt a loneliness in the pit of her stomach – an emptiness that was proving hard to fill. Even though it felt like Gary wasn't around much, she still missed his presence. All the time while they were together, it was like he had a new life somewhere else. Maybe she'd driven him to 'that' woman and maybe she'd been the cause of his anger. Even though she'd left him, the thought of him being with the other woman sent her stomach funny. There was so much she still didn't know about his affair. Where did they go? Her place, a room at a hotel, a shag pad somewhere?

She thought that the yearning, upset and pining would've passed, but it felt like it had just entered a new phase. She deleted the message. Deleting helped, until the next text.

There was a knock at the door.

'I'll get it.' Libby hurried to greet Tim. The guilt of rejecting his dinner date subsided a little when she saw his smile and the box of beers he held. 'Come in, make yourself comfortable. This is Tim,' Libby shouted, introducing the man to Olly. There was something different about him; Libby found herself staring at him, at his face, his eyes. He caught her. She looked away embarrassed. He looked away, then she looked back. Glasses – it wasn't those. New haircut, that's what it was. His brown hair was slicked down. He'd made an effort with his new-looking jeans and open shirt, exposing a crisp T-shirt. He was trying to impress her. Did she want to be impressed? She would have said no earlier but right now, she wasn't sure.

'Nice to meet you,' Olly shouted over the music as she looked Tim up and down. Tim smiled as he took a beer from the box before sitting on the sofa next to Olly. Libby swayed to the music, enjoying the wine and the euphoria it brought with it. She hadn't felt this free for a long time and it felt good.

As time passed, the music got quieter. Olly laughed as she tried to impersonate Kirsty's accent.

Libby kneeled on the floor between Tim and the window as the others laughed and joked. He'd gone quiet. 'Can I get you another drink?'

'No, I'm good thanks. I've got to be up early in the morning. My mum needs some toiletries.'

Einstein entered with a meow and he hurried towards Tim. He picked the cat up and stroked him. Within a few seconds, Einstein pawed him until his eyes began to shut. Libby smiled.

Einstein had never warmed to someone that quickly and he never sat on Gary's lap in that way.

'He really likes you.'

Tim smiled. 'I like him too.'

'I invited Mr Bull to the party, thought he'd like to come and get to know the neighbours, but he didn't reply.'

Tim twirled his fingers in Einstein's hair and the cat purred. 'That doesn't surprise me. When he first moved in, I asked him if he fancied a beer at the pub one night, he said yes but it never happened. He pretty much keeps himself to himself.'

'What's he like?' Libby asked.

Tim shrugged. 'Pretty average.'

'Is he tall, short, black hair, blond?' Libby wanted to know more about the neighbour she'd never seen.

'Yes, I've always wondered myself. The man's like a ghost.' Michaela knocked back a vodka and jokingly winked.

Tim cleared his throat. 'He's average height, wears a suit to work. I think he's a salesman of some kind as he carries a smart bag and holdall when he goes out. And that's it. I don't know any more than you do. If you find anything out, share it with me.' He laughed and leaned back. Libby enjoyed seeing him relax in everyone's company.

'He must have a really good job. I bet he's a spy or something.' Kirsty burst into a fit of drunken giggles. Michaela and Olly joined in, snorting with laughter.

'Yes, that would be hilarious, wouldn't it?' Libby said, as she laughed too.

'If the glove fits. He could well be MI5.' Tim couldn't hold back the escaping laugh.

As the party began to die down, Tim gently popped Einstein onto the floor. The cat shook and took up residence in Olly's lap instead. 'Right, I must be going. Busy day tomorrow. I hope you ladies enjoy the rest of your evening.' He stood and looked at his watch. 'Thanks for a good night.'

As they all muttered and slurred their goodbyes, 'Jingle Bell Rock', blasted out of the speakers and no one could be bothered to tell the device to skip. Olly got up and staggered to the table, where she poured herself a vodka and Coke before grabbing a cheese and pineapple stick.

'Tim's alright, isn't he? I've never got to know him before but Mr Bull sounds hot. I fancy myself a bit of mysterious spy.' Michaela howled with laughter, her freckles coming out as her face reddened with laughter and alcohol.

'Let's drink to hot, sexy spies. You never know, Lib, he could be the very man to shag while you get Gary out of your system.' Olly grabbed a bottle of wine and topped up their glasses.

'Hey, hands off. He's mine.' Kirsty scrunched up her wide nose.

The vodka was down to its last inch, the food had barely been touched and it was almost eleven thirty.

'Are any of you lot here, in this place, I mean room, going to eat my stuff? That food I made.' Libby struggled to be articulate, the drink was winning. The others explained that she'd been asleep for the past twenty minutes.

'No, we're going to head off. I've got crappy work in the morning. It's alright for you lot stinking in your pits until the hangover wears off but Tesco needs me.' Michaela swayed as she stood, then she leaned on the wall to steady herself.

'And I feel sick. Shouldn't really have had the vodka after the wine. I need to get downstairs. Another drink and I won't be able to manage even that.' Kirsty wiped a string of drool from the side of her mouth.

The more sober Michaela helped the staggering Kirsty across the room towards the door.

Kirsty grabbed a sandwich as she passed the table leaving a trail of lettuce as she left the flat. 'God, I needed that.' She took another bite as she was led out.

The two sisters were now alone.

'We should go to bed. Did I tell you that we have to share?'
Libby nudged Olly.

'Oh great. I hope you're not going to do the drunken snoring
thing.' Olly nudged her back. Einstein flitted off her lap and
scarpered into the bedroom.

'Can't make any promises there.' Libby tried to stand.

They helped each other to the bedroom, treading on the
lettuce as they passed. Libby undressed to her bra and pants,
exposing a fresh cut to her thigh.

'Oh, sis, you should call me when you're down. Your leg
looks like it needs tending to.'

Libby's hand instantly clasped the side of her body where
the bruising had been. She hadn't checked. It must have gone
but just in case, she didn't want Olly to see it. 'It's fine, the cut
was an accident. Anyway, I'm not down, I'm good. I've never
been happier.' She slipped into bed.

'Whatever. I know you're not. You know I'm always there
for you, anytime.'

'I know.' Libby yawned. 'Did I thank you for finding me this
place?'

'No need. I didn't really find it, just passed on a lead. Facebook has its uses.' Olly leaned in and cuddled her shivering
sister. 'It's bloody cold in here. Shall I shut the window?'

'No, Einstein likes to come and go. He meows all night if I
trap him in. He needs to go out and do cat things all night. I
need my slip.'

Olly reached under the pillow and pulled out the pink
slip. 'Sit up a minute. Let's get this on you.' Olly dressed her
like she was a little doll. 'You know that Tim has the hots for
you.'

'I know, sort of. Maybe I should go there. What do you
think? Or maybe not.' Libby laughed. 'I'm not ready for another
relationship. He's alright though. I like him.'

'So you don't fancy a bit of spy man, like Micky?'

'No, my heart belongs to nobody. My heart has been broken.' Libby laid her head down on her pillow.

'It's a good job you've got me,' Olly whispered as she slipped into bed next to Libby. 'And for what it's worth, I think you need to find out who you are now and a man won't help you to do that.'

Libby snuggled up to her sister, like when they were kids and used to sleep in each other's beds when they got scared. Olly reached over Libby and turned off the lamp.

'Olly, why didn't Mum and Dad want us? They left us.'

'Don't think about them now. You'll only get upset. They're not worth it. They left us and we're survivors.'

'I feel like we have no one left in the world.' Libby held on to the arm that Olly had draped over her. 'I know they were fifteen when they had you and I came along a couple of years later but they could have tried.'

'I was so scared they'd put us in homes and we'd be separated, Lib. I never let that happen.'

'Thank you, for always being there, Olly.' Olly's early years before Libby had come along were worse than anything Libby had ever experienced, but her sister would never speak of them. Libby often wondered what it was like for Olly before they had each other.

'Will you stroke my hair like you used to when I was scared in the night?'

'Of course.' Olly lovingly stroked Libby's hair.

A chinking noise came from the window. 'What was that?' Libby bolted upright, sitting up in the dark.

'Something just hit your window. Have a look.'

'No way.' Libby stared at the curtains as they lifted up with the breeze. 'Okay, I'll go.' She crept across the floor and gulped before she yanked the curtain back. 'It must have been Einstein.'

The cat meowed at the sound of his name and he emerged

from under the bed. She peered over at the roof and saw the small jagged-edged stone lying on the flat roof.

'What is it, Libby?'

'I think Gary knows where I live. I don't know how but someone threw something at the window. It has to be him.' She gazed into the darkness but there was no movement and she wondered if he was out there, watching her. Shivering, she pulled the curtains closed.

FIVE

LIBBY

Friday, 11 February

Libby stared at the rain pelting against her office window. Closing her door, she leaned against it so that no one could barge in. For just a moment, she needed time alone to make sense of all that was going on in her head. She slid down the smooth wood until her bottom reached the floor. Her salary would now be paid into her account and for once she'd have to manage her own money. She wondered what the payroll team must have thought when they paid her salary into an account in Gary's name every month. Not any more. The idea of managing everything was overwhelming but she could do it, she knew she could. No more pocket money. She could see now how ridiculous that was. Her eyes ached for rest, a symptom of many early starts after being on call all night. Top Staff Recruitment was unusually busy for the time of the year and the large order on her desk was making her head pound as the word failure kept eating away at her.

25 production workers and 2 welders wanted from tomorrow until the end of April. Saturday to Wednesday shifts. 8-hour day shifts.

Chrissie entered, sweeping Libby away from the door. Libby brushed down her trousers as she stood. 'Is everything okay, Chrissie? I was just—' She had no excuse for being on the floor. It was easier to shut up.

The woman leaned against the filing cabinet. Her usually neat French pleat was starting to lose its shape. She tucked the smooth grey hairs behind her ears. 'Yes, I just wondered how you were. You haven't seemed yourself this week. Everyone else has gone home so I thought I'd check to see you were alright.'

'I'm okay. My head is banging, that's all.'

'Is it about that order, the one that just came in? That would give anyone a headache. When I saw it, I thought, Libby is going to stress at that.'

Libby nodded. 'I can't get that many people at such short notice, especially on a Friday evening. It's impossible, especially as the company won't approve more funds to recruit more people.' She had to try again. She got up, walked across the office and slumped in her chair. Her only option was to put it out on social media again, at least it was free. Chrissie sat in her visitor seat as she carried on listening. 'I've got seventeen production workers and two welders. I had to tell them I was stuck for the rest. I bet they're calling one of our competitors as we speak.' No matter how long she stared at the spreadsheet, it didn't get any better.

'You've done all you can, love.'

'Have I? Bentons love Trevor. I haven't called him yet.'

'There's no way that man should ever be allowed to step into this office again.'

Libby shrugged. 'I know, but management say otherwise.

They want him on the job so we don't lose the contract. Bentons are worth too much to us.'

Chrissie shook her head. 'I hate them sometimes. They don't know what we have to put up with. Shelly was distraught after he charged in, going mad about his wages. I know she underpaid him but it was ten pounds, she offered to put it right and have it in his bank the next day. The man is unreasonable and when he's had a drink, he's downright scary.'

Libby remembered that day well. Trevor's dilated pupils staring into her eyes, followed by the acrid smell of stale whisky on his breath. 'He came into my office that day, before he had a go at Shelly. I thought he was going to attack me. I've never seen eyes that wide and heard such venom in a voice. I froze, Chrissie, and I don't want him to come back in here. I love this job, you know I do, but I don't know if I'll be working here in another year.' She flinched as she remembered Trevor's fingers circling her neck as she froze. His words still haunted her. *Just watch your back. You skanking cow. I'll be looking out for you.* Of course he couldn't remember any of that. He called up the next day asking if they had any work for him. It was like he was two different people. Drunk Trevor and sober Trevor.

Chrissie came around to her side of the desk and placed a hand on her shoulder. 'We need to win the lottery, don't we? Get out of the rat race and sip cocktails on a beach all day.'

Things were meant to be getting better for her. She had the new flat and her independence. 'We certainly do, that sounds like the dream.' She paused. 'I can't afford to fail, I need the commission. I want to buy my own place one day and if I leave it too late, I won't be able to get a mortgage. All I see is time slipping away from me and it's like I'm running uphill on a treacle-clad path. I guess I need to pull my socks up and try harder. What do I do, Chrissie? If I call Trevor, he might be having a good day and all might be fine. If I don't, management will be cheesed off with me. I can't win.'

A moment flashed through her mind. She definitely saw a yellow jacket disappearing around the corner from her flat window, when she thought someone might be watching her. Maybe Trevor was making good on his promise to keep a literal eye on her. She shook that thought away. Trevor always wore a yellow jacket whether working or not and lots of people wear yellow jackets. It could have been anyone. Or, maybe Trevor got drunk and was trying to play with her head. Hanging around and throwing stones at her bedroom window would certainly do that.

'I don't envy you. Sometimes I'm glad I work on reception. Consultants have it hard, especially in the industrial section. You'll get through this. In a week or two, it will be history.' Chrissie sat on the edge of Libby's desk. 'How are things with Gary? Is that lying toerag still messaging you all the time?'

'Yes, I don't reply. I blocked him on Facebook too.'

'Good for you.'

'I can't stop thinking about the woman he was sleeping with, or might still be sleeping with. It's like my mind doesn't switch off. I don't know what I did wrong.' It was easier to let Chrissie think that it was only his cheating that had been the problem. There was no way she could talk about it with anyone. She fanned her burning cheeks with her hand.

'It's his loss, love. You were the best thing in his life and he blew it.'

Libby nodded and wiped a tear away. She realised how little she knew about Gary's life or why he hurt her like he had. He was never home and although his job didn't pay him dizzying amounts of money, he had a little bit of inherited wealth. Where had he been on all those days, nights, weekends he went missing? She no longer believed he was at work. He had a fifty-hour a week contract and she didn't believe him when he said he had to cover at the other hotels in the chain occasionally. When she quizzed him about it, the anger came.

'I was such a fool believing him, Chrissie. I know now that I never knew Gary.' She literally had no idea who he was and what he might be capable of.

'Well, love. We never truly know another person, however close they are to us.'

'You're so right.' She never knew Gary or her parents. 'When the people closest to you also let you down, it becomes hard to trust anyone.' A little sob emerged from her mouth and the tears began to spill. 'I'm sorry.'

Chrissie leaned over and hugged her and Libby lay in the comfort of her arms, taking in what a motherly hug should feel like. 'You don't have to be sorry. Tell me if there's anything I can help you with.'

'Thank you for being there. It means a lot.'

'Oh, love, we've worked together for a while and I care about you. I don't like seeing you upset. You're such a good-hearted person and you don't deserve what you've been through. Gary is a pig and so were your parents. And you know what else?'

Libby shook her head and pulled away from the teary patch she'd left on Chrissie's blouse.

'You know what your problem is? You're working too hard. I watched my son go through a huge breakdown because of work. You need to lighten up on yourself a bit. Go out with your friends and have a good time. Everyone here knows you work really hard and if you don't totally fill the order, it is what it is. You can't perform miracles.'

'Thanks, Chrissie. I think I'm going to head off home and have a nice soak in the bath. I'm sure I'll feel better then. I just need to clear my head.'

'Glad to hear it. You've got some workers turning up in the morning. See how it plays out. Do you want me to drop you home? I have the car today.' Chrissie pulled the keys out of her pocket and jangled them in front of Libby.

'That's really kind of you but I think I need the walk to clear my head.' Libby forced a smile. She didn't want to take up any more of Chrissie's precious time. She had a husband she'd want to get home for.

'Alright. I'm going to wait in reception for you, just to make sure you really do go home. I'm not having you breaking down.'

Libby scooped her belongings into her handbag and shut down her computer, accepting that Chrissie knew best. She always did.

She glanced out of her office window, down at the busy street. That's when her stare met his. It was as if Trevor was waiting for her as he clung to a lamp post to stop himself falling into the gutter.

Her stomach began to churn at the thought of leaving. A gust of wind caught the bottom of his open yellow jacket and it billowed menacingly. Beckoning her to go down those stairs, right into the path of her aggressor.

SIX

LIBBY

'Chrissie, I need to leave out the back. Could you please unlock the door?'

'Of course. Everything okay?'

'No. Trevor is there waiting and he looks drunk. I can't face him when he's like that. He was staring at my office window looking all creepy.'

As they walked through to the back of the building, half climbing over several boxes of stationery, Chrissie punched in the code to lock up the building and they stepped out into an icy breeze.

'See you Monday and don't over-worry about Bentons.'

She would worry but she'd taken up enough of Chrissie's time. A white-hot pain flashed through her head and her stomach screamed with emptiness. She'd once again been too busy for lunch and she couldn't remember when she'd last had a drink. 'Thanks, Chrissie. See you then. Drive safely through the chaos.'

Chrissie smiled as she hurried up the hill towards the multi-storey car park.

Libby hurried past a huddle of people smoking outside the

Rep Theatre whilst they waited for their show to start. Others were dressed up in their best evening clothes as they headed towards Symphony Hall. Libby loved the city she'd adopted as home. Seeing all the life around her had lifted her mood. Soon she was taking the bridge over the canal, glancing at the lit-up restaurants that were starting to fill with diners. She glanced through the windows, taking in the warmth. No longer able to feel her fingers, she pulled out her gloves and slipped them on.

Her stomach let out an almighty grumble and nausea was building up. The smell of the chip shop lured her in. As she gripped the warm bag under her arm, she tottered up the final path to her flat, eager to eat them before having that hot bath.

As she pulled the keys from her bag, she dropped her bag of chips. 'Bloody hell.' Her fingers were too fat in her gloves to hold her keys. As she bent down to pick them up, she flinched as she felt someone brush past. 'Here, I got those.' Tim grabbed the chips.

Libby laughed and held a hand to her chest as she straightened up. 'You made me jump.' After removing her gloves, she checked her post.

'Sorry, I didn't mean to. I'll get the main door.'

'Great, I have another letter addressed to a Miss B Falco. I best return that to sender.' That was the third letter received with an Italian postmark. At least the return address was on the back. She shoved the letter into her bag. Tim was still standing next to her, smiling. 'Do you know where she moved to?'

'I haven't a clue. She must have forgotten to tell everyone her new address. This happens a lot. I still get post for someone who lived here years ago. Mostly junk. I've had a couple of people leave and not tell their credit card company. That was fun.' He pushed his glasses further up his nose and laughed. 'I was wondering...' He stalled.

'Yes.' Libby continued to walk ahead of Tim up the stairs.

'I know I've already asked you and I know you're busy but

would you like to go out for dinner next week? As friends, I mean. I'd love to go out to some of the restaurants around here but it's weird going alone.' As she approached her front door she turned and looked at Tim.

She remembered Chrissie's advice to get out, do new things and make new friends. They were so close that she didn't know whether she could feel the warmth of the chips or the warmth of his body. The caramel tinge around the edge of his irises kept her looking. 'You know, Tim, I haven't made many new friends around here yet and it's about time I did, so dinner would be great.' She didn't want to offer him false hope but there was something about him, something beyond his physical appearance that prickled her skin with desire, but it was too soon after Gary to jump into anything.

'Great. Is about seven on Tuesday okay? I have a light workday. If Tuesday's no good for you, I'm good for another day.'

'Tuesday's good.'

'Can I surprise you? There's a place I'd love to try but I'll have to see if I can book a table first.'

Gary had never surprised her with anything except the first day he hit her. It wasn't much, just a swift slap on the cheek. She cleared her throat and pushed that thought away. Tim wasn't Gary. 'Of course. Thanks, Tim. I can't wait to see where we end up. I think you'd best give me my chips back or I might have starved to death by Tuesday.' Her stomach let out an embarrassing growl. 'I really need those chips tonight.' She giggled.

His cheeks went a little pink. 'Of course, sorry. I forgot I had them. They were keeping me warm.' He placed the chips into Libby's spare hand.

'See you Tuesday then.' They lingered for a few seconds, both not knowing what to say or do but Tim turned away first, letting himself into his flat. 'Tuesday.'

As she entered her flat and closed the door, she kicked her

shoes off. While picking chips from the bag, she ran the bath and focused on the more positive aspects of her day. She'd finally made an effort to get back out there and get a life. She was even looking forward to going out with Tim, as a friend of course.

As she went to grab her large fluffy towel in the airing cupboard, she realised it wasn't there. She opened it wide, pushing the clothes horse aside and stepping right in. She was sure it had been hanging up on that clothes horse. She got down on her hands and knees and felt at the back of the cupboard but the towel wasn't there. Her fingers brushed on the wall as she tried to get back up. Peeling wallpaper. She brushed it back down, not wanting to tear it anymore. Brows scrunched, she hurried to her bedroom and it wasn't there either. The window was wide open and Einstein was nowhere to be seen. She pulled it to a little, leaving just enough room for him to squash through. Maybe it had blown open in the breeze. That had to be it. No one would go to the trouble to get onto a roof and climb in just to steal a towel. She ran to the living room. Her laptop, tablet and television were still there. Then she spotted the towel folded up on the arm of the chair.

She picked her bottom lip as she thought back to this morning. She couldn't remember leaving it there. She must have done. The stress of work and Gary were making her forget things. That was the only explanation. She grabbed the towel and hurried to the bathroom as the sound of water trickling over the bath panicked her. *No one has been here, stop being over the top, Libby*, she kept repeating to herself.

SEVEN

LIBBY

Tuesday, 15 February

Libby ignored Einstein's purrs for attention. She'd booked a last-minute day off work and hadn't overthought her dinner with Tim, until now. She glanced at her work emails. There had been no major repercussions from Bentons. They were willing to take the workers she had and wait for the others but once again, they'd asked for Trevor. She bit her nail as she reread the email then she closed her laptop. It should have been a relaxing day but all she'd done was stew over what still needed to be done.

Was she right to have accepted dinner with Tim? She nodded and smiled. She'd made it clear enough that they were just friends going out for a meal, but it was obvious to both of them that there was chemistry. She hurried to her bedroom and checked out her outfit in the full-length wardrobe mirror. Her chosen outfit was smart and showed off her figure but it wasn't over the top. She smoothed down her smart skinny jeans and took in a side view of the rose patterned top that was pulled in with a chunky belt. Hair up or down? She ruffled her blonde mane. No, it was better up. She grabbed a crocodile clip and twisted her hair before securing it up. She pulled on her low-heeled black boots and zipped them up. Something poked into the side of her breast. She prodded the underwiring back into her bra. Ready to go, she grabbed her bag and paced up and down the living room waiting for the knock on the door. Her heart thrummed. *It isn't a date*, she kept telling herself. *It's just dinner with a neighbour.*

Tim knocked on time. She turned the lights off, grabbed her red woollen coat and went out.

He'd left his glasses behind tonight. 'Wow, you look amazing,' he said.

Tim's long overcoat was open enough to see the well-fitted patterned shirt he had on. His dark jeans and brown shoes finished the look. There was something about him, he shone like someone with more money than her.

'Thank you. I feel a little underdressed though. Maybe I should have put a dress on.' She glanced down at her cheap boots and the only thick coat she had, wondering if she looked like the poor friend of someone who seemed to wear things a little more fitted.

'No way. Why would you think that? You seriously look great so stop worrying.'

She smiled and took his compliment. Feeling like she didn't shape up was a by-product of being with Gary. She shouldn't have said that to Tim. 'Worry has left the building. Where are we going?'

'I've booked a table at Saddlers in Brindleyplace. They do a broad range of Mediterranean cuisine. I've never eaten there but always wanted to so I thought, why not? I know they have a great vegetarian menu so that sealed it really,' he replied as he led the way down the stairs and the smile on Libby's face was all she needed to tell her that she'd done the right thing by accepting his invite.

The walk to the restaurant was bridged by small talk, mostly about work and when spring would break. He led her across the square and stopped outside Saddlers. The frontage was small, which is why she'd probably missed it in passing, but it went back far and had an upstairs. Just the look of the cosy, candlelit restaurant had her excited.

'This looks like a lovely place. Here I am thinking we might be going for a curry or something.'

'Curry, no, I'm more than happy to venture out for a curry on my own, but here, you really need to be with someone.' He opened the door, letting her in. On entry, a server wearing black and white took their coats and showed them to the reserved table by the window. The rustic tables glimmered like gems with the candles in jars taking centre space. Subdued lighting set the mood. The more Libby ventured towards their table, the more it felt like a date. The man serving pushed her seat in as she sat. Classical music played softly in the background.

'Chopin, how lovely,' Tim said.

Libby wouldn't know Chopin from any other composer. She wondered if she and Tim were worlds apart but still, they both lived in a cramped flat in a shared house, so maybe not. But his family owns it, that's the difference. She concluded that they were worlds apart but she wouldn't let that stop her enjoying what was anticipated to be a wonderful evening.

'What would you like to drink?' Tim held out the wine menu.

She glanced through it, not knowing what would be a good choice or a bad one. When she went out she normally ordered a cocktail, maybe even a vodka and Coke or the odd shot, but this wasn't the type of place to down a Sambuca after drinking six Bacardi Breezers. 'I, err, I don't know.'

'Do you prefer red or white?'

'Either. You choose.' She glanced at the price. The cheapest bottle was over thirty pounds and the menu didn't look cheap either. She'd have to put whatever her half cost on her credit card.

'Could we have a bottle of claret, please?' The server smiled and nodded. She watched Tim as he studied the menu. His square jaw, handsomely perfect and that smile that made him look quietly confident. She wondered what it would feel like to run her fingers through his thick, perfectly styled hair.

As the wine flowed Tim began to loosen up. 'Anyway, my mother was fine when I visited her the other day. Still never remembers who I am but she's in good physical health. Where do your parents live?'

She swallowed, wondering if she should tell him the truth or tell a lie. The truth wasn't pretty.

'They live in Spain now, both work in a bar that one of their friends bought a few years back. They're in Benidorm.'

'I thought you said you were from Redditch. Is that where they moved from?'

'No, it's where I moved from.' Libby looked down as she cleared her throat.

'I'm sorry if I've intruded on something personal. I didn't mean to upset you.'

She shook her head and forced a smile. Just the mention of her parents had killed the atmosphere. 'You haven't. My parents have but you haven't. Olly and I lived in Redditch with our great-aunt. She brought us up. Our parents weren't around much. They were still at school when they had my sister. I guess they weren't ready for the responsibility of two children at such a young age. It was either go into care and get split up or be carted off to relatives.' She knew he could see the misery of her past written on her face. Hating her vulnerability to be so exposed, she forced a smile. She'd shared her heartache with Gary. He knew how insecure and abandoned she'd felt but he still let her down. 'Our great-aunt was wonderful though. We were both devastated when she died.'

'Why don't you tell me about Redditch then? Were those happier times?'

She appreciated him moving on from her parents. He'd obviously had a lovely childhood from what he'd told her. Middle-class upbringing, a mother who loved him and a sister. 'Redditch was okay. It's got its fair share of pubs and the great big shopping centre. As teenagers, Olly and I would always hang around up there. We spent hours playing in the woods, jumping in the streams and messing around, as kids do.'

'So, did you and your sister go to school in Redditch?'

'Yes, she was three years ahead of me so I was left to my own devices. I always found school difficult. It was tough for kids like me and Olly. We never had nice things, our shoes were always shabby. Kids can be cruel.'

'I'm sorry you had it so bad. They hated me too, mostly. I had these awful glasses that my mum used to make me wear and...' He waved his arm and laughed. 'I'm so glad to be all grown up now.' He ran his fingers through his hair. 'Tell me something else about where you grew up.' He topped up their wine glasses. 'Wait, I remember that great unsolved case. The girl in the well, wasn't that close by. I still think the father did it.'

She smiled as she took a swig. 'Yes, it's all we're remembered for really. Horrible to think that. I was quite young but it was all over the news.'

'Horrible thing to happen.'

'I was about eleven and didn't take much notice at the time. I remember my sister telling me about some girl from her school who was found in a well. Our great-aunt wouldn't let us out for ages after that news broke but we used to sneak out. They never found out who did it. It was probably her dad. A girl was killed and no one has ever been charged.' She shivered.

'That's some news. Was your sister a friend of hers?'

'No, I don't think so but they were in the same year.' She shouldn't have said anything. The murder in Redditch was something that Olly didn't like to talk about. Louise wasn't a close friend but she had bummed Olly a few cigarettes. She shivered as she thought of Louise's body, sprawled out in the bottom of the old unused well in Beoley. Someone had taken the school bully down. 'If you see Olly again, please don't mention it to her. She doesn't like to talk about it.'

'I definitely won't. I wouldn't blab about anything you told me. Anyway, that's given me the shivers. I don't know how we got onto the subject of murder. So, how's your job going?'

After managing to divert the conversation away from her past, she now had to talk about the other thing in her life that was grating on her – work. 'My job's fine.'

'You seem to be doing a lot of hours.'

'Yes, I'm trying to save up a bit.'

'It can't be easy, you must be tired.'

'I am. Tired, harassed, suffering lack of support from management, but I'm sure that's how most people feel about work.' Thoughts of Trevor and not meeting her targets went through her mind.

'What's been so bad? Feel free to have a sound off. You might feel better.'

While picking at a breadstick she began to feel more at ease with Tim. He listened and seemed genuinely interested in what she said. Gary never took the time to listen to her. 'We get the occasional angry worker but instead of showing them the door, we end up giving them work, over and over again. The management are awful, but I love the actual job. I won't be there forever so I bide my time. Sorry to bore you but that's all there is to it.'

'You're not boring me. I am hungry, though. Have you chosen what you want for main?' The suited man approached to take their order.

'Yes, I'd like the Mediterranean vegetable stack. And it's

topped with loads of grilled cheese. My stomach is already begging for it.' Libby giggled, the wine starting to make her giggly. She really needed some food before she got wasted.

'I'll have the same. I do love cheese.'

'If you want a meat dish, don't mind me.'

'I thought I'd try something new. The stack looks great.'

Libby was genuinely warming to Tim. With every bite of the meal she felt more at ease in his company.

The next hour passed quickly, the conversation flowed and the food was much enjoyed. They'd even had a brandy to finish the meal off.

As the evening concluded, the waiter placed the bill down on the table. Libby placed her credit card in the dish. Tim placed his hand on hers. 'It's my treat.'

'No, don't be silly, I'd like to pay my half.' Her cheeks radiated heat and she knew that the tipsy redness had spread up her neck, and onto her cheeks and nose.

'I insist, it was me who asked you.'

'I know but I like to pay my way.'

'Okay, if you insist you can pay next time but don't worry, really. I've expensed it. Besides, you footed the cost of a party at yours and I was grateful for the invite.'

'Next time,' Libby said, laughing as she removed her hand from under his. Had she just committed to a next time? Her credit card catastrophe had been delayed for a short while. That gave her a bit more time to get the commission rolling in.

They left the restaurant and chatted whilst walking along the icy paths towards home. Libby burst into laughter as she almost slipped backwards as they crossed over the canal bridge. Several people on a pub balcony jeered as Tim caught her just in time. Moonlight glistened on the surface of the canal's rippling waters.

'I've got work tomorrow,' Libby hiccupped.

As he led her past the restaurants, she flinched as she saw

Trevor stumbling out of a pub. His gaze immediately locked onto hers. He'd placed his black woollen hat on crookedly and it almost covered one eye. His yellow jacket was half hanging off his shoulders and he looked more like a seventy-year-old man than his fifty-five years.

'Who's that man? Is everything alright?'

Trevor stumbled towards them and she gripped Tim's arm. He wiped a stream of mucous from his bulbous nose.

'You missed me out again, bitch. I know, I see things. I see everything.'

His slurring was making it hard to hear exactly what he was saying.

'Trevor, please go home, you're drunk. You don't want to say or do anything you might regret.' She grabbed her phone, ready to call the police but the man stepped back, holding his hands up.

'Just remember, I know where you live. You should never feel safe.' So she had seen him lurking around by Canal House. The thought of him being there made her want to bring her wine up.

Tim let go of her arm. 'How dare you threaten her, now piss off.' He shoved the drunken man. Trevor fell to the floor and laughed at him. 'Are you okay, Libby?'

Tears filled her eyes and she shook her head. 'Let's get out of here.' She didn't want to look at Trevor for a moment longer than needed.

Tim went towards Trevor again but Libby grabbed him. 'Leave it, he's not worth the bother. The man's got a drink problem.'

'You'll get what's coming to you,' Trevor shouted as they walked away.

She wanted to get home as quickly as possible. She needed to get back inside and lock herself in her flat, where she was safe. 'Let's go, now.'

EIGHT

LIBBY

As they entered Canal House and hurried up the stairs, Libby exhaled. For a moment, she'd almost sobered up after being confronted by Trevor but now, it was as if her head was swimming. She checked her phone. It was eleven, which was late enough. There were no unread messages so Gary had left her alone all day.

Tim stopped outside her door. 'Would you like to join me for coffee? You look tense and I can understand why. That man was an arsehole. If I see him around, I'll call the police. Who was he?'

'He's done a lot of work for us. When I said I had some work problems, he is those problems. I'll get it sorted. He'll soon get bored and move on.'

'He was threatening you.'

'I know but it's just because he was plastered. He'll be different in the morning. I really should get to bed. I've got work tomorrow.'

'And you can sleep, after that?'

She shook her head and smiled. 'Thank you for being concerned but crap like this is all in a day's work for me.'

'Well it shouldn't be.'

'Tell that to the management,' she mumbled. 'Actually, you're right. I won't sleep. I will have that coffee and I won't let that man ruin what was a lovely evening. Let's not talk about him again.'

'Okay.' He pulled his key out and opened his door.

Realising it was the first time she'd been in Tim's flat Libby tried to take everything in. The flat was old-fashioned but neat and it was much bigger than hers. It was as if he had all the same furniture and pictures that his mother would've chosen. In the corner of the lounge sat a computer on a desk. The three-piece suite was covered with a huge blue throw. As she trod, her feet sunk into the thick grey shag pile that had a new smell about it.

'Take a seat.' He pointed to the couch. She closed her eyes and laid her head back on the couch, trying to ignore the fact that the room felt as though it was spinning a little. As the kettle clicked, she listened to the water being poured into the cup. She needed this coffee to counteract the wine. Tim came back into the lounge and handed Libby a mug of hot coffee.

He sat in the chair next to her and she exhaled slowly before taking a sip of coffee. 'Nice place.'

He laughed. 'Come on, it's awful. My mother decorated it but I intend to do it up when I get a gap in my work. I can't be surrounded by this level of chintz for much longer.'

She laughed with him, then took another sip of coffee. 'I'm feeling a bit merry. It's probably best I go before I make myself look stupid.'

'Oh, Libby. You're a bit merry, I am too so who cares. I had a great night. Next time, you chose where we eat. I like McDonald's by the way.'

She leaned forwards and jokingly slapped him.

'Right.' She placed the cup on the coffee table and stood. 'I am going to bed.'

'Of course, I'll show you out.'

As he helped her through the hall, she spotted a calendar on the wall. 'It was Valentine's Day yesterday. Were you trying to get me on a date?' She giggled, unable to believe she'd just said that to him.

'That was yesterday. It's gone.'

'Good, 'cause we're friends, okay.' She opened the door and stepped out.

'Course. Are you okay getting into your flat?'

She scrunched her brow and pulled her key from her coat pocket. 'I'm a lock opening ninja.' His nose creased a little as he laughed. They'd had such a good night. She leaned in to give him a peck but instead, her mouth reached his and before she knew it she was kissing him hard. As she pulled away, she knew something felt wrong. Even Tim looked a little shocked by her action. 'I am so sorry. I'm an idiot. I've just come out of a really bad relationship and now... I didn't mean that.'

'Libby, it's okay. Just go home and have a good sleep. Everything will feel better in the morning.'

'Thank you for being so understanding.' She hurried into her flat and closed the door.

Einstein tangled his body around her legs. 'Not now, Einstein.' She hurried to the kitchen and hit the work surface. Why did she always ruin everything? She slammed her fist down again, harder this time, then again. 'Ouch.' One of her bones made a cracking noise.

Shaking, she lifted up her fist and stared at the throbbing knuckle. The skin was grazed and a small fleck of blood began to pool around the cut's opening. She watched the pool grow into a small ball before it split and trickled down her wrist. Breaking down, she slid to the floor and sobbed. Einstein lay next to her and purred, unaffected by her outburst. A release washed over her and her breathing slowed back down to normal. As her tears subsided, exhaustion took over. She'd ruined a perfectly good night. She didn't want a relationship and Tim hadn't said he wanted one either and on top of that, Trevor had to be there to ruin everything.

She stood and poured a glass of souring wine that was left over in the fridge. Taking it through to the lounge, she grabbed her tablet. A bit of browsing might calm her down a bit but it wouldn't get rid of the burning shame she felt. *Idiot.*

Logging on to Facebook, she scanned the meaningless comments of other people's days. She'd missed the live update of Cara going to bed, and Eleanor's dog throwing up. Ellen had tagged her in a picture of the Spice Girls. She smiled, remembering when she used to pretend to be Baby and Ellen used to be Ginger. Then, her shoulders slumped as she spotted a friend request from Gary. He'd set up a new account. Even blocking him hadn't kept him away. She sensed that he was probably looking at her wall using his new account details. Then her phone beeped.

> *Libby, I love you. I can't live without you. I know I took you for granted and I hurt you. Stop ignoring me! Please. It hurts too much.*

He was never going to leave her alone.

She clicked onto her profile settings and blocked everyone except her close friends from looking at her page. Although it pained her to keep him blocked out of her life, she wasn't in a position to talk to him, let alone forgive him, and she was confused. Why had she kissed Tim? She turned her tablet off and threw back her wine. Reaching for the phone, she began to cry as she dialled Olly. Her sister answered. 'It's just me. I'm sorry it's so late.' She wept as she poured her heart out. 'Everything is going wrong.'

NINE

LIBBY

'You alright, Lib?' Olly's voice always soothed her.

'I just needed someone to talk to.' Libby pressed her mobile tight against her ear.

'Are you tipsy?'

'Yes. I've had a few wines.'

'Wait a sec, I'm dying for a drink. It's been a hectic night at the restaurant. Right, I'm all yours. What's wrong?'

Libby took a deep breath. 'I've done something really stupid.'

'Okay, you haven't taken the tosser back, have you?'

'No, nothing like that. I went out with Tim tonight, just for a meal as friends.'

'I'm listening.' Olly swigged her drink.

'It was a lovely night until that man I told you about, who comes into the agency.'

'Trevor?'

'Yes, he was drunk outside a pub and he saw us. He went off on one. He knows where I live. It scared me.' Libby placed her shaking hand in her lap.

'Seriously, you need to have it out with management. He can't do that to you.'

'Well, that's not the worst part of it all.'

'It gets worse?'

'I got overwhelmed and Tim was so sweet. When we got back, I kissed him, properly kissed him. I feel like such an idiot. I don't want to be with anyone at the moment. I feel as though I don't know myself and I'm confused and depressed. I don't know what to do.' The message from Gary kept milling around her mind. How could he say he loved her one minute then send a tirade of horrible texts another?

'Lib, it was just a kiss. He's a grown man. I'm sure he doesn't expect anything from you. I've lost count when it comes to regretful snogs in my life. Don't worry about that.' Olly went quiet.

'You okay? How's Scott?' Libby realised that all she'd talked about was herself.

'So-so.'

'Are you guys okay?'

'Yes, I'm sure we'll be fine. It's nothing. Just the stress of the prospect of setting up our own restaurant.'

'You know you can talk to me too, Olly.' Her sister always put a brave face on everything. Ever the protector.

'I know. We'll see each other soon so we can talk then. Do you want to stay here for a bit? I hate the thought of you being depressed and harassed.'

'I can't right now. I have too much on but I'll come and stay soon. I promise.'

'Right, well call me if you need me. My phones always on, you know that.'

'Love you, Olly.'

'Love you, sis.' With that, Olly hung up.

Tears slid down her cheeks as she walked over to the window. Peering through the gap in the curtains, she couldn't see anyone. There was no one out of place, no one around, so why did she feel so exposed?

Trevor – that's why. She glanced back at her Facebook, knowing that she'd done the right thing. No one could peer into her life any more, except the people she allowed in. Gary was history and she expected that soon even more messages would come and they wouldn't all say that he loved her.

She scrolled through Olly's profile. She clicked 'like' on a dessert photo that looked like it had come straight from a cook-book. A pink dessert, decorated with rose petals. She popped a like on Ellen's tag.

The bang from beneath almost made her fall off the chair. Then it was followed by another, then another. It was as if Mr Bull was downstairs declaring war on his furniture. A flashback hit her. Gary, angry that he'd seen her having coffee with a male client. She shook as she thought back to that day. The day he tore apart her favourite work dress in a jealous rage, then smashed her vanity mirror on the back of the chair. All that jeal-ousy when it was him having the affair. She'd put up with his behaviour for far too long. It wasn't as if he was like that when they met. He was the sweetest man ever. The changes had been so gradual. It began with him grimacing at what she wore, telling her that she was bad with money and that he could manage it for her. Then there was the slap, the one he was so sorry about. That slap turned into a push a few weeks later, then a punch a while after that. Another bang came from below and she flinched.

She lay down on the carpet and listened as the man bashed something repeatedly against the wall. So much rage. She imag-ined chair legs flying. She lay there, weeping as she wondered if she was ever going to find anything better in life.

You can't shut me out, Libby. What are you trying to hide? Whatever it is, I will find out. You can't hide anything from me.

That was the last thing she wanted to see on a text. He was never going to leave her alone. Lying there on the carpet, she wept as Mr Bull smashed glass below. Was he as angry as Gary was? Was there a partner out there who was bearing the brunt of it all? She was sick of everything. Tomorrow had to be a better day, otherwise what was the point of carrying on?

TEN

UNKNOWN

She's completely shut me out. How dare she? I have lost my
eyes on her. There has to be another way in.

I check her posts again on my camera roll. Thankfully I had
the foresight to take snapshots of everything. Grabbing another
beer, I down it in one. I'm so wasted, I can barely see the words
on the screen but I'm capable, more capable than she thinks
I am.

There's an old post from her friend, Ellen, asking if Libby
had seen anything from an Ian Linden, as she wants to trace
him. Libby replied, saying it would be good to see him again but
she hadn't heard from him. Reading further, it appears that Ian
had been Ellen's first real kiss. Maybe Ellen's marriage was
going sour and she couldn't resist the urge to contact an old
flame.

What I need to do is clear now. I set up an email account in
the name of Ian Linden. After that, I set up his profile on Facebook, supplying the bare minimum of details. There would be
no photo, of course.

Libby would definitely want a conversation with Ian. I can

be Ian and she can talk to me. From reading Ellen and Libby's walls, I know quite a lot about him.

After doing my coat up, I turn the light off and lock up for the night to go home; to my real home.

I will never give you up, you will not make a fool out of me. I thought you were special but now I wonder if you're just like the rest of them.

ELEVEN

RICARDO

Thursday, 17 February

'We therefore commit this body to the ground. Earth to earth, ashes to ashes, dust to dust.' Father Bernard bowed his head as the coffin was lowered into the earth. Ricardo kneeled down, tears clouding his vision. He threw the flowers that Maria had grown on their Naples estate into her grave. She'd lovingly tended to them and he didn't even know what they were called. Moments later he was joined by well-wishing relatives. Ricardo looked up and thanked God that Maria had been sent off on a day when the sun shone golden rays all over the earth in front of him.

He remembered his promise to her. He had to go and look for Bettina, that's why he'd booked the flight earlier that day. His letters were being constantly returned and that had worried him. He would leave Italy to visit the place that she last lived, Birmingham in England. The flight was booked and nothing would stop him.

The last day he'd heard from his lovely daughter, Bettina, was at the beginning of March, last year. Their words weren't pleasant. Refusing to come home and being the free spirit that she was meant that they'd argued, both saying things they didn't mean. He replayed some of that conversation in his confused mind as he'd done so many times before. *Isn't it time you came home and stopped being childish? Following this silly dream, it's no good for you. We have everything you need here. It doesn't look good, my daughter, working in a bar when we have all this. You're bringing shame on us. Come back, work here for a while and then study. You need to start acting like a Falco.*

He remembered her reply. *So you're ashamed of me now?* He'd even got Father Bernard on the phone, to try and talk some sense into her and when he took the phone back, she said *Fuck Father Bernard.* Those were the final words he heard from her but not the final words she'd heard from him. He wished in that moment that he hadn't put Father Bernard on the phone. Things went from bad to worse.

Maria always said that he should give Bettina some space but he couldn't. He always worried about her; she wasn't the tough girl everyone thought she was. He did love her but her troublesome teen years had made it impossible for him to show it. This time he wanted to find her and tell her once and for all that he loved her, and he also had to tell her that her mother was in heaven.

Standing alone by Maria's grave, everyone had left Ricardo to mourn alone. It was strange that Bettina hadn't called. Even when they argued in the past she still checked in with her mother once a week to say that she was safe. She had even sent regular letters and postcards to her brothers in the past. But not since that day, that phone call. Since then, there had been nothing. It was as if none of them knew her any more.

Please find Bettina, promise me you will go and find Bettina.

His wife's last words repeated in his head, in a haunting whisper. Until he found her, he wouldn't stop hearing them.

'I miss you, my love, I'm going to find our girl and I'm going to tell her how sorry I am. What I said to Bettina was unforgivable. I didn't mean it. She has to know that. I'm so sorry, Maria. There are things I never told you and I hate myself for that. I know you will never rest in peace until I have made this right.' He was going to find their daughter and he would beg for forgiveness.

TWELVE

LIBBY

Friday, 18 February

Agreeing to go out with her colleagues had seemed like a bad idea earlier that day. She'd refused several times but eventually Chrissie persuaded her to go. The last time she had a drink she had ended up kissing Tim and the last thing she wanted was to embarrass herself again.

Several drinks later and a lot of dancing, she felt freer than ever. Trevor had left her alone and even Gary's messages had calmed down. Maybe this was the start of things improving.

As she danced alone in the middle of the floor, drink in hand and sticky bodies all around, Chrissie tapped her on the shoulder. 'I'm taking the grandkids out in the morning so I'm heading home. Enjoy the rest of the night, love.'

'I love it, Chrissie. Thanks for persuading me to come out.'

For once, she didn't have to turn invites down because Gary wouldn't have approved. If she had gone out, he'd have called her all night to say how much he missed her, or ask when she was coming home. Eventually, it wasn't even worth trying to go out and have a good time. Chrissie hugged her and blew a kiss as she left.

Shelly and Verity giggled while doing some sort of funny dance that made them look as though they were trying to fly. She'd missed this and she'd missed going out with them. One club music number rolled into another and she loved them all.

Shelly waved and placed a hand to her mouth, mimicking a drink.

Libby smiled and shook her head. She'd already had too much. The drink in her hand would definitely be her last.

As she headed towards the loos, Libby weaved her way through the many bodies that were all packed together. The smell of sweat and sweet scents hung in the air. The stark lights of the foyer made her squint and she poked her ears, hoping to get rid of the ringing.

'Libby.' Turning around she saw a man waving behind another man. He slowly revealed himself as the crowd shifted and her heart began to pound.

'Gary. What the hell? Why are you following me? I want you to stay away from me.' She turned and ran into the ladies' loos where he couldn't follow her. The only thing she could do was to wait him out. He couldn't loiter outside the loos all night. She paced, took a few deep breaths and washed her hands. The smudged mascara down her cheek and the sweaty strands of hair that had fallen out of her clip were all she could focus on in the mirror. Wetting her hands, she teased her hair back into place and wiped the make-up from her eyes. Then she shook her head. No more was he going to influence how she wore her hair or dressed. She undid the clip and popped it in her pocket, allowing her sweaty hair to fall messily over her shoulders.

Two women barged in, one running behind another who looked like she was about to be sick. Libby didn't want to be around to hear her retch, fearing it may start her off.

She peered out of the toilet door before fully opening it, hoping that Gary had got bored and gone somewhere else. No such luck. He leaned back on the wall in front of the toilets, looking directly at her with the saddest eyes he could muster.

'I'm so sorry about everything. Give me a chance to explain.' He walked towards her with his arms out, ready to embrace her.

Pushing him away, she barged past him. 'Get off me. I don't need anything from you. I wish you would go away, stop messaging me, and stop harassing me.'

'Harassing you?'

'Messaging me. Throwing stones at my window and loitering by my flat.'

'What? I haven't been throwing any stones or loitering.'

She didn't believe him. The man was a born liar.

The bouncer walked over.

'Do you need some help?'

Libby shook her head. 'I got this.' No more shrinking violet, Libby. If she didn't stand up to him, he'd never leave her alone. 'How could you? And how could you lie to me? I asked you over and over again to tell me the truth. I knew you were seeing someone else and you made me believe I was crazy. I found you out though, Gary. I read every single one of those messages and she hated me when she should have hated you.'

'I'm sorry. I know I made a mistake but I need a second chance.'

'No, you blew it. If only it was some sort of fling, that wouldn't excuse you hurting me. No one will hit me ever again. Not you, not anyone. I don't want to go back to being the person that can't go out or feels like I have to beg to be able to do overtime at work. It's pathetic. I was pathetic. I'm not that person any more. You turned me into that person with your manipulation and lies and now you're trying to make me feel sorry for you. All of this was your fault.'

Gary looked down at her with his big brown eyes, the ones

she'd fallen for. Then he spoke in his proper English accent that had always in the past put her to shame when she attended his family functions and had to speak. She never did feel like she was good enough for them and him. 'I know I was wrong but I miss you badly. I was so stupid and I would do anything for a second chance, I mean anything. I need to be able to make it up to you. I'll have therapy, we can do couple's therapy. Don't throw away what we have.' It was all lies and Libby knew it.

'Had. What we had is over. I am not a punchbag and what about her? If you loved me so much you wouldn't have shagged her. You thought I was that stupid I'd never see the messages if you called her John.'

'She meant nothing, I promise. I know I lied and I know I have anger problems but I'll do anything to make it up to you. Anything.'

'Despite how you were, I was ready to spend the rest of my life with you, have your children and...' She broke down into a flood tears. Gary moved closer and tenderly held her.

'Get off me. I never want to feel your hands on me ever again.' She pushed him away and walked towards the cloakroom, ticket in hand in readiness to retrieve her coat. As the attendant handed it over, Gary came up behind her and tried to take it.

'Let go.' Rage fired within her as she yanked it back.

'I was going to help you, that's all.' He paused. 'Please, just let me help you.'

'I don't need your help.' She hurried as fast as her heels would allow, out of the club and past Brindleyplace. Her hands trembled and she was doing all she could not to stumble.

'Libby, stop.'

She grabbed her phone from her pocket. 'I'm calling the police. I'll do it.'

He reached over and snatched it from her. 'Don't be ridiculous. You don't want to do that.' He gripped her wrist. 'Just come home with me now, Libby. We can talk about this tomorrow, then we can collect your stuff and the cat. You've kept this up for far too long. You've made your point.'

She shook his hand away and snatched her phone back. He could tell she was visibly shaking at his presence as she stepped back slowly. The very thought of walking into that luxury prison of an apartment of his filled her with the sickest feeling ever. She'd rather stay at Canal House forever. Her breath quickened as he reached for her again. She stepped back and kicked off her shoes. Without hesitation, she grabbed them and ran as fast as she could. She wasn't going anywhere with him. Not now, not ever. She'd rather die. As soon as she reached the chip shop, she turned. 'I'm going in there right now and if you don't leave, I'll tell them you tried to attack me.'

He held his hands up and grinned. 'You always were a manipulative little bitch. I come here to tell you how sorry I am and how much I love you and you pull this little stunt. I will never let you go.' With that, he turned and walked away.

Reaching down, Libby could tell that there was blood on her feet. Maybe she'd trodden on a stone or a bit of glass. Her heart pounded as she thought of how intense the last few minutes had been.

As she approached Canal House, she regained her breath and stood for a moment, trying to calm down.

Mr Bull's lounge light was on. She glanced back to double-check that Gary had left, and he had. All she wanted to do was slip into bed but her curiosity got the better of her. She wanted to know more about the troubled man who threw his furniture around. Peering through his net curtain, she took in the sparsely furnished room. There was only a table with a desktop computer on it and a leather office chair. Her gaze landed on a pile of broken chairs in the corner of the room.

Not being able to see enough, she got closer. As she did, she slipped on a loose stone that forced her to fall against the window and knock her arm. Shaking, Libby remained still, hoping he wouldn't venture out of his flat for a look, but everything remained quiet. She moved so that she could get a glimpse from the side of the window, and that's when she saw a shadow on the floor. Whoever was there was getting closer and closer. Transfixed, Libby's mouth opened as she saw Einstein chewing on a spider in Mr Bull's lounge. She waved at the cat but he wasn't taking any notice.

She moved away and quietly unlocked the main door wondering if she should knock and ask for her cat, but then he'd know she'd been snooping through his window. No, she'd knock and ask if he'd seen her cat.

She knocked, gently at first but louder after, but there was no answer. He had to be in, he'd left all his lights on. He was either not answering or he'd just nipped out, but why was Einstein in his flat? She crept up the stairs, not wanting to wake anyone else, then she dashed into her flat before exhaling with relief and holding a hand to her thumping heart.

THIRTEEN

RICARDO

Wednesday, 2 March

Ricardo buckled up as he saw the seat belt sign flash above him. An announcement was made and the cabin lights were dimmed.

The plane began its descent and his ears popped. On the ground below, he marvelled at the rows of orange street lamps. The dense city roads were like light snakes weaving amongst each other. 'We are about to land at Birmingham International Airport, we trust you've had a pleasant journey and hope to see you all again soon. The time is eight fifteen this evening.'

Following the rest of the passengers, Ricardo showed his passport to the officer and he then continued forward to the luggage carousel. He tapped his foot and waited patiently as the carousel cranked up. Bags trundled on the conveyor belt through the flap and the other passengers fought their way to the front, all wanting to be first. With no apology, a red-faced bald man stepped on Ricardo's foot to get in front of him. He could never understand why Bettina had chosen to come here and leave behind their beautiful Naples estate that he and his ancestors had worked so hard to keep. To live here and work for next to nothing in a bar when she had it all made for her. Was it his overprotectiveness that had driven her away or was it him not trying hard enough to protect her that made him lose her? He was now in Birmingham, England, to answer that question. It was a question that had been plaguing him for a while. He had to find his daughter and bring her home. She didn't even know her mother had died.

A red case flashed past his eyes – he'd missed his luggage. Running towards the back of the crowd, he raced the carousel to the end to get his luggage before it went back through the flap. He pushed his way to the front and crashed between a couple, grabbed his case and stepped back. 'I'm really sorry,' he said in his rich Italian accent. He gave a friendly nod as he pulled his case out of their way. After breezing through the *Nothing To Declare* walkway, he left the airport and stepped straight into a taxi. 'The Cropton Hotel.'

As he buckled up, he laid out his plan in his head. Tonight he would get his bearings. Tomorrow, he would visit Canal House, the last address he had for Bettina. He needed to find his daughter and tell her how much he loved her. She'd been gone too long. He fought back the palpitations in his chest as he wondered if she'd ever forgive him. He thought of Maria. Had he told her what he'd said she would never have forgiven him. He wondered if she was looking down on him now with hatred in her heart.

FOURTEEN

LIBBY

Thursday, 3 March

'Olly, I've been avoiding him since I kissed him like some pissed up lush. I'm so embarrassed.' Libby knew she shouldn't have told Olly about bumping into Gary at the club, it was more trouble than it was worth and she had excluded the bits where he snatched her phone and tried to take her back to his.

'Don't change the subject on me, Lib. Forget Tim, we were talking about Gary. I'm telling you, don't let him change your mind. I don't want to go back to the times when you visit and all he does is call and accuse me of covering for you. I can't believe he had the nerve to make out you were having the affair and he had the whole second life going on. I mean, that woman thought they were getting married and he was going to leave you. That's not even a fling or a one-night stand.'

Libby bit her nails, sick of the lecture. Olly might be her older sister but sometimes she came across like a lecturing mother and this was one of those moments. 'Ah, Olly. I can hear the bin lorry and I have a smelly bag in the kitchen. Got to go, see you later. Love you.' She placed the phone back in its cradle before Olly could say another word. There was no bin lorry coming but she did have to take a bag down. It was only a half lie.

She tied the bag and crept down the stairs hoping that Tim wouldn't hear her. Not once had he bothered her but it felt awkward. Halfway down, the buzzer made her jump. As she stepped out into the chilly morning she spotted a man sitting on the dwarf wall. She could see that the top of his head was generously covered in grey-flecked hair. His head was hunched over into his hands. Underneath his leg, there was a small, unwrapped bunch of daisies. Curious, she walked closer to the man. He didn't seem like the usual type that hung around these streets. The usual types were smoking teenagers and people needing a rest on their way back from the many pubs. He seemed out of place. 'Excuse me. Did you just ring?'

The man lifted his head and turned to Libby. 'Yes, do you live in this building?'

She could see the sadness in his red-rimmed eyes. He held his glasses in his hand. As he rubbed his temples, he placed his glasses back on. She wondered if he was Spanish or maybe Italian with an accent like that.

'Yes, who are you looking for?'

'My daughter, Bettina.' He stood and was a little taller than Libby. His starch-pressed pale-green shirt with perfectly fitting jeans and leather shoes were smart in a classic way. The large brown leather coat hung down, undone. He straightened up the leather satchel that crossed his chest.

'There's no one living here by that name. Are you from around here?'

'No, I've come all the way from Naples in Italy and I need to find Bettina.'

The man unbuckled the straps of his satchel and pulled out

a photograph of a young woman. 'That's my daughter, Bettina. The young girl standing at the front.'

Libby took the photograph from the man and gazed at it. The older man was clearly the man in front of her. There were three more people in the photo: a stout, pretty woman of about his age, a younger man and the woman. Bettina was about Libby's build. She had almond-shaped brown eyes and beautiful olive skin. Her dark-brown hair cascaded over her shoulders, layers reaching as far as her elbows. The girl wore a pair of khaki shorts, a lightly printed blouse and brown leather sandals.

'What a lovely family photo. I hope you find her soon. She must have moved.'

'The last address I have for her is this one. I'm so sorry I haven't introduced myself. Ricardo Falco. Please call me Ricardo.'

'Wait, I recognise the name now. I'm Libby and I've lived here since January. I never met your daughter but I do recall returning some letters with her name on. She must have moved out before I got here.'

'I sent those letters.'

He looked deep in thought before speaking again. 'I haven't heard from her for a year. We had a bit of a disagreement, we were always having disagreements.'

He picked the daisies up and placed them on the damp wall. Libby began to shiver in the cold. There was a bitter chill in the air that had made her fingers and nose go numb, that chill was ebbing ever closer to her core. She checked her watch, it was only eight fifteen. She didn't have to be in work until lunchtime that day so she had a bit of time to listen to a man who was looking for his daughter and if she could help, she would.

'Can I offer you a coffee? It's a bit warmer inside. We can talk in there.' Libby's teeth were beginning to chatter.

'Thank you. That's very kind of you. I don't want to... what is the word? Impose?' He furrowed his brows.

'You're not imposing. Please, come in out of the cold.' Libby led him upstairs to her flat.

'Take a seat. I'll just make a drink.'

The man went through to the lounge before sitting on the sofa. Moments later Libby came in with a tray containing two coffees, milk and sugar and placed it in front of Ricardo. Ricardo took his coffee black. She kneeled on a floor cushion on the opposite side of the coffee table. She wasn't sure if she'd done the right thing by inviting a stranger into her home but there was a warmth about the man. Then again, there had been a warmth about Gary when she first met him.

'You were saying that you haven't heard from your daughter since last year?'

'No. I had planned to just wait. I hoped that it wouldn't be long before she came home. But Bettina wanted to travel. She had spent several months in Paris, a few more in Madrid. She was meant to be coming back to Milan last September to take up a university place. But she didn't start. I know she had been dating a man here, I assumed she'd taken up with him. I tried to call her a few times but her phone rang out. She was angry when we last spoke, angrier than I have ever known her to be. I was quite rude, telling her to grow up, things like that. She said to me that she never wanted to speak to me again but I need to find her now. Things have changed.'

'I'm so sorry. That's terrible.' She saw in Ricardo what she would like to have seen in her own father. From what he was saying, he'd had his differences with his daughter, but this was a man whose heart was now breaking. Libby felt tears welling up in her eyes; she looked away and willed them to go. She wiped away the wetness with her sleeve and smiled at the man. Silly, she knew, but any time she came across parental love, it set her off.

'I have tried you know. I should have done more, calling wasn't enough. I've failed her. I should have been doing this a year ago. I let her go.' He lifted his glasses up to wipe the tears from his eyes. Libby moved to the other end of the sofa and she placed a box of tissues between them.

'Look, I'm sure you had your reasons not to come. I've had non-stop troubles with family of my own so I'm not about to judge you.'

'You don't understand. I would have come here last year. But after our argument, my wife was diagnosed with terminal cancer and before she passed away I promised her that I would find Bettina, and this flat was her last home.' He looked up with teary eyes that had disappeared and had been replaced by a look of determination.

Libby shivered at the thought. Who would disappear like that and not give a forwarding address to a family that loved them? 'Yes, I'm really sorry for you and your family's loss.' Libby leaned back into the sofa and hugged one of her cushions hoping that it would provide some comfort, but the chill in the air was spreading despite the heating being on. 'What was Bettina like? Maybe that will give us some clue as to where she is now.'

'She was a clever and creative girl. She had a place to study fashion in Milan. We were all so proud of her.' Ricardo smiled as he swigged his coffee. 'She's passionate and knows her own mind. I wish I'd appreciated that more than I did. She told her mama and me that she was deferring her place in Milan to travel for a couple of years. I begged her not to go, I know the dangers all too well but she has always been stubborn. She said she was going and she went.'

'So she eventually ended up here in Birmingham?'

'Yes. I wanted her to come home. I constantly asked her every time she called but she refused. I had everything for her. I'd hoped she'd study fashion and then come to work with me.'

He paused. 'There was a boy, maybe a friend or a boyfriend. I don't know his name but I need to find him. Has anyone been here, asking for her?'

'No, sorry. Where did she work last? It's probably worth asking the people she worked with if they know anything about where she's moved to or the boyfriend.' Libby inhaled sharply. Maybe Bettina had left because of the boyfriend, just like she had left Gary.

'A pub called the Sun's Rays. She said she could walk to it from where she lived.'

'I know it. It's not far from here.'

'I can't believe she used to live right here, in this flat. She must have looked out of that window, ate breakfast at that table.' He gazed across the room, his expression haunted by Bettina's ghost.

'I'm sorry. It must be hard for you being in here.' Libby felt the weight of the air change as she imagined Bettina sitting on her couch, sleeping in her bedroom. Where had she gone?

'On the contrary, it is comforting. It's a start to me finding her. I knew she was no longer here because you returned all the letters, but I thought people would know her and be able to tell me where she went after.' He finished his coffee.

'I'm sorry I don't know any more.'

Ricardo stood. 'It's my fault. I shouldn't have left it so long to come here. Something has happened. I think I need to talk to everyone else in this building and visit the Sun's Rays. Someone must know where she is.'

'If you need any help while you're here you know where I am.' She walked Ricardo to the door.

'Thank you. You know something, she was around the same age as you and there's something in you that reminds me of her.' He furrowed his brows. 'It's her smile. Bettina always lit up a room with her smile. Thank you again.' Ricardo handed the daisies to Libby. 'They were for Bettina. She used to love these flowers as a child. Thank you for your kindness. I am a stranger yet you help me.'

The man headed to Tim's door and knocked. There was no answer. 'I'll have to come back later.' Libby waved him out after he tried knocking on the other doors but everyone was out.

With half an hour to spare before she had to get ready to leave, Libby put on her trainers. She hadn't jogged for a while. Keeping fit was something she used to do with Gary and it was one of the things she'd missed.

She called Einstein from the window but once again, he didn't come. It had been two nights since she saw him last. He'd done this before a couple of times and she found that he'd been going in through a neighbour's cat flap and eating their cat's food. She already knew that he'd sneaked into Mr Bull's place.

Before leaving, she glanced out of the window one more time. The sound of shuffling below sent her hearing on high alert. She shivered as she imagined someone splayed flat against Mr Bull's wall below, just out of sight. 'Einstein.' There was a bang of the gate and whoever was in the garden had fled. They were running down the alley alongside the house. She rushed to the living room and stared onto the main road. Whoever was there had left. She hurried back into the bedroom and made sure the window was securely closed.

FIFTEEN

LIBBY

Friday, 4 March

It had been a long week and a much-needed soak in the bath had been most welcome. Actively placing Trevor back on their books yesterday had almost made her heave. The very thought of that man coming into her office after all that he'd done was unthinkable. She watched as the water gurgled into the plughole.

As she stepped out of the bath her phone began vibrating across the toilet seat. 'Hello.' She wedged the phone between her damp ear and shoulder as she grabbed a towel and wrapped it around her body. There was no reply. Whoever called her had hung up. She checked her call register, the number was withheld.

It rang again. Libby stared at the phone and answered again. 'Hello.' Once again no one spoke. The call however remained open. She couldn't hear anyone on the other side but the timer on the call was still going. She listened carefully, not knowing whether someone had accidentally called and not known. 'Hello,' she shouted. Again no answer. There was a rustling sound, then the phone call went dead. She lifted the bathroom blind up and peered out. There wasn't a soul in sight. Once again the phone rang but this time the number came up on the caller display. It was Gary. She grabbed the phone. 'What?'

'About that night at the club. I just wanted to say I'm sorry. I shouldn't have chased after you. I was wondering if you fancied dinner next Friday so we can talk properly.'

'No, I don't fancy dinner. I want you to leave me alone and stop calling.' She didn't want to go anywhere near him so that he could threaten her again. 'Were you at my place yesterday, spying on me?'

'What. You're being paranoid. No.'

Maybe she was being paranoid. It could have easily been some loser trying to find a shed to rob. She couldn't picture Gary hiding in a garden to stalk her but then again, he had made her life a living hell. He must have followed her to that club. He was capable of more than she could imagine. She knew nothing about the man she once lived with.

'Libby, we have things to sort out like our joint savings account. I need your signature to close it then you can have your share. I also need your name off the utility bills so I need to give you a list with the account numbers so that you can call them all up. I'm being practical here. I know you hate me but we need to get this sorted if we're to move on.'

She thought of the savings account. It had three thousand pounds in it and half of that was hers and she needed it. 'I suppose.'

He paused and she heard him licking his lips. 'I hate that you're scared of me. I swear to you. I'll bring the bank stuff and the account numbers. We can discuss it over coffee, in a public place if that's better for you. On neutral ground. Anywhere you like.' She didn't know if she could trust him. He'd given her no reason to. 'What the hell do you think I'll do in a coffee shop? I would never hurt you.'

He already had but she didn't want to go over all that again. The less said at this point the better. She didn't want to antagonise him. All she wanted was to get her share of the money in the account and to never speak to the man again.

'Okay. Coffee, forms and that's it.'

'I'll text you later when I'm looking at my shift schedule. We can decide where and when to meet.'

She exhaled and ran her hand through one side of her damp hair. Maybe one last meet up would be a good thing, especially if it was to finalise the relationship. That didn't stop the jittery feeling she had about it all. 'Okay. By the way, did you try calling me earlier on a different number?'

'No, this is the first time I've tried all day.'

'Are you sure. It was from an anonymous number.'

'I don't have another number.'

'Okay.' She ended the call, not quite believing him. Abrupt maybe, but she didn't want to give Gary the wrong idea. She shivered at the thought of the silent call. As she wrapped her hair up in a towel she scurried out of the bathroom to the front door and tested it to see if it was locked. Gary would know that calls like that would unnerve her. Maybe he thought he could make her that scared, she'd go running back to him. She looked at her bedside clock, it was ten to eight. Kirsty and Micky would be knocking soon and she didn't want to be standing there wearing a towel. Grabbing her baggy jeans and a jumper, she quickly dressed.

There was a knock at the door. They were early. She scooped her wet hair up into a clip. It was only drinks with the neighbours in her flat, she didn't see the need to dress up or care what she looked like.

As she opened the door, Tim was standing there holding a

box. 'I bought too many cakes earlier and they're cream. I wondered if you wanted some of them. They'll only go in the bin otherwise.'

'Thanks, Tim. How are you doing?' He was being kind after she'd ignored him for ages. It was time to confront the wall she'd put up. She took the box.

'I'm good, thank you.'

'Look, Tim. I am so sorry about that night, what I did after dinner.'

'Libby, it was a drunken kiss. You don't have to apologise. I liked it, a lot, but I respect that you've just come out of a relationship.' He smiled. 'You don't have to avoid me.'

'I wasn't—'

'It was a fun night. Anyway, I have so much work to do.' He turned to walk away.

'Tim?'

'Yes.' He glanced back.

'I thought I should say something. I think I heard someone loitering in the garden yesterday.'

'Right, thanks for letting me know. I must have left the gate open. I'll make sure it's locked in future. I've had the shed broken into a couple of times. Probably just some opportunist thief seeing if it was open.'

'Oh, and also a man came by the house looking for his daughter who was a previous tenant. Bettina Falco. She used to live in my flat. Do you have a forwarding address?'

'I don't. She left in the middle of her tenancy without paying all her bills.'

'She never said anything to anyone?'

He shrugged. 'Not that I know of. It wouldn't be the first or the last time a tenant has left like that.'

She smiled and closed the door before pouring a vodka and Coke. Einstein still hadn't returned and she was getting worried. She hurried to the bedroom and opened the window a little. It was strange that he hadn't meowed to come in. Maybe leaving the window open would encourage him. There was another knock. This time it would be Kirsty and Micky.

As she ran to the door, she couldn't help feeling unnerved. People don't just up and leave without giving a forwarding address unless they are in trouble. What kind of trouble was Bettina in?

SIXTEEN

LIBBY

Two empty bottles of wine sat on the coffee table and Libby topped her third vodka and Coke up with just Coke this time. As hard as she tried, she couldn't get Bettina out of her head.

Michaela had relayed several funny stories of her past, telling them about a disaster holiday romance. The conversation now turned to Libby. 'Did we see you go out with Tim the other week?' Kirsty wiped the lipstick off her front tooth.

'I might have done. It was just dinner.'

'Is there something going on we should know about? Only I said to Micky that it was the day after Valentine's night.'

'Precisely, the day after. He wanted to try this place and I did but neither of us wanted to go alone, so we went together.'

'He's a bit of alright. Did you sleep with him?'

Libby threw a cushion at Kirsty. 'No, I did something so stupid though.'

'You can't stop there,' Micky said as she put her red hair back into a ponytail.

'Well, it was a bit embarrassing. I was a bit drunk and I kissed him. What an idiot. I told him it was a mistake. I've spent days avoiding him but tonight he finally knocked and I apologised again. I feel so stupid.'

'Libby, you care too much. Are you going to get the cream cakes out?'

She hurried to the kitchen and brought the box over. They all picked one out. 'Here, tuck in. I haven't told you the rest.'

'There's more?' Kirsty took a bite of an éclair.

'I've agreed to go for a coffee with my ex, Gary, next week. We have some things to sort out. Finances, that sort of thing.'

'Wow, are you sure about that? Didn't you say he keeps sending horrible messages?' Micky leaned forward on the couch.

'Yes, but they've stopped. I think he's finally accepted that we're over.'

'If he starts on you, anything like that, just remember you can walk out at any time. Don't stand for any nonsense. If a man had sent me messages like that, I'd never want to see him again.' Kirsty dropped her usual smile. It was lovely that the two women below cared so much. She'd well and truly found some friends there. 'If you feel threatened in any way, call one of us. Have us on speed dial.'

'Why did you leave him in the first place?' Michaela asked.

'He cheated on me.' Libby put her cake down on the table and looked into her glass.

'Well he deserved to lose you, hun.' Kirsty shook her head.

'He works in a hotel and he cheated on me with the receptionist. He then spent months lying to me. You know when deep down you know, and they know you know, but you just can't get them to tell the truth? Anyway, I found all the evidence I needed so I left him while he was at work one night. It was the morning I moved in here.' Libby sat silently in thought. 'He promised her everything. Something doesn't ring true either. At first I thought it was a fling but the more I dug, the more I found out. I got hold of his bank statements.

He had a whole new life on the go. I saw a payment marked rent. He had a shag pad. I mean, who does that to another person?'

'A complete arsehole,' Michaela said as she opened another bottle of wine. What started off as a fun girly evening was now hanging in awkward suspension. Michaela stopped and stared at Libby as if weighing her up. 'Was he always so horrible, like with the way he messages you?'

Libby bit her bottom lip. People were seeing through her. Leaving him in the middle of the night was the act of a woman scared and they knew it. 'Yes, he has a temper.'

'Did he...?' Michaela couldn't seem to bring herself to finish the sentence but Libby knew what she was asking.

She nodded and took a deep breath. The atmosphere was falling as flat as the wine that had been fizzy on opening the bottle. 'I really don't want to talk about it. Do you mind?'

'Sorry. I should learn to mind my own business. Just know that we're here for you. If he comes around, call one of us. We're only downstairs.'

'Thanks.' Trying to steer the conversation away from her problems, Libby brought up the subject of Ricardo. 'I saw a man sitting on our wall outside yesterday. He was really upset so I invited him in.'

'You picked up a stray.' Kirsty laughed.

'No.' Libby playfully tapped Kirsty's arm. 'He said his daughter Bettina used to live here a year ago. She's disappeared and he's looking for her, he's travelled all the way from Italy.'

'Oh, we know,' Kirsty replied. 'He knocked on our door earlier. Neither of us has met her. Your flat was empty when we moved in. She must have moved out before then.'

'I hope she's alright.' Michaela topped up her wine. 'Or maybe she had a better offer. These flats are miniscule. We could do with something bigger.'

'But, she didn't tell her dad she was moving.'

'Yeah, that's strange.' Michaela bit the edge of her thumbnail.

'When did you two move in?'

'Last September. Kirsty moved in with me in October. We decided to share to keep our rent costs low. We're saving so that we can travel around South America next year.'

'Now that sounds interesting.' Hearing about their travel plans would definitely lighten the night up.

'Hang on, rewind. What more do we know about the missing girl?' Michaela asked.

'Well, I don't know. He said she left without a word and that she used to work at the Sun's Rays pub.'

'Well I hope he finds her, that's really sad.' Kirsty stared into her wine glass.

'Yes, me too. He seemed distraught and he'd just lost his wife. Bettina doesn't even know that her mother has died. Anyway, hopefully he's caught up with her.'

'If he hasn't, I wonder if Mr Bull knows anything, he's been here ages. He would at least know of her.' Kirsty scrunched her nose.

'You may be right but saying that, what does he know about us? Nothing, because he can't even be bothered to get to know anyone here. Anyway, I'll probably never see the man again.'

'Talking about the bull man. Did you hear the banging coming from his flat a short while ago? It sounded like he was trashing the place. Something must have upset him.' Michaela leaned in over the coffee table.

'I did hear a few bangs. They made me jump.' Libby realised that her eyes were getting heavy. 'I'm so sorry, I've had a really long day and I've been on call this week. I occasionally get angry people calling me in the night when their staff don't turn up for the early shifts. The joys of the job.' She yawned and stretched before throwing what was left of her cake back into the box. The cream wasn't sitting well with the alcohol.

'That's okay. I'm getting tired as well. Kirsty, I forgot to tell you, your mother called earlier and asked you to call her back.'

'Thanks for telling me now. She'll be worried sick. My mum does worry. Anyone would think I've left the country,' she said. No one laughed. 'Wales. You don't get it, do you? Anyway you're right. Let's get going so I can call her back before she goes to bed.' Kirsty laughed as she stood.

The two women left their empty glasses on the table and said their good nights. Libby forced herself to stand and see her guests to the door. Every bone in her body felt heavy, a combination of tiredness and the lactic acid build up in her muscles from her run the other morning.

She ambled back into the living room and began placing the empty bottles in the kitchen doorway, then she noticed a chunk of cake under the coffee table. Bending down to retrieve it, her hand brushed on something powdery. She shifted the table along the rug and saw a few specs of powder, like a small pile had been brushed over. She picked a bit up between her fingers and rubbed it. How had it got there? The place had been deep cleaned before she moved in.

She wondered if Kirsty or Micky had brought something in on their shoes. She pulled the table back over it. Forcing her stiff body to walk to the bedroom, she undressed and slipped into bed knowing she would sleep. She nodded off as she watched the curtains billowing in the wind. Shivering, she pulled her heavy duvet over her shoulders and sunk into its warmth.

She woke, startled by the floorboards creaking in her room. Sitting up, she couldn't see anything. The moon's light beams faintly lit up one side of the room by her wardrobe. Her heartbeat quickened. The floor creaked once more and it was followed by a heavy thud on her bed and a loud meow. Einstein had come home. 'Hello, stranger. You scared me to death,' she said as her heart rate began to return to normal. She beckoned the cat over, snuggled him under her arm and laid her head on the pillow. There was a weird smell. Musty or maybe slightly rotten, like bin. Running her fingers through his fur, she felt the same gritty texture in the powder under the table. She couldn't for the life of her work out what Einstein had done. It had to be him. He must have sneaked in at some point when the window was open and brought the dust in.

She turned over, unable to deal with the stink coming from him any longer. As she closed her eyes again, all she could see was the young woman in Ricardo's photo. Lying on her back, she stared at the ceiling and wondered how many nights Bettina had stared at the same spot. Had she been scared and wondering what her next move should be? Maybe she'd lain awake, like Libby had at Gary's, trying to fathom out her next move. Kirsty was right, the only other person here that lived in the house at the same time as Bettina was Mr Bull. Maybe he saw and heard things; interactions between Bettina and her boyfriend; shouting; debt collectors; anything. He had to have heard something and if Bettina hadn't been found, Libby knew she had to catch him in and ask him.

SEVENTEEN

LIBBY

Friday, 11 March

Arriving back at Canal House, Libby looked up at Gary. She didn't want him to walk her home after their coffee but he'd proven to be hard to get rid of. The money in their account was much needed and she didn't want to risk him dragging his feet.

For the first time since the rush of love when they'd met, he'd been charming, and complimentary but she knew he was wearing a mask. Even though she knew he was manipulating her, there just wasn't much she could do about it. That money was a game changer and he knew he was in a prominent position when it came to the game they were playing.

'You don't look so well, Lib.' They passed the chip shop and she wished he'd just go away. He went to place his arm around her shoulder.

'Stop.' She threw it off and walked a few paces ahead. This time she had her flat boots on. If she needed to run, she could.

'Gary, let's not pretend that you care about anyone but yourself.'

His stare intensified as they stood under the light of a lamp. 'I can't believe you sometimes. I've made an effort all night and this is what I'm faced with. What does a man have to do?'

'I don't know.' She shrugged. 'Maybe not have a relationship with a colleague and set up a shag pad. Maybe not promise her the world when really, you were playing us both. You made her hate me too. What did you say to her that caused her to call me all those names in the texts?'

He smugly laughed and ran his fingers through his hair. 'I guess you got me out just for the money and I thought we'd talk about us and how we can move forward.'

'Gary, look at me. The infidelity, that was bad, but you hit me.' She stared straight into his eyes, adamant that he wasn't going to see how scared she was. 'There is no us any more. The only reason we set tonight up was to sort out the money and the bills. Half of that money is mine, of course I want it.' It was no good. She turned to walk away but he caught up with her.

'I'm sorry. You're right.' As they reached Canal House he ran around and stepped in front of her, preventing her passage into the house. 'I do want more and yes, I used the money to meet you. She meant nothing, Libby, and I know I hurt you. I promised you I would get help for my anger. I want to change but I can only do it with you in my life. You're the woman I want to marry and to have children with.'

She shook her head. 'Why did you do it? All of it? I didn't deserve to be cheated on, then made to feel like I'm going crazy and to be attacked.'

'I... err.' He leaned against the door frame. 'You're not blameless. The amount of hours you were putting in at work and with my shifts, I felt like we weren't connecting, then when you had a spare weekend, you'd go off and see your sister and we all know the stupid bitch doesn't like me so I couldn't come.

I got angry, I thought you were trying to punish me by not answering your phone.'

'Punish you. When you call me every half an hour, of course I'm going to stop answering. It was all too much. You are too much and how dare you call my sister that name. She's been there for me all my life and she was there for me when you put me down, when you cheated, when you spoke to me like shit. She picked up the pieces. No wonder she doesn't like you and I haven't even told her about the other things. If a person loves you, they don't hurt you. You don't know how to love.'

He shook his head and stared at his feet. 'The problem is, you don't love yourself. This isn't about me. You're insane, the way you cut yourself, the way you sob in the night. It's embarrassing, Lib. All I wanted to do was to help you and you pushed me away. It got frustrating and I lashed out. I thought some tough love might help you.'

'Tough love, that's what you call it. Have some of your own tough love back.' She brought her hand back and slapped him across the face. The shock on her face was as apparent as the shock on his. She'd never slapped anyone in her life. 'Get out of my way.' With trembling hands she nudged him and he obliged.

'Well, I never knew you had it in you and everyone thinks I was the problem in our relationship. Look at you. You're a bag of bones and a mess. Run away, go cry like a baby and cut yourself.' She ran and he followed.

Tears slid down her cheeks. All she wanted was for him to go and leave her alone. She glanced through the windows wondering if Michaela or Kirsty would come to her assistance if she knocked on their door, but there wasn't even a flicker of light behind their curtains. She looked over to Mr Bull's window and saw that his flat was in darkness too. Tim didn't appear to be in either. It was her and Gary and she now saw joy spread across his face. She grabbed her phone but he nudged it back into her bag.

'What you going to do, Libby? It's just me and you.' He leaned in and wiped the trailing tears from her cheek.

'Please, Gary. Go back to her.'

She exhaled as he held his hands up and moved aside. Leaning against Mr Bull's window, he nodded. 'If that's what you think. You've got it all wrong. You don't know who I really am and what I'm capable of and you don't want to find out.'

Coffee had been a mistake. The messages and texts were one thing but right now with him in front of her, it felt like things had shifted to a whole new level. She was never going to see her money and right now, to make him go, she'd give it up and let him have it despite how much it would help her. With her key outstretched, she took her chance and slotted it into the door. Just as she turned it, he gripped her hand so hard she thought he might break her fingers. The warmth of his breath made her neck tingle with fear as she held her breath. 'Let go of me,' she whimpered.

With that, he unravelled his hand and stepped back towards the wall. Wasting no time, Libby ran into the hall and slammed the door behind her before running upstairs and letting herself in. She threw her keys onto the settee and hurried in the dark to the window where she stared out, hoping to see Gary leave. There was no sign of him anywhere.

The old wooden window juddered as she opened it. Leaning out, she couldn't see him anywhere. He must have gone as soon as she closed the door on him. She held her breath as she listened out for him. Maybe he was lurking in the alley or heading around the back of the building.

She'd left the bedroom window open.

She started to run but screamed out as she bashed her shin on the corner of the coffee table. Hobbling to the bedroom, she shivered as an icy breeze filled the bedroom. The curtains flapped and the window squeaked on its hinges as it slammed back and forth. She leaned out and listened once again for Gary but she couldn't hear a thing. 'Einstein,' she called but he didn't respond. She slammed the window shut and closed the curtains.

Her phone beeped. Grabbing it from her pocket, she was relieved that it was a message from Olly.

See you tomorrow, sis. Can't wait. X

She swallowed. There was no way she'd mention that she'd gone out with Gary. The last thing she needed was a lecture. She thought she knew what she was doing, but he'd scared her. That would never happen again. Maybe she'd only tell Olly that they'd spoken.

Inhaling, she held her hand over her mouth and nose as a putrid smell caught her nostrils. Following it, she turned on the kitchen light and the first thing that hit her was the upturned bin. It had to be Einstein. He'd come back and trashed the place. Half-eaten sandwiches mingled with brown lettuce and eggshells littered the floor. Then she noticed that he'd been sick. The gnarled innards of a mouse lay there, turning her stomach. 'Einstein.' He didn't come. There was something going on with him but she couldn't put her finger on it. She knew he was being fed by someone else but he'd also turned cold on her, like he was no longer her cat and now he'd gone again.

As she went to grab the kitchen roll, a loud crashing noise came from the flat below, filling the room as objects struck the wall. She'd seen her cat in the flat below. Did Einstein prefer Mr Bull to here even though he was so angry?

She began to cry. Everything that Gary had said flooded through her. Was she insane? She felt insane. With racing thoughts, the dark cloud was flowing ever closer. Once again, she'd screwed up. She tried to handle herself, stay assertive but when it came to it, Gary could see that she was still scared little Libby. Sobbing loudly, she let all her feelings come out. The pent-up sadness flowed down her cheeks and landed in her lap. How had she become so screwed up and what the hell was it with that cat? Everything in her life was a mess.

Sitting on the kitchen floor staring at a soggy half a cucumber, she wondered how her life had come to this. She reached up and slid open the drawer. The first thing she laid her hand upon was the corkscrew.

Pressing the tip into the top of her arm, she watched as a tiny globe of blood appeared. She pressed harder as the tears fell and the incision began to bleed. It was a small cut, she could blame the cat if anyone saw it. Angry with herself, she cried harder. Blame the cat, who was she kidding? Gary was right. She was insane. Pressing hard on the cut, she held her arm above her head. It was time to stop this juvenile nonsense. No one saw, no one cared and no one felt sorry for her. She grabbed a tissue, wiped her eyes, compressed the cut and waited until the bleeding stopped.

A roar that sounded like it was coming from the underbelly of the house filled the room. Indistinct in all ways, the animalistic noise was followed by banging and slamming. She laid her head on the floor and listened for more, maybe the sound of his voice but that was all that he was giving her for now. Maybe he was in as much pain as she was but instead of cutting himself, he destroyed things.

Maybe they were both insane. Two people living two different painful lives, separated only by a few inches. She placed her palm on the floor wondering if he could feel her presence.

EIGHTEEN

LIBBY

Saturday, 12 March

After cleaning her wound, Libby laced up her trainers. She stuck a small plaster over the tiny cut on her arm hoping that it would mask the memories of her mood the evening before. Placing her leg on the worktop, she stretched those muscles out. Gary had always made her do a warm-up. Gary, her mind had wandered back to Gary again. All she wanted was for him to go away. She slammed her hand on the worktop. Angry that she'd allowed him into her head again.

All she needed right now was a run to get Gary out of her mind. The sun shone but the air was chilly, perfect for her run. The best thing she could do was clear her head ready for when Olly arrived. She wanted to feel the force of nature providing resistance for her to break through. She walked to the bathroom and instinctively placed her hand into her clutter basket, reaching for her hair clip, it wasn't there. Reaching the back of the shelf, she pulled down the basket and pushed around all the bits and pieces. Necklaces, tweezers, a wrapped up bar of soap, but no clip. Annoyed, she grabbed an old bobble and pulled her hair up. Where had she put the clip? She gazed around the flat one last time and she couldn't see the clip anywhere. She'd lost it, but how? With furrowed brows, she stared and pursed her lips.

Without wasting another moment, she grabbed her water bottle and locked the door. It would turn up.

As she walked down the stairs, she heard Michaela shouting at Kirsty. Funny, she could never imagine them having an argument. They seemed happy as flatmates when they spoke of their travel plans and they seemed to know each other well. Not being able to quite hear what was being said, she placed her ear against the wall. 'I wish you wouldn't touch my stuff, you lose everything,' shouted Michaela.

'I was only doing the washing. If you didn't leave your pants on the floor, I wouldn't need to pick them up. Sometimes I think I live with a pig.' Kirsty's loud voice travelled through the door.

'I know I live with one. First you touch my stuff and somehow lose it and I know you eat all my food when I'm out.'

'I didn't think you minded sharing, only that's what happens when you use all my perfume, Micky.'

'I don't use your perfume.'

'Oh and I put your stupid knickers in the washing machine with my stuff. I then hung all the stuff on the clothes horse to dry and went out. It's not my fault you've moved them and forgot where you put them and don't bloody worry, I won't touch your dirty clothes in future.'

The lounge door slammed. Libby heard a tap on the door then she heard Kirsty crying. She'd never heard Kirsty get upset and she'd never heard Michaela shout. It sounded like they were as bad at misplacing things as she was.

Libby crept down the last few steps and opened the main door.

She felt the chilly breeze on her face and began jogging. She ran past the canal bridge, down the steps and along the towpath. She passed people on barges cooking breakfast and others on foot walking their dogs. She soon approached the canal-side restaurants where people were sitting in the window seats drinking coffee, reading papers and talking. The barge café was open too. A woman with a little boy waited outside the hatch and an ice cream was passed through the window. Libby thought it wasn't really ice cream weather, but the boy didn't seem to care. She passed the barge and ran up the steps and over the bridge. Pounding the pavements, she carried on past the Art Museum, then she passed 'The Floozy in the Jacuzzi' statue. Realising that she'd jogged in front of a tourist holding up a camera, she held her hand up in apology.

The argument she'd had with Gary kept running through her mind. Throughout the night, she'd checked her phone expecting a tirade of texts but none came. He was up to something. After the way their end-of-relationship meeting had gone, she knew that wouldn't be the end of it. Probing further into her thoughts, she turned to her own faults. In a way she could see it from his perspective. She'd worked hard, been on call a lot, been tired and turned down most of his advances for both love and sex. She realised that he'd probably felt unwanted, even unloved. Pounding the streets harder, she thought of Olly. Her sister would tell her never to make excuses for him. Always the stronger one, Olly had guided her through all of her boy troubles in her teens but Libby had 'never really learned properly,' Olly would say. She was too soft, too forgiving and too bloody sentimental, that was another of Olly's favourite words she always used in a derogatory context – sentimental. She loved her sister immensely but she wished she'd go a little easier on her sometimes, but she claimed to always have Libby's best interests at heart and didn't want her to get hurt. Anyway, tonight she would have to decide whether she would tell Olly what had happened.

Libby ran past the Tesco store where Micky worked and turned off down a side street. Realising she was close to the Sun's Rays, she then thought of Bettina.

Her legs ached heavily. Slowing down her pace, she concentrated on her breathing. She hadn't run that far and fast for ages. She'd jogged with Gary for miles some days in his quest for optimum fitness and she'd enjoyed going, but it was mostly to spend time with him after he complained that they never did anything together.

She reached the pub. Breathing heavily, she stopped and bent over. After getting her breath back she walked over to the window and gazed through. The clock on the wall said ten thirty, which meant it was a bit early for the pub to open. She saw a man setting up the bar area. She'd never been in this pub, she normally opted for the more modern pubs that had emerged in recent years.

The Sun's Rays was an old drinker's pub, painted out in dark greens and reds. Mahogany tongue and groove split the walls in half and the dark upholstered benches and chairs made the snug even darker. An open fireplace with fireside tools to match sat neatly against one wall. The walls were covered in framed pictures of the pub and the shelves were filled with trophies for winning at darts. Behind the bar, she could see another room. The shared central bar split the two rooms up. The man looked up from his work and saw Libby looking through the window. 'We open at eleven,' he mouthed while pointing at his watch. Embarrassed, Libby stepped back from the window and waved as she jogged away.

'Libby.' She heard her name being called from behind. Turning, she saw Ricardo. The man jogged towards her. Libby wiped her brow with her arm and swigged her water. 'I was hoping to catch up with you again.'

She smiled. 'Have you found Bettina?'

'No, I did go back to the flats and to the pub. No more from the others that live in Canal House but someone at the pub said that there is only one person who worked there when my Bettina did. His name is Liam but he's on holiday so I have to come back in a few days. I was told that he and Bettina were close but he wasn't her boyfriend.'

'It's a shame that you have to waste time waiting.' Libby clasped her foot against her buttock and stretched her right thigh.

'I was meaning to come and see you. I think I need some help.'

'I'm not sure what I can do but if I can help in any way, I will.' They walked together, not anywhere in particular, just walking.

'I think she was seeing someone, I am not too sure but she seemed to become withdrawn the last time we spoke. She was argumentative, troubled, and I think a lot of troubles come with love. She was very evasive when I asked her things. I'm not sure if she held back because she knew I wouldn't approve or if there were other reasons.'

'Love can do that to a woman. I've felt troubled and withdrawn more than once in my life over love,' Libby replied with a smile.

'I managed to speak to the landlord after seeing your neighbours, the two women. He said that Bettina was asked to leave because of the noise complaints.'

Tim hadn't mentioned that to Libby when she'd seen him. All he had said was that she'd left mid-tenancy and he didn't know where she'd gone to.

'I wondered if you could try to find out more. Bettina was never noisy at home and she certainly wasn't brought up to disrespect the home of another. Something doesn't seem right. I know my daughter.' He stopped walking and looked at her.

Libby wondered who lived in Kirsty and Michaela's flat before them. 'Of course I will. I'll see what I can find out.'

'She mentioned another man who lived there. Maybe you could ask him.'

'Mr Bull?' Libby asked.

'Yes, that's the one, I couldn't remember his name. I knocked at his door but he didn't answer.'

That didn't surprise Libby. 'I've haven't met him yet. I know he works away a lot and he isn't there often.' The man looked ahead in thought as they walked. She wondered if Mr Bull would be there when she got back home.

'Maybe you could ask the landlord about this Mr Bull if he isn't there. You could ask how he was with Bettina.'

'I can try.' She knew from past conversations about Mr Bull with Tim that he hadn't really given her much information. 'I'll ask Tim about him next time I see him. Can I have your phone number?'

'Here are my details.' He pulled out a business card and a pen from his pocket. On the back he wrote Cropton Hotel, their phone number and his room number, then he passed it to Libby. The card had Italian writing on the front and a little picture of a shoe. 'The one I've underlined on the front is my mobile number and the one on the back is my contact number for the hotel where I am staying.'

'I'll do my best to help you.' Libby truly meant it. As she took the pen off Ricardo, she ripped the edge of the card. In small writing, she wrote her number on it and passed it to him.

'Thank you.' He placed it in his inside pocket and patted it. She could see the loss and pain in his face. Her father would never have come looking for her. She hadn't called her parents for over eighteen months and they hadn't made any effort to contact her either. They were probably still knocking around in Spain, working the bar with their friend and getting drunk all the time. She shook all thoughts of them away.

'Thank you and God bless you.' The man took her hand and kissed it, before turning away and walking back in the direction he came from.

Once again she ran. It was time to head back and prepare for Olly's arrival. Tonight she would attempt to cook a heart-warming meal, which she thought might soften Olly up before telling her all about Gary. She'd decided to tell her sister about what happened and it wasn't going to be easy.

Then there was Mr Bull. Had he been seeing Bettina? She thought of Mr Bull and the frustrations he was displaying. Could he have been her lover? Maybe he'd made the complaints because she rejected him.

NINETEEN

LIBBY

Olly was due any minute. Libby hoped that the vegetarian lasagne she'd prepared would be tasty; she could smell the cheesy aroma oozing out of the oven as she checked it for crispiness. She hid the ready-made béchamel and tomato sauce jars at the bottom of the bin, then tipped a generous heap of pre-packed salad onto the plates.

All day she'd listened out for Tim and Mr Bull, but neither of them had been home. She'd messaged Ricardo to keep him updated. She opened the bedroom window and called Einstein but once again, he didn't come. A pang of sadness flushed through her. She missed how he was before they'd moved. Did he hate her for removing him from the comfort of Gary's flat?

The doorbell rang. Libby dropped the bag of salad, bolted to the door and ran down the stairs.

Olly hugged her and followed her upstairs. 'Yum, smells good in here. I'm literally salivating.'

'I hope you like it. I've made veggie lasagne. Anyway, how have you been?'

'Great, I've been on a course all week, master classes in French style pastries. In fact, I've made you one.' She pulled a twisted pastry out of a bag. Libby inhaled the butter and flaked almonds that tantalised her nostrils.

Libby couldn't resist a bite. 'Wow, it's absolutely delicious. You're going to be disappointed with my lasagne now.'

'Nonsense. It's always nice to be cooked for after you've cooked non-stop all week. Not that I'm complaining of course. I do love my job. No news on the restaurant yet but I should have some soon. I want my own place, sis. One I can call my own. You could come and live there and work with me. I cook, you do front of house.'

Libby chuckled. 'It sounds like a dream. Wouldn't I be taking Scott's job?'

She shrugged her shoulders. 'Who knows?'

'Are you okay, Olly?'

'Maybe, maybe not. I don't want to talk about it. I need to chill out.'

'Of course.' Libby made a zip motion with her fingers. Things were obviously a bit strained between her sister and Scott. Olly would fill her in on it all when she had something to say. 'Here, let me take your coat. Go and have a seat at the table while I dish up.'

Libby threw Olly's biker jacket onto her bed and hurried to the kitchen. A few minutes later, she took the dish out of the oven and evenly split the lasagne on the two plates alongside the salad and carried them into the lounge where they sat at the cramped kitchen table. 'Right, tuck in, then we can chill out.'

'So what's been happening then?' Olly sliced up her lasagne.

'Not a lot. Same workload, busy as usual. Chrissie has been lovely. I told you about her, didn't I?'

'Yeah. She seems nice.' Olly ate a mouthful of salad.

'I've started jogging again.'

'Not with that knob I hope?' Olly stared at Libby.

Libby shook her head. 'No, on my own.' She paused and

wondered whether she should tell Olly about Gary. She decided it was best she did. 'I met Gary for a coffee. We had to discuss a savings account and the bills.'

'You met him in person? You didn't have to see him to sort that out. The man's a snake.' Olly placed her knife and fork down.

'We talked. Nothing else.' She decided that telling Olly about last night would be a bad move.

'I hope you told him what a loser he was. Is he still seeing that woman and how about the property he was renting?'

'I don't know. We didn't talk about any of that. I signed the things I needed to sign and that was it.' Libby pushed her food around the plate.

'I'm worried about you. You're too gullible. I bet he said a load of crap about how he was sorry and what a mistake he's made and I bet you went home and justified his mistake with, oh I wasn't a good girlfriend, and it was all my fault. That's the sort of thing you do. I want you to start sticking up for yourself.'

'I did actually. We argued and I slapped him. I don't know where it came from but I can see through his lies now. I'm not the person I was, Olly,' Libby shouted as she put her knife and fork down. She needed to change the subject. Gary wasn't going to ruin another night for her. 'Anyway, have I told you about my naughty cat?' She wanted to enjoy her sister's company, not spend the whole night being lectured about how she handled Gary.

'No, is he alright?'

Libby filled her in on how Einstein had been since the move to Canal House.

'Whoa, I suppose you've just got to ride the storm with him. It's probably just the move that's turning him into a bad cat. Fancy tipping the bin over? I wonder where he is.' Olly licked a bit of sauce from her bottom lip.

'I hope I haven't driven him away. Someone is looking after him better than me.'

'No one could look after him better than you. You love him like a baby.'

'You're right. Okay, someone is feeding him more tempting food than I am.' She thought about the mouse the cat had brought up. Maybe he was turning more feral. She wasn't going to gross Olly out with that over the dinner table. 'Oh, he stinks too.'

'Stinks. What of?'

'I don't know, damp, mouldy and muddy, I guess. Just horrible. I had to wash him in the sink and he hated it.'

'That's probably why he's hiding from you. Probably thinks he's going in the sink again.'

Libby thought back to her clip. 'And I keep losing things. I swear, I think I'm going mad.'

'I keep telling you, you need to book some holiday and come and stay with me, that's what you need. Are you still getting a load of hassle from that idiot who's always in looking for work?' Olly undid the top button of her jeans.

'Not as much.' Again, she didn't want to open that can of worms over the dinner table. The last thing she needed was to worry Olly and she hadn't seen Trevor for a while. As she collected the plates up there was a knock at the door.

Libby opened the door to Michaela. 'I wasn't expecting you. Come in,' Libby said as she opened the door. Kirsty stomped up the stairs, catching her up.

Michaela passed Libby a bottle of wine. 'We heard Olly's heels tapping up the path so we thought we'd come up and say hi.'

Showing them in, Libby popped the wine on the table. She'd hoped it would just be her and Olly but the more she thought about it the better it was to let them in as they could distract her sister from asking any more about Gary. She wanted to forget him for now. 'Michaela and Kirsty are here.' Libby grabbed the corkscrew and some glasses. The two neighbours joined Olly. She listened as they exchanged pleasantries and opened the wine. The music channel went on and she heard laughter fill the living room. Libby piled up the dirty dishes and joined the others.

After a while, Olly turned the television up and The Prodigy blasted out. Mesmerised by the telly and the warmth of the flat Libby relaxed more and closed her eyes. She was sure she heard a bang above the noise. 'Is there someone at the door?'

'Maybe your spy man neighbour has come to complain.' Olly laughed.

Libby hadn't heard him move about at all that day. She hoped it was him coming to complain as she'd finally get to meet him and she could ask him about Bettina.

Libby hurried to the door. 'Hey, Tim. You okay?'

He smiled and scrunched his nose as if what he had to say was going to be awkward. 'I wondered if you could turn the music down.' He held his phone up. 'Mr B underneath you has messaged me moaning about the noise. Sorry.'

'Yes, I'm really sorry. Olly?' Libby called. 'Can you turn the telly down?' The sound of the music quietened. 'That's better. I'll make sure it stays down. Should I apologise to him?'

Tim read the message. 'He said he's in bed with a bad head, so probably best not to disturb him.'

'I really thought he wasn't in. I wouldn't have turned it up that loud if I'd have known.' She sighed.

'Well, none of us can tell when he's in. I wouldn't know either. Anyway, thanks for turning it down. I'm sure he's grateful. Oh and I've got your tenancy agreement here. You never did sign one, it's just a formality. It was my fault. With all the paperwork I have to do, it slipped my mind.' He shrugged and rolled his eyes. 'I need one for the file. If you have a look at it maybe you can pass it back to me tomorrow or when you get five minutes.'

'Of course I will. Why don't you come in and join us?' Libby opened the door wide to let him in.

'That's really kind of you but I have so much work, you know how it is? Maybe we can have a drink sometime soon or do something?'

'I'd like that,' she replied. She was so over that awkward drunken kiss. He liked her, she could tell.

'Great.' With one hand tucked into his jean pocket and the other dangling down, he smiled as he left.

'Who was that?' Olly asked.

'It was Tim, just popped by to give me a tenancy agreement, which I've never signed, and to tell us to turn the music down because Mr Bull has a headache. Whoops.' Libby grabbed her drink and took a swig.

Michaela smiled. 'Did you tell your sister about your meal with Tim?'

'Briefly. He's okay with me. I said I'd go for a drink with him at some point.'

'You like him.' Kirsty pointed and grinned.

Libby shook her head. 'I don't know what I want at the moment. I have too much on my plate. The more I think about him and about me and what I want, the more I know it's not him. He's attractive but I don't feel as though there's any chemistry. Maybe I'm not in the right place. Actually, there are no maybes about it. I'm not in the right place.'

Olly placed her hand over Libby's. 'I agree. You need to look after number one for a bit. You've just come out of a bad relationship.' Libby squeezed her hand. If only Olly knew exactly how delicate she was. Bad relationship was an understatement.

The three women talked about what they were doing and their future plans for about an hour, then Michaela announced that she was going. 'I've got to get up early tomorrow, work again,' she said with a laugh. 'That's why I didn't bring the vodka. I hate getting up early.'

'I'm going to get on too. It's been a long day. We just thought we'd pop by and see you while you were here.' Kirsty stood and embraced Olly.

'Oh, Libby,' Kirsty said. 'You haven't seen a necklace lying around, one with a twist pendant on it. Micky said she hasn't but I know I saw her wearing it one day.'

'Was not.' Michaela shook her head.

Kirsty nodded slowly. 'Anyway, it's gone missing. Didn't know whether you'd seen it in the communal lounge or the washing room.'

Libby shook her head. 'No, but it's funny you say that. I've lost a hair clip.'

'We've lost a few other things too. It's getting weird.' Kirsty sighed.

Olly giggled. 'You don't think the bull man is sneaking into your places and nicking your stuff?'

Kirsty sniggered. 'No, it probably fell behind the bed or down the sink. I've got to forget it. Right, we'll leave you two to catch up.'

'It's been lovely seeing you both again, take care.' Olly slouched back on the couch.

As Libby showed her neighbours out, she couldn't help but think of what Kirsty had said. More than before, she was now sure that her towel had been moved that day and that her hair clip had been taken, but she also wondered if someone had come in through the window. She shivered as she imagined some weirdo sneaking around her flat. From now on, she was going to be more careful.

TWENTY

LIBBY

After seeing Michaela and Kirsty out, Libby returned holding a large chocolate bar.

Her hair clip was a nothing item but still it was missing. Was she being ridiculous because right now she couldn't swear that she hadn't worn it outside and dropped it? She shook her fears away. Everything that was happening with Gary and even Trevor, was getting to her. No one was sneaking through her window. The person in the garden was just a burglar, hoping that the shed door would be open. Tim said it himself. He'd had the shed broken into before. A fleeting thought stopped her in her tracks. What if Bettina still had a spare key and was coming back? Could she be looking for something? She shook that thought away.

'Shall we share this, like when we were kids?' Libby switched the lamp on and turned off the main light.

'Oh, yes, I thought you'd skimped on dessert.'

Libby snuggled next to her sister and halved the chocolate bar.

'What was it like when I was little, you know, the bits I don't remember?'

'You don't want to know.' Olly picked the edge of her fingernail.

'I just wondered why Mum and Dad never bothered with us. Don't you ever feel as though you've missed out?' The closest Libby had felt to any semblance of parental care was Chrissie with her fussing and comforting words.

Olly placed the chocolate on her lap, stopped eating and stared out of the window. 'They were hard times. I try to forget about them. As far as I'm concerned I haven't got a mother or father. They abandoned us, Libby.'

Libby looked at Olly's reflection in the window and saw tears trickling down her cheeks.

'I'm sorry. I didn't want to upset you but all I really remember is great-aunt Alice, we lived with her for years. I remember she always let you have your friends over and you used to let me hang out with them.'

'She was a good woman.'

'I was thinking about Louise the other day, was she one of them? I can't remember.' Libby thought back to how she'd spoken to Tim about the girl in the well. That's what Louise would always be known as.

'That was a long time ago, Lib. Louise was horrible. I only invited her around once then I avoided her like the plague. What happened to her was awful but... never mind. Let's not get morbid.'

Libby hadn't wanted to get morbid but she was trying to piece together their childhood. It was obvious that Olly didn't want to talk about that part of her life. Libby knew she wouldn't which is why she was now wondering why she had to go and ruin the atmosphere by mentioning it.

'Sorry for being snappy. I just don't like remembering that. In my mind, what happened to her could have happened to any one of us. I remember we weren't allowed out because of the killer on the loose. We were scared back then.'

'Sorry, Olly. I shouldn't have brought that up.'

'It's okay.' Olly ate a square of chocolate. 'Do you remember living in the foster home with Frank and Chris?'

'No.'

'They were so neglectful. I remember sneaking down to get you milk and cheese in the night, you were a skinny toddler. They didn't look after you and I knew you'd get ill. One night I got caught so he threw cold water over me and locked me in a cupboard. I was about five. I cried and cried, not because I was upset about being cold but because I thought they'd hurt you. Before that we lived with Nan, she was nice but as you know she died when you were eighteen months. We were lucky that great-aunt Alice took us away from them.'

Olly cried like she had never cried before and buried herself into Libby. Libby wept too.

'I didn't know. Why didn't you tell me about them?'

'I've never told anyone the things that happened at that house before. I hate our parents.'

Libby held her sister, knowing that this woman had grown up far too young. She always remembered Olly as being like her little mother. She wondered how many bad things Olly had protected her from and how many punishments she'd taken to protect her. Aunt Alice was sweet enough but she never reared them when they were little. She gave them food and a bed. It was Olly who helped her to get ready for school, Olly who bathed her and Olly who would sit up all night with her when she was ill. She had a lot to thank Olly for.

'I love you, Olly.'

'I love you too. We'll always have each other I promise you that.'

The next morning, Olly was up and ready to leave for the train station before Libby had even properly got up. Her sister had helped herself to coffee, had a shower then woke Libby. As they opened the door, Tim was just about to come back in with his post. Libby did up her dressing gown.

'Morning,' he called out before heading back into his flat, not giving them a chance to reply.

Olly scrunched her brows. 'He was in a rush.'

'He has a lot on.' Libby went to follow Olly down.

'I can see myself out. You get back inside. It's cold out here.'

'Okay, but message me when you get back so I know you got home safely.'

'Will do.' Olly hugged her tightly before rushing off to catch her train.

Just as she closed her door, she heard a piercing meow coming from downstairs. Hurrying down, her bare feet cold on the hall tiles, she ran into the communal lounge. There were a few magazines scattered on the table. She kneeled down and gazed under the settee but he wasn't there. 'Einstein.' Maybe he was stuck.

She ran over to the shelves and opened the cabinet doors underneath. He wasn't there either. Then came another meow. It was coming from the laundry room. Hurrying, she opened the door and was led to his scratching. Opening all the cupboards one by one, she followed the noise until she reached the last one. As soon as she opened it, the bedraggled cat darted out and ran into the communal lounge before jumping onto the couch and licking his paws. Libby hurried over to pick him up but as she got close, he scratched her and hissed.

'Einstein, naughty boy.'

He must have been trapped in the cupboard since he went missing. Someone else must have done laundry since. They must have heard him. She reached out again but this time Einstein let her pick him up. Carrying him upstairs, she placed him on the floor and stared at his matted fur. 'What have you been up to?' He hissed again before running to the kitchen and nudging his bowl. As she went to stand, she spotted a small box of chocolates on the coffee table. She'd thank her sister later.

As she poured the cat food, Einstein greedily snatched at it before she could even get the food into his bowl. She stroked him as he ate but his hackles went up and he began angrily swishing his tail. She withdrew her hand, wondering what exactly had happened to him. Instead of fussing him, she grabbed the chocolates and lifted the lid off them. They looked handcrafted and for a moment, Libby wondered if Olly had made them. She popped one into her mouth allowing the truffle to melt over her taste buds. As soon as the cat finished, he ran straight to the bedroom and crawled under the bed. That wasn't like Einstein at all. The last time he seemed that nervous, it was the night Gary pushed her into the kitchen table while shouting angrily. Her cat was scared.

TWENTY-ONE

LIBBY

Monday, 14 March

Libby styled her hair into a bun. She looked at the flowers on the worktop that Gary had sent to her. Several pink roses, what did that mean? She snatched them and plunged them straight into the bin. She didn't want him and she didn't want his flowers. The smell wafted up, cloying in her nostrils. Roses had never smelled so unpleasant. Einstein scarpered back under the bed. It was as if he could smell Gary on the flowers.

She heard the main door bang followed by someone running up the stairs. Knowing that it was probably Tim, she grabbed her tenancy agreement off the table and hurried to the door. As she opened her door, his closed. It was now seven thirty, early enough to hand it over to him before work. She checked her hair and make-up one more time in the mirror and buttoned up her suit jacket. With a day of interviewing candidates to fill a big staff order she'd received, she had to look nothing short of professional.

Grabbing her laptop bag, she left and knocked on Tim's door. Behind the door, she heard him shuffle from one room to the next before he opened up. 'I thought I'd just pop the tenancy agreement back, it's all signed.' Libby handed the document to him.

'That's great, thanks. Sorry again, for taking so long.' He took it and opened his door wide. 'Come in a minute, I'll just photocopy it for you.'

Libby followed him over to the end of his lounge where his computer sat on a desk. He placed the page into the printer and pressed the copy button. 'I'm sorry that I haven't been around much lately. My mother's been really ill. The visits are draining me at the moment.'

'I'm really sorry to hear that. I had no idea things were so bad.'

'It is what it is. Do you want a coffee?'

Libby could spare a few minutes before she had to walk to work. 'That would be lovely.'

Tim grabbed the copy of the tenancy agreement and handed it to her. As he went into the kitchen she ran her finger over the edge of his desk. On it were some accountancy analysis pads, a few paper files with names on them and a framed photograph. Libby picked up the photo and looked at the woman who was probably in her fifties. An elegant woman, wearing a blouse that was buttoned up to the top. In the background was a picture of a lounge, a flowery settee and a coffee table neatly dressed with a lace tablecloth. She imagined that the woman in the photo had helped to dress the very room she was standing in. It had to be his mother.

Shoved behind the printer was a picture of a little girl aged about three who was looking into her lap and a boy who looked to be about six. Libby picked up the photo for a closer look. The photo was worn and the creases in it had caused distortion of the whole picture and the faded colour didn't help. A loud clashing of pans coming from the kitchen made her flinch. She almost dropped the picture. She placed it back down. The kettle boiled ferociously before it clicked off.

In the corner of the room stood a bookshelf containing files. Libby walked over and noticed that the top shelf was labelled 'tenants.' She read the names that were written on the spines of each box folder. There were folders for Michaela and Kirsty, Mr Bull with no first name, herself, and a few other names she didn't recognise. At the end of the shelf there was one marked Bettina Falco. Tim had details of Bettina on his bookshelf. As she went to pick up the folder, Tim walked into the room holding a tray, Libby's heart jumped as he caught her looking at his files.

'My work, not very interesting, is it?'

'Sorry, I didn't mean to be nosy.'

'That's okay, as long as you're not reading them. My tenant and client activities are confidential.' He laughed and placed Libby's cup on the coffee table. 'Also, they don't make good reading. Totally boring.'

'I couldn't help noticing the file on Bettina.'

'Oh yes. I keep files on all the tenants.'

'Bettina's father still hasn't found her. He mentioned that you said she had to leave because of the noise she was making. When we spoke, you said she left mid-tenancy.'

Tim sipped his coffee. 'Sorry, I didn't think that her father would like me furnishing you with all the details so I just gave you a quick overview. Now that he's mentioned it to you, I suppose I'm okay to talk.'

'So you had problems with her?'

'The biggest problem I had were the noise complaints. And then there was the unpaid rent. She left owing me a few hundred pounds, which I've written off. I asked her to start looking for somewhere else and I felt bad, but it was hard having her here. She didn't have to rush but I sensed that she didn't want to stay after that. I had intended to ask her for a forwarding address but when I came back from visiting my mother, all her stuff had gone and she'd left the flat door open. The key was left on the side.'

'So she left owing you money?' Libby bit her lip.

'Yes. The place was really dirty too.'

'Do you have any idea where she could've gone or who she could've gone with?' Libby asked.

'Not really, there were always men coming and going. She liked a drink as well and she'd play this loud techno music. I wouldn't be surprised if she just upped and went off with one of them and travelled abroad. She made it clear that she was just doing the one term here before continuing with her adventures. She did say something about Milan but that's all I can remember.'

'Wow, it does sound like she's just upped and gone. It's such a shame. Her father's heartbroken as he hasn't heard from her. What did she look like when you saw her? Her father showed me a photo but I may be able to give him a more up-to-date description if you can remember.'

'Let me think.' Tim paused for a moment. 'She had shoulder-length brown curly hair with red streaks running through it.' He paused again. 'She'd recently got her nose pierced and she always wore flat boots with her jeans tucked into them. There was this brown corduroy blazer that she would always wear.'

'Thanks, Tim, that's really helpful. I'll pass that on to her father. She seems to have changed a lot.'

'She did change a lot,' Tim said.

'Just the way she looked?'

'No, in other ways.' Tim stirred his coffee and took another sip.

'How?' Libby asked, taking a gulp of her coffee. She

checked her watch; she'd been in Tim's lounge for fifteen minutes and needed to hurry to get to work on time.

'Well, when she first moved in, she seemed so nice but after a few months I barely recognised her. She didn't know many people to begin with so kept to herself. I used to hear her sewing machine chugging away, day and night. After a couple of months, she started coming back late, drunk, making a racket, falling up the stairs, bringing guys back. The others in the house used to complain, especially when she took over the communal room for her little parties. There was the loud music and not to mention the loud sex. She would always have her dark glasses on the next day, these huge bug-eyed things that almost covered her face. Other times I would see her staring into space. I couldn't swear to it but she may have been taking something, the dilated pupils were a giveaway. I don't know what went wrong.' Tim gave a sympathetic look. 'Her poor father. I didn't have the heart to tell him all this when he asked me.'

'I think I need to tell him what you've just told me. It's best to know the truth, isn't it?'

'You're right. I should have just told him. It's always best to know the truth even if it's not what a person wants to hear.'

'Anyway, I'm going to be seriously late for work.' Libby stood and placed her cup on the table. She picked up her bag and walked towards the front door.

'About that drink?'

Libby had thought long and hard about that. She looked up at him. His eyes were so kind and his smile, warm. He nervously twitched as he looked away.

'Do you mind if we don't, for a while? I'm feeling a bit confused lately and I don't want to complicate my life at the moment.' She stepped closer to him, knowing that her body language was telling him another story. His warmth, his smell, his firm arms – there was no doubt that she was attracted to him, but she didn't want a relationship with him. He was a good guy and the last thing she wanted to do was hurt him. Besides, she needed to clean up her life before she moved on in any way and to do that, Gary had to get the message one way or another.

'Course not, I don't mind at all. You know, if you ever want to talk, I'm a good listener.' His smile had her drawn in and speechless for a few seconds.

She shook her head and stepped back a little. 'Thank you. There is one thing I thought I should mention. I found Einstein trapped in a cupboard in the laundry room. However much I try, I don't know how he got there unless someone shut him in. I also saw him through the window in Mr Bull's flat.'

'That's odd. I'll keep an eye on things for you. I wonder if he jumped through the downstairs window.'

'He probably did. He's got used to using windows as cat flaps. Also, both me and the girls have had things disappear out of our flats.'

He scrunched his brow. 'What kind of things?'

'For me, it's a hair clip. I know, it's nothing major but it's just odd.'

'I lost a pen. It was my mother's Mont Blanc. But I think I may have dropped it while out with a client. But, maybe not. Are you sure you just haven't misplaced it?'

'No, I'm not sure. I think I'm just a bit jittery lately. It's probably nothing. I hope you find your pen. If I see it around, I'll let you know. Right, I've got to go before I'm late.'

'Have a good day. I'll look out for a hair clip, you look out for my pen.'

Tim led her to the door and waved her off. Libby darted down the path and walked as fast as her legs would go all the way to work. Her first interview was in thirty minutes. If she could recruit the right person, it would save the Trevor debate from coming up with management again.

TWENTY-TWO

LIBBY

Libby took another look at her notes and threw them down in frustration. She needed three welders but she'd only inter-viewed two that were suitable. Bentons' last order hadn't been supplied in full, and there was no way she'd allow herself to fail again. She counted the application forms and interview sheets. She lifted Bill's form and examined it again. He'd be good if only they'd give him a chance but with his limited experience, she doubted they would. With that thought fresh in her mind, she picked up the phone to call the company, but a tap on her office door stopped her. Chrissie entered.

'I have Trevor waiting in reception for you about the job you've advertised. He's a bit fed up that you never called him and he's being a bit gobby with everyone.'

Libby felt her heart start to race.

'I never called him because he's a pig.'

'I totally understand. At least you had six new candidates, we can tell him where to go.'

Libby exhaled. 'Only two had suitable experience. I'm up the creek, Chrissie.'

'Do you want to see him or shall I tell him you're busy?'

'I don't have a choice on this one. If I don't at least consider him, I'll be hauled in by management. Besides, if I don't talk to him now he'll just ring all day and come back later when he's drunk.' She thought about all the odd things happening to her and her heart hummed away. Trevor was a drunken nasty piece of work, and he was definitely vindictive enough to make someone's life a misery if things didn't go his way.

'I'll send him in. If you need me just give me a call and I'll hurry in.' Chrissie pressed her lips together in a sympathetic smile.

'It shouldn't be like this, should it?'

'No, love.'

'Thanks, Chrissie.' Libby placed the other applications in a folder and took a deep breath. She removed her jacket and placed it on the back of the chair before taking another deep breath. She listened to the footsteps stomping along the corridor. They stopped as they reached her office before the heavy-handed knock shook the picture on the wall.

'Come in,' Libby called.

Trevor entered. He was wearing work boots, jeans, a jumper and that ugly, stained yellow jacket. Libby never understood why he wore a high-visibility jacket when he wasn't going to work. Trevor walked in before sitting down opposite Libby, legs sprawled and open, hands on each arm of the chair.

'How can I help you, Trevor?'

'I've come about the welder job on your website, the one you never called me about.' He pulled out his phone and flashed the vacancy at her.

'I never called you because of the episode you pulled not long ago.' She scratched the nervous itch that was climbing around her neck.

'This job would be good for me, sounds like they may take people on permanent, which is what I need. Anyway, it was your company who messed my wages up so you're to blame, not me.'

'I know. It was an accident though. We put them right for you the very next day. I don't take kindly to being harassed outside work.'

He scrunched his nose up. 'Harassed. Yeah, right. A man has got to stick up for himself when the agencies try to do him over.' He paused and scratched his stubbly chin. 'How many contracts have I done for you this past couple of years?' He stared, awaiting her reply. Libby paused for a moment.

'Six, or is it seven?'

'It's nine. Shows how appreciated I've been. And has anyone ever complained about my work or me?'

'No.' Libby cleared her gravelly throat.

'So why on bloody earth can I not have this job? I need the money. You lot are just robbing me of jobs now because you didn't pay me right and on time, and because you have obviously got it in for me. I take all this very personally.' The veins on the man's neck were starting to swell and his face reddened. He enunciated every word, clearly expressing his disgust.

'We haven't got it in for you.' Libby held her arms up in frustration.

'So why the hell didn't you call me? I'm a damn good welder, you know I am.'

Libby looked at him and opened her mouth to speak. Before she got the chance to reply she was interrupted.

'You lot are all the same, you and all the other muppet agencies around. Just line your own pockets and dump people like they're rubbish. Well, I'll tell you something.' He stood and pointed his index finger at her.

Libby trembled as she stood and cut off his sentence. 'Sit the fuck down and I'll tell *you* something.' Libby had asserted herself but had no idea how she was going to follow that up. Chrissie ran in on hearing her raised voice.

'Is everything alright? Only I was just going to the photo-copier and I heard shouting.' She glared at Trevor.

'We're fine, Chrissie. Thanks though.' The woman nodded before leaving the room. 'I will not have you speaking to me like that again. Yes we made a mistake with your wages, it wasn't intentional but you came in my office and spoke to me in what I could only perceive as a threatening manner and you've been like that since. It's also not the first time; you really need to sort your drink problem out. And you know, I do have other good people registered here that work hard too. You're not indispens-able to me so get that out of your head now.'

Trevor opened his mouth to speak but failed. Libby remained silent, taking satisfaction in watching him process her last few words. Adrenalin pumped through her body and her legs began to tremble under her desk. *Hold it together, Libby.*

'I'm sorry,' he said after a pause. 'I'm just so desperate for the work. I've got problems, I know I have, but I'm getting them sorted. I've never been on the drink at work, you know I haven't.'

'You can't take whatever problems you have out on me any more. Is that clear?'

'Yes.' Sitting, he held his head in his hands and ran his fingers through his greying hair.

'I'm going to give you one last chance, Trevor. You let me down and you're history with this agency. Do I make myself clear?'

'Yes.'

'You come here when you're drunk or speak to me like shit one more time, that's it for good and I mean it. I'll text you all the job details later. You will definitely be starting tomorrow so I suggest you go home, get some rest and have a good night's sleep, and stay away from my home.' She stared at him, wondering if he'd give something away.

'Look, I know I've upset you but I'll do well, I promise. That night outside the pub wasn't me. I'll keep away from that end, I promise. They'll like me that much they'll want to keep me there.'

'Just go now and take some time sheets on the way out.' Libby smiled. As he closed the door, she punched the air. She'd handled Trevor the way she should've done all along. If only she could put her new-found assertiveness into practice in other areas of her life, like Gary. Her hands were shaking from the adrenaline surge.

Reaching the back of the filing cabinet she pulled Trevor's folder out. She'd banished him to the back after his outburst the other week. She placed his file in front of her, called up the company and got through to the person who booked the welders.

'I'm sorry,' her contact said. 'I was just about to call you. We've had word from head office that we aren't allowed to recruit as planned. Sorry to let you down.'

She'd now have to tell Trevor there was no job to go to tomorrow. Picking up the phone she dialled his number. She slammed the receiver down before the call connected. She couldn't face Trevor yet. All that was fixed in one part of her life was now undone because someone couldn't call her soon enough. Libby banged her closed fist on the table. Chrissie came in with a cup of coffee.

'Are you alright?' Libby couldn't find the words to reply. 'Was it him?'

'No, it's this bloody job. I managed to get all three people. I even managed to get Trevor to chill out and gave him one of the positions and now what do they do? They go and cancel on me and I have to tell Trevor there's no job. I'm in for a bad day. Why can't things ever go right?' Libby shouted. Tears of frustration began pushing their way out.

'Oh don't let them all upset you.' Chrissie walked around to Libby and hugged her. 'Things will be alright. It's not your fault that the jobs are cancelled, you're stressing too much. The people that work for us are fully aware that this happens.'

'They used another agency, I know it. We're losing them and there's nothing I can do about it.'

'We can't win them all, really.'

'I know, but I just got things right again. Is it too much to ask for things to stay right for more than a week?'

'Of course not, love.'

Libby's phone rang. 'No peace for me.' She didn't recognise the number. 'Hello ... oh hello, Ricardo. Yes, I can meet you in about half an hour. Yes, by the baked potato stand on New Street.'

'Ooh, tell me more,' Chrissie said, with a smile.

'It's nothing. He's just someone I know. Nothing like that. Looks like I'll be out for lunch. Can I pick anything up for you? Cake?'

'Best not.' She patted her stomach. 'You have a nice lunch with your friend and don't worry about this place,' she said, emphasising the word friend as if she didn't believe that Libby was meeting a man on a platonic basis. 'I best let you freshen up.' With that, Chrissie left.

Libby pulled her hand mirror out of her bag and checked her appearance. Her eyes looked a little red and her eyeliner had started to smudge. She rubbed the make-up off and reapplied a fresh coat. Her eyes were still red but she looked a bit better. Grabbing her jacket and bag, she locked up her office as she left. Trevor could wait until later. What she really wanted to know was what Ricardo had to tell her.

TWENTY-THREE

LIBBY

As she hurried out, she saw Trevor hanging around smoking. Instinctively, she ducked down the alley and waited.

'Alright, Trev,' shouted a man who staggered past.

'Alright, my mucker. See you in the pub later. I got some things to sort.' He dropped his nub end onto the ground and squashed it with his work boot.

Hurry up and go. Libby tapped her feet on the floor. What she should really do is walk right up to him and tell him about the job cancellation but she couldn't. Not out here without Chrissie or anyone else around who would have her back in this situation. She exhaled as he began walking away.

She hurried up the main walk, passing shop after shop as she pushed through the lunchtime crowds. Ducking under a row of scaffolding, she grabbed her phone. No more messages. Her fast walk turned into a jog, then a run until she spotted Ricardo standing at the baked potato stand.

'Libby, thank you for coming.'

She smiled as he kissed her on both cheeks. 'Shall we head to the café?'

He nodded. 'Yes, it's a bit chilly for being outside. I miss Naples, it's not so cold there.'

In the café Ricardo walked over with two coffees and placed them on the table. 'Would you like anything to eat? My treat.'

'No, I'm fine, thanks. Just the coffee will be lovely.' Just the thought of knowing that she had to speak to Trevor again was enough to turn her stomach.

'Did you find anything else out?' he asked her.

'I know you spoke to the landlord, Tim, but I was at his and we got talking.'

'And?'

'It's not all good.' She didn't quite know how to tell Ricardo.

'I need to know. It might help me to find her.'

'He said that Bettina hadn't kept up with her rent payments but that wasn't why he asked her to leave.'

'He asked her to leave?'

'Yes. He said that the noise complaints made by the other tenants were getting too much. He mentioned that she kept bringing people back for parties. I'm really sorry but he said that she might have been taking something.'

Feeling guilty at having to break this news to Ricardo, she looked down. He needed to know the truth of how Bettina had left. She thought it might be the only way for him to piece together what had happened.

'You mean drugs?'

She nodded. 'He said that she left one day while he was visiting his mother. When he came back, she was gone. The keys had been left in the flat and her stuff had been taken. He didn't get a forwarding address but that may be because she still owed rent.'

'Why didn't he tell me all this?'

'He said he felt bad for you.'

'That doesn't sound like her, something isn't right.' He

rubbed his temples. 'If she needed money, she knows she could have called me at any time.'

'Maybe she wanted to sort it out herself, I don't know.' She sipped her coffee. 'He also said she changed her appearance. Maybe the crowd she socialised with changed her.'

'In what way?' Ricardo removed his thin scarf, folded it and placed it next to his coffee.

'He said, before she left she'd had her nose pierced and her hair cut. When he last saw her, it was shoulder length and curly with red streaks.'

'That sounds even less like her. Although she was into fashion, she was never keen on piercings. She was scared of needles.' He scrunched his brow.

Libby didn't know what to say next. It seemed he was taking the information badly and not accepting that his daughter may have changed. 'It must be a shock.'

He stared at the wall and his cheek twitched as he ground his teeth. 'I'm scared I'll never see her again.' She placed her hand over Ricardo's and tilted her head. 'I wish I'd been a better father.'

'You're a really good father. You've come all this way to look for her because you love her. Only a good father would do that.'

'I cast accusations on her reputation. They weren't nice. I called her some names. All because she wouldn't come home. I was angry and stupid and I didn't mean any of them. My wife argued with me a lot even when she was ill, saying it was all my fault that Bettina wouldn't come home. I now have to live with her voice going through my head saying those things over and over again. I dream about it while asleep and I think about it while I'm awake. My wife died blaming me for driving Bettina away.'

The man wiped his eyes with the back of his hand. The more upset he got, the stronger his accent became. 'I didn't mean to though, my family are very old-fashioned and like

things to be done traditionally when it comes to relationships.'
Libby nodded, prompting the man to continue. 'Although she
wasn't a bad girl as such, I came down on her hard. When she
wasn't at home I'd always want to know where she was, I would
check. I didn't do the same with her brothers. She thought I
wasn't fair. But I know what men are like. I only wanted to
protect her and I lost her.'

The man broke down. Libby passed Ricardo a napkin off
the table. A couple of men on the next table stared at them.
Libby stared back at one, then they looked away.

'Ricardo?' The man looked up. 'I don't know how we're
going to find her but we will.' Libby knew that she had a
connection with this man and felt it was her duty to do whatever she could to help him find Bettina. The love he exuded for
his daughter made her feel so warm. Although she hadn't
known him long, she enjoyed Ricardo's warmth and she wanted
to befriend him. She'd met so few good, honest people in her
life, she felt he was worth her time.

'Thank you. You're a kind woman, Libby.'

She saw the loss etched in his face. He was probably a handsome man a few months ago but now he looked tired, confused
and lost. His jawline was perfectly chiselled and his eyes were
warm and friendly, but the bags that hung underneath them
told another story.

'Would you like another drink?' Libby asked. 'I'll get these.'

'I'm fine, thanks. I should get back soon and get myself
together for later.'

'What's happening later?' Libby wondered if he had a lead
to follow up on.

'I'm going to talk to a man at the bar. Apparently the man
who knew Bettina is back from his holiday and will be at work
tonight.'

'Let me know how you get on. I really hope he can help
you.'

Ricardo put his scarf back on and stood. 'I will let you know. She'd really like you, I hope you can meet her one day.'

'I would love to meet her one day. For now, you have to go and find her.' Libby followed him back out into the cold. She had given him a lot to think about.

'Could I meet you for lunch again tomorrow? I can tell you how I get on at the bar.'

'Of course. Would twelve be okay?'

'Twelve would be great. Thank you, I don't know what I'd do without your support. Staying here, away from the rest of my family is so draining, it helps to have you to talk to.' Ricardo opened his arms and embraced her. Libby normally felt uncomfortable with physical contact, especially with strangers, but Ricardo was different. His embrace was so fatherly. 'I will call you when I know something and thank you once again. If you hear anything else that's important, please let me know. I'll see you tomorrow,' he called as he walked away.

Libby checked her phone and saw she'd received a text message.

No wonder you've been keeping me at arm's length, you could've told me there was someone else. I'm gutted and isn't he too old for you!!!! You know where you can shove the flowers. G.

Glancing up and down, she doubted she'd even spot Gary in the huge crowd but he was there. Somewhere, watching her. She deleted the text and put the phone in her pocket. It rang, she pulled it back out. Gary was trying to call. She looked around to see if she could spot him, he was nowhere to be seen. She pressed the cancel button, placed it back in her pocket and started walking back to her office. She'd go back to work, ignore her mobile phone and deal with Trevor.

She watched as a figure in a dark coat slammed a phone box

door and ran. She jogged over to the phone box that was now a quirky cashpoint and was taken aback by the stench of urine. This was an all-time low for Gary. On the tiny shelf a newspaper rustled in the breeze. She picked up the *Birmingham Mail* and stared at the edge of the paper. Her name had been written in capital letters around the edge. She grabbed her phone and typed out a message. Gary had gone too far this time.

I hate you, Gary. Stay away from me or I'll involve the police.

It had to be Gary lurking by her new home, getting into the back garden. She wouldn't put it past him to take Einstein for a few days. Maybe he'd broken into Canal House and shut the cat in the laundry cupboard. She was finally getting to know the real Gary now that she'd left him and she didn't like what she was seeing. What scared her the most was that she didn't know what he was capable of. She also knew that she didn't want to find out. He was becoming scary and unpredictable.

Her phone rang. She snatched it up. 'Olly.'

A friendly voice was just the thing she needed.

'Lib, the restaurant is mine. I'm just working through a few things with my solicitor and I'll be able to take it over.'

'That's the best news ever, sis. We are going to have to celebrate very soon. Oh, thank you for the chocolates by the way.'

Olly paused. 'What chocolates?'

'The truffles that were on my table when you left.'

'I didn't leave you any chocolates.'

Her heart rate began to race as she gazed through the sea of people. Someone came into her flat and left chocolates on her table, but who? An unpleasant tingle worked its way along the back of her neck.

TWENTY-FOUR

LIBBY

Libby checked the time – it was just gone four and she wondered how much longer she could delay speaking to Trevor. The thought that Gary had gone as far as breaking into her home in such a way made her skin crawl. He had to have entered through the window. He was certainly fit enough. Even the most stupid of burglars could get onto that extension.

She flung her files across the desk, leaned back in her chair and stared at the phone. Right now, she had to focus on Trevor and telling him about the contract cancellation. She chewed the end of her pen as everything happening in her life gnarled her. She flinched as it snapped in her mouth. The plastic shards cut into her bottom lip and blood trickled down her chin. Grabbing a tissue out of her top drawer, she wiped away the blood and placed the tissue on her desk.

She swallowed, it was now or never. She opened Trevor's file and dialled his number. It rang and rang, no answer. Relieved, she left a message.'Hi, Trevor, really sorry. The client has cancelled so unfortunately there's no work tomorrow. I'll let you know as soon as I have something else for you. Once again I really am sorry.'

As she placed the phone down her mobile rang. It was a withheld number. Libby grabbed the phone and answered. As before the caller stayed on the line. She couldn't hear any background noise. 'Stuff you,' she yelled as she continued to leave the call open. Two minutes passed then a loud bang that sounded like a slamming door broke the silence. Libby dropped the phone. Her heart hammered against her ribcage. As blood pumped through her body it began once again to seep from her lip. She lifted the phone off her desk and cautiously placed it to her ear. The caller had gone. Slamming the phone down, she picked up the tissue and dabbed her lip again. The phone beeped. This time it was a text.

Are you fucking a grandad? Wow!

With shaking hands, she threw the phone onto her desk. That text had confirmed everything she'd suspected. The office phone rang. 'Hello, Top Staff,' Libby said, as she picked up the receiver.

'You've given it to someone else, haven't you?' Libby froze. It was Trevor. 'I've been celebrating getting this job all afternoon.' In other words, he was drunk.

'No, the job hasn't gone to someone else. The client cancelled. Nothing I can do about it. You know the score. This is an agency and you signed up for temp contracts.'

'Yeah, right. I know your type. And I'll call you tomorrow and the day after until you bloody well get me a job,' he slurred. 'I'll be there, I'll be everywhere, watching and waiting. You won't get rid of me that easily. Watch your back.'

'Trevor. Do one,' she shouted as she slammed the phone down. He'd led her down this argumentative route so many times she was past falling for it any more. She knew he got off on arguing. 'I wish they would all just do one,' she whispered under her breath as she wiped her seeping lip. She placed her elbows on her desk and leaned into her hands. Yawning, she allowed her eyes to close.

Chrissie entered with a tray of coffee cups. 'I thought you could use a drink. Oh goodness, what's happened here? Shall I get the first-aid box?' She placed the tray on the desk.

'I'm alright. I just cut my lip on the pen, that's all. Serves me right for biting it.' Libby picked up the bloody tissue and tossed it into the bin.

'You look like crap and I don't mean that in a nasty way.'

'I feel it, my head's killing and now I have a fat lip.' She smiled.

'You should go home and tend to your wounds, my love.'

'I think I might just do that. Thanks for the coffee. I'll finish off a few bits I have to do here, drink my coffee and I'll head off home for a soak in the bath.'

'That's the best thing you could do. Are you alright getting home? If you don't feel too good, I can drop you off. Don't want you passing out in the street like.'

'I didn't lose that much blood. I'll be fine, thanks anyway.'

Chrissie placed the cup of coffee next to her and left. As she sipped the warm liquid, her lip was stinging. She flinched, it was hopeless. She couldn't even successfully manage to drink a cup of coffee now. She slammed her drawer closed and grabbed her coat. Her mobile phone went again and once again the number was withheld. This time Libby grabbed the phone and rejected the call. *That'll teach you to bother me, whoever you are.* She threw the phone into her bag. She suspected it was Trevor playing stupid games and she decided if it was, she wasn't joining in. Turning off the light, she locked up her office and left.

As she stepped out into the grey evening, a few drops of rain began to fall. Her phone beeped again. She was sick of hearing from Gary and she didn't want to hear another thing from

Trevor. She reached into her pocket, fishing through the tissues and keys to get to her phone. She gazed at the friend request.

Ian Linden. It had been a long time.

TWENTY-FIVE

LIBBY

Libby walked through the front door, threw her keys onto the kitchen table and headed through to the bathroom. Gazing at her reflection, she could see how nasty the cut was. The open wound on her lip glistened but the bleeding had stopped. She picked the delicate scab that had formed and it lifted from the skin. She covered it with antiseptic cream and began to run a bath. Dropping her clothes to the floor, she was determined to wash away the troubles of the day. She'd have a nice long soak, call Olly, and then she'd imagine that the ready meal for one she had in the fridge was a gourmet meal for two. Who with? She didn't know.

As the bath water swirled around, the rose scent from her bubble bath filled the room. Stepping into the soothing water, she allowed it to wrap its warmth around her body. She reached for her phone off the toilet seat and dialled Olly's number, hoping she'd have ten minutes to chat. The phone rang out – no answer. She placed the phone back on the toilet seat and sunk her whole body under the water.

Head immersed, she heard the vibrations of a loud scraping noise coming from beneath her. Mr Bull was in. Lying silently

in the bath, she listened. Again, she heard the scraping noise, it
sounded like a chair scraping across the floor. Then footsteps
followed. They were coming from the kitchen. She heard the
cupboard door close and things being placed heavy-handedly
on the worktop. Maybe the bull was cleaning. Then she heard a
cupboard door being opened before being slammed shut. After
the cupboard closure there was no more noise. She waited for
the noise to return but it didn't. The rest of the house was in
silence.

Resting her head on the curve of the bath, she closed her
eyes and slowly drifted off into a deep sleep.

Her mobile phone rang and vibrated across the toilet seat,
waking her. Heart pounding and disorientated, she looked
around the room. She heard a loud bang in her bedroom and
then nothing. The phone continued ringing. Not answering,
Libby listened for more noises. 'Meow.' Einstein entered the
bathroom wailing with his tail in the air. That was his usual
hungry sign. The phone still rang. She grabbed it off the toilet
seat just as it was to about to vibrate onto the floor. 'Hi, Olly,
sorry, I nodded off in the bath.'

'That's okay. Sorry I didn't answer earlier I was just doing
some prepping. We have a full restaurant tonight. I've managed
to grab a quick break though. Are you okay, you sound like
you've been running?'

'Yes, the phone just startled me, that's all. Sounds like
you're busy at work.' Libby placed a hand on her racing heart.
There was no way she'd tell Olly about her weird dream.

'I'll be working really late for the next four nights.'

'Poor you. How's Scott?'

'I don't know.'

'Why do you say that? I thought you two were fine.'

'We were. I should've told you everything when I came to
stay but I didn't want to put a dampener on things. We're
having a trial separation.'

'Oh God, I'm so sorry. Do you want me to book some holiday and come up for a couple of days?'

'No. I'm not sad, Libby. I'm actually happy. It's for the best when you both want different things.'

'But I thought you both wanted the same things. What about the restaurant you're opening together?'

'He changed his mind. I want a Michelin star, he wants some kids. I just don't think I can do it, Libby. I still have a lot to prove and I really don't want to be a mother. We've grown apart.'

'I understand. I'm here if you need me any time of the day and don't forget that.'

Libby listened to Olly talk for a few minutes and Libby told Olly about her day, about her cut, about Ricardo, about Trevor. 'Olly, I'm sorry for bringing up Mum and Dad and the girl in the well last time you were here. I know it upset you to talk about all that, about our past.'

'It's okay. I can't stop thinking about it all since you mentioned it. It was like it was yesterday.' Olly paused. 'I remember the news at the time, with her dad being a suspect and everyone attacking his house when the police let him go.' Olly went silent for a moment.

'I remember you taking me to that place a couple of times, through the woods in Beoley. It was there, wasn't it?' Libby asked, not remembering too clearly.

'Yes, you were only about nine, I used to take you along with me.'

'I can't really remember the other kids. They were your friends, not mine.'

'I didn't know them that well. I gatecrashed a couple of times and Louise told me I wasn't welcome any more. I was scared of her so we didn't go back. I'd stand up to her now. If only we had the chance to go back.' Olly paused. 'That was weird, saying that. She was killed.'

Libby felt the weight of the silence between them. She knew it was hard for Olly to talk about. 'It's not weird at all. Things could have been different. Remember when you were sick on my shoe?'

Olly chuckled. 'We hung out there for a couple of summers, all the kids did. That's where I first tried a cigarette, remember? That's what made me sick and we had to clean it off in the brook on the walk home so Aunt Alice wouldn't know.' Olly laughed. 'But we never returned after what happened. Libby?'

'What?'

Olly paused. 'Nothing.'

'What is it?'

'It's silly. Ignore me. Right. Yes, Aunt Alice didn't suspect a thing.'

'I remember we had a lot of fun at the time, didn't we?'

'And we still do, and we still will,' said Olly. 'Anyway, I have thirty people to feed and they'll all be arriving shortly. I'll definitely catch up with you soon. And don't worry about me and Scott, I'm not. Did you get to the bottom of who left you the chocolates?'

Libby knew that Olly was trying to change the subject on her. 'Yes, it was Micky.' Libby also didn't want to discuss that any further, that would involve talking about how bad Gary was getting. 'Olly, what did you want to say just then? I feel as though you're hiding something from me.'

'Honestly, it's nothing. Just me and Scott, that's all. Speak soon,' with that Olly hung up.

Libby knew her sister too well. Her silent thoughts were nothing to do with Scott. She grabbed her phone and scrolled through Olly's Instagram and Facebook. All it contained were food photos and pictures of her in her chef's whites. What wasn't Olly telling her? Another crash came from below and the cat shrieked before darting back out of the window. A gust billowed through the flat and the bathroom window flew open.

Libby stepped out of the bath and grabbed a towel. As she closed the window, she noticed that the airing cupboard had come open slightly. Creeping towards it, she pushed it open. A couple of pillowcases had slipped off the pile and fallen to the floor. As she went to grab them, her hands brushed over the peeling wallpaper. Shivering, she pulled it back further and saw some writing.

> *Ho paura, tanta paura. Mi guarda sempre.* He's always watching me.

She typed it into Google. It was Italian and the translation sent a shiver down her spine. 'I'm scared, so scared.' He was always watching her.

TWENTY-SIX

RICARDO

Hurrying back towards the hotel, Ricardo couldn't help thinking that everything he thought he knew about Bettina was wrong. He remembered the time she had to have a tetanus shot after being scratched by a stray cat. She gripped him for dear life as the thinnest needle ever came her way. She screamed the surgery down and that was when she was fourteen. She'd sobbed and hated him for days as he'd been the one to hold her. Libby had not described his Bettina.

He remembered back to when Maria offered to go with her to have her ears pierced and Bettina had been adamant she would never put herself through that. She said she'd never travel to any countries that required her to have jabs, the fear in her was that strong. What had happened to her since leaving Paris? He no longer knew her.

Ricardo passed a cake shop and knew the turning to the Sun's Rays was coming soon. A scuffle behind him caused him to glance back. It looked like a man had bumped into a child and the father was shouting at him.

Eventually, he reached the Sun's Rays. The smell of bin lingered outside. He glanced to the side and took in the over-spilled bins. Out of the corner of his eye, he spotted the back of a man. Coils of smoke filled the air.

He almost pressed his nose against the window as he checked out how busy it was. As he entered, the beery smell felt inviting. He pushed the lounge door open.

There were two young women looking at the jukebox and a couple sitting down doing a crossword together. The man he was looking for wasn't in this room. As he headed to the bar, a man almost bumped into him before hurrying into the lounge. He caught sight of the coat and it was the same person who knocked over the child and was outside smoking.

Ricardo pushed open the bar door and smiled at the server.

'What can I get you?' she asked.

'I know I'm early, but is Liam here?' He stared through to the other side of the bar into the lounge. It was so quiet he could hear people in that room chatting away.

'Not yet, lovely. He'll be in later. Come back about seven.'

He didn't want to come back later. Everything was taking too long. He stared at the top shelf, wondering if a couple of brandies would help his nerves. No, if he had one, it would lead to more and he couldn't afford to get drunk, not with what he had to do. 'Did you know Bettina, she used to work here?'

'Nah, sorry. I've only been here a few weeks. Maybe she worked here before my time. I have heard Liam mention her. They were friends. He's been trying to contact her.'

He pulled a card from his pocket. 'If you hear anything else, can you call me? She's my daughter and I'm worried about her.'

The server nodded, her topknot bouncing on her head. 'Yes, of course.'

'I'm staying at The Cropton for a while so I'm close by.'

'Great.' She placed the card in her pocket.

Ricardo swallowed. Liam had to know something that could help him.

A jittery feeling began to fill his chest. 'I... err, I'll come back later. Thank you.' Hurrying out of the pub, he took a few deep breaths. The Sun's Rays was the last place that he had for Bettina's whereabouts and if his investigations came to nothing, he had nowhere to go.

No, he had to think he would find something useful out later. As he hurried up the main drag, he stopped at a scarf cart. Lots of brightly coloured material hung in strips. Bettina must have seen this every day. He stepped closer and felt drawn to a green scarf. It had to be a sign. Bettina often used this colour when she was making her creations. He passed some money over to the market trader and took the scarf. When he saw her, he would give it to her. He swallowed again. He had to have hope that she hadn't deserted him forever.

He hurried up the steps past the huge statue in a bath before turning off the main drag towards his hotel.

'Any messages for me?' Ricardo smiled at the receptionist.

'No, none I'm afraid.' She held out his room key.

'Thank you.' As he was about to step into the lift, he spotted the man again. Unable to see his eyes under the peak of his cap, Ricardo reached through the gap of the closing lift doors and levered them open. Running across the lobby, past the entrance hall, he emerged out of the front door, but the man was nowhere to be seen. The smell of cigarette smoke lingered in the air, taking him back to outside the pub. If only he'd walked right over to that man there and then. He'd lost his chance. One thing was for certain, he'd be looking out for him later.

TWENTY-SEVEN

LIBBY

Although the volume on the TV had been low, Libby heard Mr Bull's back door creaking. Running to the kitchen window in her comfy pink pyjamas, she looked down towards the extension. The security light hadn't come on, making it hard to see. She knew she needed to report that to Tim at some point. Maybe at the same time, she could ask if a cat flap could be fitted to the communal lounge, but that might be pushing it. Leaving the window open gave her the creeps with all that had been happening. If she kept closing it, Einstein would definitely abandon her for whatever good thing he had going somewhere else.

The gate slammed but she couldn't hear any footsteps. Libby switched the light off – she didn't want him to catch her spying. Her eyes hadn't adjusted in time to get a glimpse of her mysterious neighbour. He was gone. The only thing she did see was Einstein scarpering off the flat roof below before he disappeared into the darkness of the backyard.

If only she'd got out of the bath when she knew Mr Bull was in. She could have introduced herself and asked him about Bettina. That message hidden under the wallpaper sent a shiver through her. Was Bettina scared of him? She doubted whether he'd come back that evening and she doubted he'd even answer the door to her. He didn't seem to be the most sociable neighbour she'd ever had. She yawned, ambled back to the sofa and grabbed the TV remote. There was nothing but rubbish on the television and she couldn't call Olly as she was busy at work. She pressed the mute button on the remote.

Glancing around, she couldn't help but feel a presence of the woman before. Who was always watching her? The boyfriend? Mr Bull? The same person who had thrown a stone at Libby's window? Libby always felt like she was being watched too. A gust of wind rattled the flimsy window frame and the curtain rustled, casting moving shadows of the lamplight around the room. She stood, then darted to the bathroom and flung the airing cupboard door open. Getting down on her hands and knees, she threw aside the washing that had fallen on the floor, crawled into the huge space and felt in each corner where the carpet met the skirting board. Her fingers brushed over something plastic. A chocolate bar wrapper. Closing the cupboard door, Libby sat on the floor in silence, knees under her chin, hands wrapped around them. To write that note, Bettina must have been right in the cupboard. Had she felt so unsafe she'd taken to shutting herself in and staying there?

He's always watching me. Is this the only place he couldn't see her? Libby shook her head. Maybe it was the drugs. She could have been suffering from paranoia. If that was the case, why did Libby feel the same? Bettina was right. The cupboard felt safe. She nudged the door open and went back to the living room.

Picking up her phone, she scrolled down her contacts list. She had no one to call for a chat. Even Michaela and Kirsty had gone out, so a drink with them was out of the question. A distraction was what she needed. Obsessing about Bettina would get her nowhere and as soon as Ricardo caught up with her, they'd have all the answers they needed.

She turned her computer on. Maybe Facebook or Instagram could take her mind off things for a bit. After neglecting her account for a while, she started by clearing down all the requests for games that she wasn't interested in before checking her notifications. There was that friend request from Ian Linden. She'd forgotten about it earlier.

Accepting immediately, Libby looked at his profile. There were no photos at all and he only had one other friend, Ellen. He must be new to Facebook. She clicked on his details. There was nothing apart from an email address and a location. He was living in the West Midlands, UK. *Big area,* Libby thought. She posted on his wall. 'Welcome to Facebook Ian!' She turned on her chat. Ian was unavailable. At least Ellen would be happy. She'd been looking for Ian for a long time. Libby only wished he'd put more information on his profile. She wondered how he'd look nearly twenty years on, if he had a family and what his interests were.

Gazing at the mundane wall posts, her finger hovered over the letter G. Before she knew it, she'd done a search on Gary's name. She couldn't find her Gary then she remembered she'd blocked him. She bit her thumbnail as she imagined him posting pictures of good times with her – the other woman. It shouldn't bother her or hurt now, not as she'd left him, but it did. It wasn't like she could just turn off a switch despite what he'd done to her. Curiosity was getting the better of her. Maybe she should unblock him for ten minutes, just enough time for a sneaky look at his wall. She hoped that he and that woman were together, then he'd leave her alone. The mouse hovered over the unblock tab. To stop herself from delving any further she logged out and went to the kitchen. She pulled her meal for one from the fridge, pierced the lid and placed it in the microwave. Not even knowing what she was eating, she pulled the sleeve out of the bin; ravioli filled with spinach and goats cheese. Ravioli was good, not a patch on the quality of Olly's ravioli but it would do. It would divert her attention from Gary.

Ping – it was done. She placed the container on a plate and took it through to the lounge. She opened her mouth to take her first bite and the phone rang. Gary, she almost tipped her dinner off the tray as she ended the call. After what he'd been messaging, she didn't want to talk to him

Her phone rang again. She ended the call but it rang again and again and again. 'What?'

'Who is he?'

'Gary, please leave me alone. I said I'd call the police and I mean it.' Her hands trembled.

'You want to know the truth, about her, about why I did it?'

She did. She wanted to know everything but all she would get was a vile speech from Gary.

She shook her head as if he were there in front of her. 'No.' Why didn't she hang up? Just end the call. Something kept her gripped to the phone. He always did have that power over her.

'We were going to get a place together. She's so much more fun than you because let's face it, Libby, you were never fun. You didn't do spontaneity. You lacked adventure and you spent all your spare time with your sister like a little girl following big sis. You gave me nothing.'

'I gave you everything,' she shouted. She'd given up her friends, her social life and her own self to try to be perfect for Gary but no, she would never have given up her time with Olly. He was right about that. If he was decent, he'd have never expected her to but he was so jealous of what they had.

'It didn't feel that way. You drove me to her. If you look deeply enough, you'll see that this situation wasn't my fault but despite that, I can't imagine spending the rest of my life with anyone else. I did do everything wrong. I found another place that I was going to do up and I stayed there sometimes to work on it but you, you didn't even question where I was going. It was like you didn't care as you coasted through life with your blinkers on. The first thing I knew about you caring was the pile of crap you left on the worktop before you went.'

'Gary, stop. It was more than that and you know it. You hit me.'

'I've said I'm sorry about that. You make me angry and you know it.'

'I make you angry. That's your excuse?'

'I'm getting help.'

'Whatever.'

'See, you're doing it again, Libby. I'm trying to be totally honest with you here.'

'Okay, so tell me why you make those silent calls from another phone and why you hang around my place and throw stones at the window. You tell one lie after another and you get angry when I call you out on them.'

'That's because I don't have another phone and I don't throw stones at windows.'

'I saw your other phone, the one you used to keep in your bed drawer.'

He paused. 'You went mooching through my stuff. Do you know how that sounds? That's what crazy women do.'

He'd driven her to it, to all of it. She'd searched every inch of the apartment, looked through each number he'd called on his bills. The only thing she could never manage to do was access his work emails. 'Where were you staying, Gary? I saw the rent payments going out.' She needed to know that he wasn't closer to her than she thought. If he was paying for the flat below, she had a right to know.

'Give me another chance and I'll tell you everything.'

'Where, Gary?'

He didn't answer. It was no good, she wasn't getting

anywhere and he was enjoying the fact that he'd managed to keep her on the phone.

'When you pushed me and slapped me, I thought, maybe he's going through something. Pressure at work possibly. I can't believe I made excuses for you. If you're getting help, good for you. No, good for her. I guess it's only a matter of time before you show your true colours and she will leave you too.'

'Shut up, Libby. You always thought you were better than everyone else. That was half the problem. You. Little Miss Perfect. But, you're not perfect any more. You're as much to blame for everything. Were you with him before you left me? Is that what made it so easy for you? Is it the old man or the other man who lives in your house?'

It was easy for him to point the finger when he'd ruined everything. 'You will never know, Gary. Maybe it's both of them. Send the money you owe me to my account and get out of my life.' She ended the call, tears welling up, knuckles clenched. Only then did she realise that her dinner had slid off her lap onto the floor, face down on the rug.

She stared at her phone in disbelief at how nasty he was getting. Olly would be at work now. Her friends downstairs weren't in. She'd never felt so alone. She clicked on Ian's profile again but he was offline. So was Ellen. She tried Chrissie's number but her answerphone came on. Her sobs filled the room. What was the point in it all? Right now, she had no one. Her phone rang again and it was the withheld number.

'Leave me alone.' She listened to the sound of cars going by and muffled speaking but the caller didn't say a word, then came the breathing, then the pause. It was like the caller wanted to say something. 'Just say it,' she yelled.

'He who deserves the truth, gets the truth.' The distorted hushed voice sent a shudder through her. Man or woman? Who knew? It could have been Gary, Trevor or even Beyoncé. The caller hung up leaving Libby with those creepy words in her head.

She ran to her door and checked that it was locked, then she closed the window. Staring out into the orange light speckled darkness, she gazed over the garden and beyond at the high rise and the many other buildings. Someone out there knew her every move and it was someone close. Maybe she'd been a bit over the top in thinking that Gary had rented the flat below. It was too much of a coincidence. But Gary could have been renting one of the flats opposite, in the distance. She could imagine him there with a telescope. His other pad could be down the road or by the canal, or... She closed her eyes. Or, maybe her instincts were right. He could live beneath her and all this time he'd been able to see who came and went. She had to confront Mr Bull for her own peace of mind.

A sick feeling travelled slowly through her. The answer lay with her mysterious neighbour. She didn't know how she knew, but something was stale when it came to him. He couldn't hide from her much longer. She was watching and waiting. Seeing him would clear a lot of things up, if nothing else.

TWENTY-EIGHT

RICARDO

Ricardo unbuckled his seat belt as the taxi pulled up outside the Sun's Rays. He paid the driver and stepped out into the darkness. Music and laughter spilled out as a couple left and the smell of kebab hung in the air. Hurrying in, he waited at the bar for a man to be served, then the woman from earlier smiled at him as she came over. 'What would you like?'

'I'm okay for a minute. I need to speak to Liam.'

'He'll be about ten minutes, he's running a bit late.'

'Actually, I'll have a Courvoisier with ice, please.'

His fingers had a slight tremble to them. The thought of someone following him earlier had set him on edge. He gazed around wondering if his pursuer was in the pub but he couldn't make out who was in the lounge on the other side of the pub. That person wasn't in the bar. The jukebox stopped playing and all that was left was the hum of voices.

'There you go.' As the server placed the glass down, the ice chinked before sinking to the bottom of the glass. He took the seat right next to the fire and undid the top few buttons on his coat, enjoying the warmth. He and Bettina had enjoyed a post-dinner brandy together in the past. Back home they had a huge open fireplace that crackled on the winter nights. He had no one to share that with any more with his sons now married and Maria dead. The fire's light reflected a beautiful spectrum of colour as he swirled the ice.

He glanced at his watch, noticing that fifteen minutes had passed and Liam still hadn't turned up. 'Hey,' the server shouted. 'Liam's just passed the window.'

'Thank you.' He looked up, waiting for the young man to come in.

The twenty-something, long-haired student type walked in and fist bumped one of the customers he called Derek.

'Liam, there's a chap here to see you.'

He turned and looked at Ricardo, taking him in.

'I'm really grateful you're able to speak with me, can I get you a drink?' Ricardo asked the man.

'A lager would be great.' He took his sweater off to reveal a T-shirt that said 'Sex God' on the front. His face was pale and sickly on a skinny body. Ricardo wondered if Bettina's friend existed on cheap lager and pot noodles.

Ricardo got up and ordered the man a drink as well as another brandy. 'Make it a double,' he called out as the woman was about to pour it. With the couple of mini-bar drinks he'd had at the hotel, he was beginning to feel tipsy but he didn't care. He watched as Liam got comfortable on the seat opposite to Ricardo's, just under the window. He placed a satchel on the floor and a book spilled out. The spine on the book mentioned the words, contract law. Liam must be a student. Ricardo hurried over with the drinks, spilling lager over his hand as he walked.

'I'm Ricardo, I suppose you know why I'm here.' He didn't want to waste time.

'Yeah. Phil said you're Bettina's dad.' Liam took a sip of the lager.

'I've been looking for her and so far I've not been able to

find her. I haven't seen her for over a year now, we fell out.' Ricardo bent his head slightly.

'That sounds like Bettina. We spent many nights locked in here putting the world to rights. We'd complain about the government, capitalism and vivisection. Anything we could heavily debate, we did and when she fell out with someone, that was it. Silent treatment for a month.' He paused. 'She's remarkable. I'd love to meet up with her again. That girl is going places,' Liam replied with a smile.

'Do you no longer speak with her? I was hoping you kept in touch.'

'I haven't spoken to her for months. She said she was heading back to Milan to study so I thought she'd gone. She got fed up with her job here. Complained about having to work every Friday, Saturday and Sunday. Said she'd saved a bit of money and was packing it in. I was a bit miffed she didn't say goodbye. I thought we were friends. I tried to call her but her phone number is no longer in existence. I really miss her.'

Ricardo looked down, sadness etched in his face.

'Did you go to her flat, ever?'

'Only a couple of times. We walked to work together. She invited me in once as she was running late and made me a coffee while I waited. I did go there to look for her when I couldn't get her on the phone.'

'And what happened?'

'I rang her bell and no answer. I went back three times in all. Later in the year I walked past and saw the "To Let" sign out and that's when I realised she'd gone.'

'Do you think she would just go?' Ricardo asked. He lifted his hand to his eye and wiped away a tear.

Liam stared out of the window, then took a long swig of his drink. He shrugged. 'I really like her. She's one of the smartest, nicest girls I've ever met. I think she's lovely and I'd love to see her again. It hurt when she left.' He paused. 'It hurt a lot. I kept thinking she might call but I knew I'd blown it. I told her I liked her but she said she only liked me as a friend. In answer to your question though, I do think she would just go. She was quite impulsive, always spoke of moving on and wanted to do everything now.' He paused again before continuing. 'She told me about her moves before, how she'd upped and left Paris when she got herself set up here.' The young man took a piece of paper and a pen from his bag and wrote on it. 'When you do find her, please give her my number and tell her to call me. Tell her I miss our debates and our drinks together. She's always welcome around here, even as mates.' He smiled.

'I will.' Ricardo looked at the young man and patted him on the shoulder. He seemed genuinely upset that Bettina hadn't told him where she'd gone. He took the number and placed it in his top pocket.

Liam looked out of the window and Ricardo looked down at his drink, staring at the rich caramel-coloured liquid around his glass. 'Did she ever mention the place she was living at?'

'Occasionally. She liked the landlord but she said the man downstairs was noisy. She'd complained about the noise. Said she'd hear him throwing his furniture around and hitting things. She felt like the place was suffocating her. The rules were becoming stricter. She said the landlord asked her to stop sewing because the knob who lived beneath her had complained. She argued that he was hardly ever there but she had to give up doing what she wanted all the time.'

'What happened then?'

'I'm not sure. I know she wasn't happy there. She became a bit worried. She went on about some cold case, something to do with a girl who was found murdered in a well. We often discussed old criminal cases. She told me my career in contract law was boring and that I should have done criminal.' He laughed. 'Us talking about things like that was nothing unusual. She hated that house, though. The security light was never working, she hated the temper tantrums from him below and she was fed up of the rules that the landlord kept imposing on her. Another couple lived in one of the flats but she said they were alright. She and the landlord had drinks together in the communal lounge, but the one who complained all the time never joined in. That's all I know really.'

Ricardo paused as he thought about his next question. He knew he shouldn't hold back. He needed to know everything even if it was hard to hear. 'I have to ask this. It's a question no father ever wants to ask but I need the truth. Was she on drugs or anything?'

'No, definitely not. She liked the occasional drink but never drugs. She was totally against them.'

'I'm relieved to hear that. Do you know the names of the couple who lived downstairs? I will need to track them down.'

'I know their second name was Bailey as it was on their postbox when I visited. The woman worked at The Queen Elizabeth Hospital as a nurse, may even still work there. Here, let me think. He worked in the train station, behind the counter, New Street Station. You could go in there and ask for him. I think his first name was Glen. Glen Bailey.'

'Thanks for talking to me. I may come back to see you, if that's alright?'

'Anytime, and call me when you hear from Bettina. I'd love to know that she's alright. You know, you should file a missing persons report. I'm really worried now, especially as you don't know where she is.'

'I will do. I must admit. I'm worried too that something has happened to her.'

'Don't jump to conclusions, try and stay positive for her. It's definitely worth contacting the police though.'

'I definitely will. I'll give them all the information I have and maybe they'll help me.'

'I have to get on now as I'm meant to be working. If there's anything else I can do, or if the police want to speak to me, give them my number.'

Standing, Liam grabbed his bag, then took his position behind the bar with his colleague. Ricardo ordered another drink, then another. One hour rolled into two and then more. Thoughts swirled through his mind. First thing in the morning, he was going to the police. Something was seriously wrong. She turned her back on him because of the things he said, but she would never have not kept in touch with a sweet lad like Liam. He knew Bettina and, if nothing else, she was a good friend to have. She'd kept in touch with people for years.

He knocked back his sixth brandy and felt the alcohol affecting his legs. It was no good. He had to go to the hotel get some sleep and be fresh in readiness to go to the police. He glanced around. A large party had left not so long ago, probably heading for a club. He was alone in front of a fire that was now nothing more than cinders cracking away.

'Hey, Ricardo. It's closing time. We have to clean up.' Liam took his empty glass.

'So it is,' he said, taking in the quietness around him. 'Thank you.'

After two attempts he managed to balance on his jellied legs. The room was a little wavy and his sight was slightly blurred. He needed a taxi. Feeling his way out of the entrance hall and onto the road, he rubbed his eyes. 'You.' The coat, the shape of the man, it was definitely him. 'You were following me earlier.'

The man remained standing by the huge industrial bin. 'I know where your daughter is.'

TWENTY-NINE

RICARDO

'If you want to know more, you have to come here. By telling you what I know, I'm in great danger and I can't be seen.'

'You were following me earlier.'

'Sorry. The right time for me to approach you never happened, which is why I'm here now. Come here out of the light.'

'I'm not going anywhere near you.' Ricardo staggered around the front of the pub. No one else was on the road. It was just him and the man by the bin.

'Fine. If you don't want to know where Bettina is, go, but you won't see me again. I can't put myself at risk like this by trying to tell you again. Liam cannot know that I'm here, talking to you.'

Ricardo staggered closer to the bins before glancing back towards the pub. The thick curtains were now closed. He had no choice but to trust this stranger. So Liam had been lying to him and he was about to find out the truth. If that lad had done something to his daughter, Ricardo would make him pay. With clenched fists, he took his last step towards the large blue bin. 'Where is she?'

'I, err.'

There was a tension in the man's face and a strength in his body. Was he trembling? Ricardo shook his head. 'Tell me where she is.' As he stared at the man, he could see four eyes and two noses all in shade. His heavy arms were held down by his drunken mind. That's when he felt the sickening crunch of what looked like a rock coming down on his head. Ricardo fell forward, trapping the man under his hefty weight. He couldn't let him go. If he got free, the man would kill him. The rock came from nowhere again and Ricardo dropped into a pile of over-spilled bin bags.

'Why?' Ricardo whispered.

'Because he who deserves the truth, gets the truth.' The throbbing in Ricardo's head was like nothing he'd ever experienced. He closed his eyes, trying to ride through the white-hot pain. That's when he felt a prick in his neck, followed by a dragging motion as his body was tucked behind the bins. His attacker crouched beneath him as his body came over tingly and he couldn't fight the exhaustion any longer.

THIRTY

LIBBY

Tuesday, 15 March

Libby checked her watch, it was gone twelve thirty. She ordered a cup of the house coffee before sitting at the table nearest to the window, that way she'd see Ricardo arriving. She hoped he wouldn't be too late as she had more interviews and placements to contend with that afternoon.

As she reached into her handbag, she felt along the seams in an attempt to locate her phone. Not able to feel it, she opened all the zips and pockets and emptied some of the rubbish out. She had a bag full of junk she didn't need but no phone. She threw the notebook, the lip gloss, hair clips and all the marketing leaflets she'd hoarded back into the bag. She couldn't even call Ricardo to find out where he was or when he was coming. Maybe he'd tried to call her. She swigged her coffee down and glanced at her watch. Twelve forty and he still hadn't arrived. It was obvious. He'd stood her up.

Still having some time left, Libby decided to walk home. There was no way she could manage the whole afternoon without her phone. She knew she'd be a little late back but Chrissie would cover for her. Scooping up her bag, she placed her chair under the table and left the café.

Managing to keep a brisk pace, Libby was soon passing the chip shop on the corner of her road. A few specs of rain landed on her face. As she approached Canal House she pulled her keys out and opened the main door, then something struck her as odd. She backed up a couple of paces; it was Mr Bull's door. She was sure there was a small gap between the door and the frame, almost like it was open. She watched and listened for movement. There was no one about. Now was her opportunity to finally meet him. Her stomach churned as she stepped closer. She imagined pushing that door open and seeing Gary. He could have left the chocolates and he could have been listening to her comings and goings. He was messing with her life and mind.

She placed her ear against the door. Maybe he was sitting in his living room reading or browsing the net. She listened a moment longer but heard nothing. As she nudged the door she half expected a man's voice to call out but it never did. Still she heard nothing. Once again, she pushed the door a little and peered through the gap. There was a door ahead that was slightly ajar, exposing only a bit of the hallway and kitchen. Maybe he was in the kitchen. Her gaze wandered across the room. This time she could clearly see the room, not like the time she came back from the club and peeped through the window. The computer was still positioned on the table and a couple of chairs were tucked in. On the computer was a screen saver. The person who was using it had obviously left it for a few minutes. Spirals upon spirals kept dancing across the screen in red, yellow and orange; going nowhere but constantly replenishing themselves.

On the floor next to the table lay a pile of rubbish. Stained tissues, a couple of empty bottles of wine and chocolate bar wrappers. A yellow jacket hung over the back of the chair. Trembling, Libby took another step forward. There was no other furniture. That blew any wild theory of this being Gary's shag pad. Whoever lived here was not living a comfortable existence. Maybe he was leading some sort of double life, maybe he was a spy. But why was he so angry? Mr Bull really was a mystery.

She crept into the lounge. 'Mr Bull.' There was no answer. If she called out it wouldn't be intruding, would it? It would be a neighbour checking on another neighbour. One step after another led her to the table where she was standing over the computer. She ran her shaking fingers over the yellow jacket and her mind flitted to Trevor.

The mouse was beckoning her. *Move me.* What to expect, she didn't know. It could be anything from stocks and shares to pornography; she had no expectations. Maybe everything she needed to know about Bettina's whereabouts was on that computer. Still the flat was in silence. She looked around once more to see if she was alone. It was just her, the magnolia walls and the sparse furniture. The truth was right in front of her, all she needed to do was build up the courage to reveal it.

As she lowered her hand towards the mouse, a huge thud came from the kitchen. Libby scurried back towards the door. She heard a patter running towards her and just before she managed to escape from the room, Einstein appeared. Embarrassed, she scooped the cat up and held him close. 'What do you think you're doing coming in through someone else's window?' The cat looked up at her, purring and content with the smell of fish on his breath. As she left the flat, she knew she'd had a near miss. It was wrong to pry and wrong to snoop and all her theories were ridiculous.

She placed the cat down as she pulled the door back to how

it was before. As her hand left the door handle, Tim came downstairs.

'Hello, Libby, no work today?' he asked with a smile.

'I, err, just popped home, I left my phone here.' Einstein ran up to Tim and began rubbing his body against the bottom of Tim's trousers, leaving a clump of hair stuck to him. 'I'm sorry about that,' she said, scooping the cat up.

'That's okay, don't worry.'

'How's your mother?' Libby asked.

'She's fine. You'll have to pop in for a coffee when you have a bit more time so that we can have a catch up,' he replied.

'Sounds lovely,' Libby said as she passed Tim on the stairs. She looked back. Tim stared at Mr Bull's door.

He quickly opened the door to grab his post and as he came back in, he stared at Mr Bull's door again. 'That looks open to me.' He stepped closer and gave it a nudge. 'I best close it, he must've gone out and forgot to lock up. I didn't even know he was in. Have you seen him?' Tim asked as he pulled the door to. She heard the door catch the lock.

'No. I did notice that the door was open and the strangest thing happened.'

'Oh, what was that?'

'My cat came out through his door so I just pulled it back to where it was. The rascal must've entered through one of his open windows. I should hang around and apologise. I bet he thinks I'm a right nuisance neighbour.'

'I wouldn't worry. He sometimes moans about noise, not really the party type, but he's never said anything about the cat.'

'That's good and I'm sorry about that other night when my sister was here. I know we made a bit of a racket.'

'That's alright. I mean he's not in most of the time so you weren't to know he was there that night.' Tim smiled.

'Anyway, I must go and get my phone and then it's back to work for me.'

'Okay, have a nice day and I'll probably catch you later,' he said as he opened the letter in his hand. A puzzled look spread across his face.

'Are you okay?'

Tim passed the printout to Libby.

She stared at the photocopied article.

'Was this the murder you were telling me about when we went out?'

She nodded. The title of the article stated all she needed to know. *Local Girl Found Dead in Well.* She read on as it mentioned Louise and how saddened and shocked the community was. 'I'm sorry. It has to be my ex, he's being a dick.' Only Gary really knew about that. Only Gary would use that to try and unnerve her. 'Is there a postmark?'

Tim turned the envelope over. 'No, and the envelope's blank.'

Libby took the envelope in her trembling hand and searched in it. Nothing. It was empty apart from that printout.

'Look, I'll throw it in the bin. No harm done. I think I need to look at security in this place, especially as we've had things go missing and now this.'

'I was going to ask. Can we get a cat door fitted in the communal room? I know you didn't bank on this when you let me move in here but I don't feel safe and I can't shut Einstein out either. I'm always leaving my windows open for him. After someone came in and left chocolates on my table, I've been constantly on edge. I still haven't got to the bottom of that mystery.' She took a breath. 'Did Bettina ever mention to you that she was scared or that she felt she was being watched?'

'No, never. Did her dad say that she was scared here?'

Libby shook her head. 'I found something.'

'Where? In the flat?'

'Yes. Bettina has written on the wall, under a bit of torn wallpaper in the cupboard. I know it's her as I had to translate the Italian writing. She said that she was scared and that someone was watching her. I think she shut herself in there sometimes.'

'That's weird. I wish she'd said something when she was here. Maybe I could have helped her.' He looked down. 'Damn, I asked her to leave when she may have needed some help.' He ran his fingers through his hair as if trying to brush his guilt away.

She placed her hand on his arm. 'You couldn't have known. If she chose not to tell you, then there was nothing you could do. It just scared me when she mentioned being watched. I feel as though I'm being watched. The house feels alive with its past, only I can't see what has happened before. Does that sound stupid?'

He scrunched his brow. 'No, and it upsets me that you don't feel safe. I'll make some calls, see if I can get someone out quickly to look at the security of the building. Of course we can have a cat door and I'm sorry to hear that someone had the nerve to come into your home. We should call the police. Do you still have the chocolates?'

She shook her head. 'I ate them. I thought Olly had left them for me, so no. I touch that window all the time. I've vacuumed and cleaned since. Thank you for allowing me to have a cat door.' It was as if a huge weight had been lifted off her shoulders.

'That's no problem. I want everyone here to feel safe. I tell you what, while they're here, I'll get them to put one in your door too so he can get into your flat too. We'll get this sorted.'

He placed a caring hand on her arm and she smiled. 'I can't thank you enough.' She checked her watch. 'Damn, I'm so late.'

'I'll update you later and I'll keep my eye out for everything in the meantime.'

Libby ran upstairs and opened her front door. She dropped

Einstein on the floor. As she rummaged around, she heard voices coming from downstairs. Tim and Kirsty. Kirsty must've finished her shift at the nursing home.

Her stomach grumbled. She opened the fridge. Yoghurt was all she had to eat in a hurry. There was a knock at the door. She answered to Kirsty. Einstein escaped between her legs. He ran down the stairs and straight into Kirsty's flat. 'I only want to know if I can borrow your tin opener. I forgot to buy one on my way home and ours has finally given up the ghost,' she said with a big smile.

'Yes, sure, no problem. I'll just get it for you.'

'Thanks, I'll give it straight back. I'll just go and get your cat,' Kirsty replied.

Libby went to the kitchen and grabbed the tin opener. She ran out of her door, leaving it ajar, ran down the stairs and knocked as she entered Kirsty's flat.

'Here he is,' Kirsty said as she exchanged the cat for the tin opener. 'If you hang on a minute I'll give it straight back to you. I only want to open a tin of spaghetti to go on my toast.' She opened the tin before handing it back to Libby.

'So, have you been up to much lately?' Libby asked.

'Work, work and more work. We have, however, booked a fun day out on the twenty-first, it's a Monday. The only day we could both get off together. We're off to London for the day, only a coach trip but I can't wait to hit the shops. Have to be at the coach station for six thirty though. That's a bit of a pain.' Kirsty laughed.

'Sounds good.'

'Why don't you come? We were planning on doing some shopping. You look like you need a good day out. Some retail therapy.'

'I do but I can't. I have to work that day.'

'You could book the day off.'

'I can't, too much to do. Or else I would have,' Libby replied, faking a disappointed look. Having so much going on in her mind, she couldn't predict what she'd be doing by then.

'Well, how about you meet us for a drink later. We're starting out at the Sun's Rays after work. You should join us, get out for a bit.'

Not wanting to seem like a complete misery, Libby agreed. She might even bump into Ricardo and find out why he hadn't turned up to meet her. 'I'd love to come. What time are you walking up?'

'About eight. I'll give you a knock before we go.' Kirsty picked up a glass of squash from the side and took a couple of gulps. 'Did you ever find out who left those chocolates on your table?'

'No, not yet.'

'That's creepy.'

'Tell me about it. There is some good news.'

'Spill.'

'Tim is getting a cat door fitted so that my window won't need to be open for much longer. I can't wait.'

'That is good news. It gives me the shivers thinking of an intruder wandering around. Do you remember anything odd on the day the chocolates were left?'

'No, not at all. I walked Olly down and when I went back up, there was a box of chocolates on the table. Whoever left them had to have come in through my bedroom window.'

'Shit. I'm going to have to make sure our windows are shut when we're at work.'

'I wish I could keep mine shut but it's the only way Einstein can come and go. Tim's also said that he's going to keep more of an eye out on the place.'

'You know you can knock on our door any time, day or night. If you feel unsafe, come straight down and make a load of noise.'

Einstein wriggled in her arms. She bumped awkwardly into Kirsty's glass as she dropped the cat to the floor, knocking black-currant squash all over her best white shirt. 'That cat, he's nothing but bloody trouble. Thank you, again.' Libby firmly grabbed him and marched back up the stairs.

THIRTY-ONE

LIBBY

Libby hurried in carrying another shirt. Time was more than against her and Chrissie could only cover for her for so long. Management would go berserk when she got back. She undid the top button on the blue shirt, ready to slip it off the hanger.

'This is all your fault, matey.'

Einstein began to wrangle his furry body around her leg. She lifted him up and kissed his head.

'I don't know. Why can't you be more dog and chase those horrid burglars away.' Burglar, that was a funny term in this situation. Nothing had been taken. 'You recognised him, didn't you? You knew it was Gary. We'll get him out of our lives soon when that cat flap is fitted.' She swallowed as she thought of the article that had been posted to Tim.

A creak came from the hallway. She ran out and listened again but there were no more noises. She stood there, silently waiting for it to happen again. She'd been agitated by the article, the weird phone calls and the chocolates. There was no one in her flat. She exhaled and hurried back into the bathroom.

The cat purred as she placed him back on the floor and

began to run the tap. She lathered up a flannel and wiped the sticky squash from her chest. As she wiped her arms, she brushed over the scars and shook her head. With all that was going on, it would be so easy to go there again, but she'd promised Olly. No more self-harm. No more cuts, prodding, scratching or playing with scabs. Every one of those things was off-limits.

Gary was not going to break her. She pulled on her clean shirt, hurried to the living room and grabbed her phone. There were no messages from Ricardo. Something felt wrong. He didn't seem the type to stand her up. She was helping him. Pressing his number, she listened to his phone ringing out before the answerphone kicked in.

As she went to grab her bag off the floor, she caught sight of something black and shiny next to the television. Her hair clip. She ran to the bedroom, racing Einstein to the window. Too late. He'd escaped before she could shut him in.

'Einstein,' she called him in the baby voice he normally responded to but the cat simply licked his paws and jumped down onto the fence, then the pavement. With that, he was gone.

No way was Gary coming in again. Her cat would have to wait in the garden until she came home. She stared at the clip, her heart pounding and her mouth running dry. She took several deep breaths that soon sped up until she hyperventilated. Her head began to swim as she gripped the dining chair to steady herself. She had to get out of the flat, right now. She grabbed her coat and ran as fast as she could out of that building. As she reached the path, she glanced back at Mr Bull's flat. The curtains were now closed, shutting her out.

She'd been so close. If it wasn't Gary in that flat, it was someone who knew him well. It had to be. The person messing with her head was too close to her. It was like they were occupying the very same space in which she was living. Those bangs below, they were bangs of anger. She was making him angry and he knew everything about her.

They happened soon after her meal out with Tim. Then again, when Ricardo came into her flat. It screamed of Gary's jealousy.

She was going to get into that flat again, one way or another. She was going in. All she had to do was work out how.

THIRTY-TWO

OLLY

Olly filed the last of the utensils in the drawer. It had been another successful evening at The Flighty Hare thanks to her new menu. *The bream had gone down exceptionally well*, she thought as she completed her food order for the next day. All this was good practice for her own restaurant. Every week, she'd gauged how successful a dish was, what worked and what drew people back in time after time. She was going to do it all without Scott.

She placed her dirty whites in the laundry bin, and then changed from her soft shoes to her small-heeled shoes. Olly glanced at her phone, at all the pages she had open. The more she stared at that photo, the more she was sure that she knew who that person was but the name and age didn't fit.

'Bye, see you tomorrow,' she called to Vernon, the front of house manager, as she passed him in the cloakroom. She'd miss him. It was a shame she couldn't take him with her but it would be wrong to poach staff from the Hare. Maybe Libby would give up her city life to come and be a part of the team. She thought of her sister and she knew that the stress of all that had been happening was getting her down.

'Hope so, keeps us all busy.' There was always a sparkle in his smile. He leaned over the counter and pored over the diary. Olly left, it was eleven fifteen and she was on her way home.

The wind had picked up, but it wasn't too cold. Feeling the need to unwind, she headed to Tenby's seafront. Leaning against the railings, she gazed at the horizon. In the distance she could hear people leaving the pubs. She hadn't seen too many tourists over the past week and they were too quiet to be tourists. She listened as the sea lapped against the sand below. The night was clear and the stars plentiful. The moon shone down on the water's surface, gently highlighting the ripples that the wind whipped up. It was a picture of beauty.

Carefully walking down the stony steps, Olly reached the sand. Her heels buried themselves deep with every step she took. She decided to take the shoes off and walk with stocking-covered feet. That would help her to unwind. The cold sand eased her aching feet. Continuing to walk, she looked across at the next set of steps. They were probably about five hundred metres away, just far enough for a late private stroll.

In the distance she could see a light in the sea. When she focused more clearly she could tell it was a fishing boat. Then she remembered how much Scott liked fishing, he'd even mentioned getting a little boat. His promise to her was that they were going to have their own restaurant, cooking the fish he caught. That was the dream, the dream he shared with her until recently. He'd changed. First he'd taken a job in a factory, then he'd said they should have children. That's when she realised they both had different dreams. What he wanted was her night-mare. She closed her eyes as tears welled up.

The wind blew and she shivered. Why did he give up on the dream? Why now, when it was so close to hand? Olly hadn't told him that she'd spotted the perfect little restaurant with twelve covers, a sea view, already decorated perfectly with a fully equipped stainless-steel kitchen. Without him knowing, she'd put in an offer on the premises and it had been accepted. All she ever worked for in life was about to be rewarded and Scott wanted out. That's why it had ended. She'd lost in love but her work was her life. Food was her art, her passion, everything she woke up for every single day.

The wind howled, almost sounded like a gale. It was a good job the steps were close by. She'd soon be back up them and on her way home. A bag blew across the beach, she hated litter. It hid behind a rock as if sensing her disapproval.

Checking her phone, she noticed that Libby hadn't called her back despite the many missed calls. She'd been thinking about the girl in the well after talking about it with Libby. Olly remembered Louise and her friends, and how they intimidated the whole school. Jayne, her silly sidekick, had crumpled when Louise got murdered. Their tirade of terror had ended only to be replaced with a subdued nothing that continued until the end of term.

Earlier that day, she'd looked through some old school fete photos and saw a resemblance she couldn't ignore. She'd hoped to tell Libby, but Libby hadn't called back. There was something strikingly familiar about that kid, a visual connection she hadn't instantly made until she looked over the photos again.

As Olly approached the rocky area under the steps, she heard someone call. 'Help. Please help!' A man sprinted towards Olly, the peak of his cap covering his eyes, his scarf reaching the bottom of his chin. 'My friend, he's fallen down the steps over there and we don't have a phone. Can you call an ambulance?'

'Of course. Is he conscious?' Olly pulled her phone out of her pocket but then nearly dropped it as the familiar man took his cap off. What was he doing here? 'No, get away from me.'

She needed to warn Libby. She was in danger. As she went to step back he whacked Olly over the head with a rock. Over and over again the rock came down, every thwack touching a nerve, sending a white pain through her body. She fell to the ground and could only watch as her phone lit up in the distance, Olly tried to shuffle along the ground to reach it. She could see Libby's name on the screen. Dragging herself along the sand, she managed to touch the corner of the phone. *Just a bit farther*, but the pain was too much. The hardest blow yet landed on the front of her head.

Through half-opened eyes she could see him placing her phone into his pocket. 'Libby,' she whispered under her breath. Her vision blurred and her eyes closed. Too weak to fight, she allowed the icy sea to lap over her, drawing her into the arms of death.

THIRTY-THREE

LIBBY

Wednesday, 16 March

Michaela giggled as she held Kirsty up. It was alright for them, they both had the next morning off work. Libby's feet ached so much. She removed her heeled shoes and continued walking on the pavement. She checked her phone again, there were no messages from her sister or Ricardo. She hadn't seen him at the pub either.

After calling Olly a while back, Libby thought she might have returned her call when she finished work. Maybe Olly had turned her phone off if Scott had been calling her, or maybe she'd just forgotten to switch it off silent when she'd left work. Either way, it was just past two, too late to call. Olly would definitely be home by now and more than likely she'd be in bed. Placing the phone back in her pocket, she decided she'd catch up with Olly in her lunch break the next day.

'Wait for me,' she called to her friends as she ran towards

them. Kirsty was sitting on someone's wall and Michaela was standing beside her.

'Hurry up then, my kebab's getting cold.' Kirsty held up the bag of steaming food. Above them, a curtain twitched. Kirsty laughed and waved at the woman.

'Sorry, my feet are killing.' Libby hobbled faster to catch them up. After a few trips and laughs they all reached Canal House. That night out was exactly what she needed. It hadn't helped her to forget everything that was going on but it had helped to distract her for a while. Had she stayed in, she'd have spent all night listening out for noises and toiling in her own head as to what Gary would do next.

'It's been a brilliant night, you should do this more often with us,' Michaela slurred as she tripped over the small step at the base of the main door. Kirsty's knees clicked as she kneeled down to help her friend. As she leaned forward, she dropped her kebab on the floor.

'I'll get it.' Libby bent down and helped Kirsty lift Michaela back up.

'I think I'm a bit wasted and I sat on my hand.' Michaela cried with laughter.

'It's definitely bed for you when we get in.'

'Are you going to be alright?' Libby asked Michaela.

'Yes, she'll sleep it off.' Kirsty led Michaela through to their door. As Kirsty struggled to find her keys, Michaela leaned against Mr Bull's door. 'Hey, Mr what's your name, spy man. I don't want to go to bed alone. Do you hear me?' shouted Michaela with a huge drunken grin on her face.

'Michaela, for God's sake.' Kirsty shushed her as she unlocked their door and prised Michaela's abnormally long limbs from the bull man's door handle.

'I think you should be careful of him. I don't trust him.' Libby picked up the kebab and followed the two women into their lounge. 'I'll just leave this here.' She placed the wad of food on the coffee table.

'Thanks for that, I best get her to bed,' Kirsty replied as she helped Michaela get to the bedroom.

'No problem, I'm off to bed myself in a minute.'

Kirsty came back out alone. 'I think someone's going to have a thick head tomorrow afternoon while she's stacking those shelves. About what you said. Do you really think the bull man could be messing with us?'

Libby shrugged. She wanted to scream out yes, she did think that. The more she went through everything in her head, the more insane it all seemed. She suspected Gary of staying there but then she saw a yellow jacket on the back of the chair. Trevor hated her. Then Ricardo goes off grid. 'Someone stole my hair clip and then put it back, and someone broke into my flat and left a box of chocolates on the table.'

'Yeah, that is a bit creepy. And we have missing pants, but then again, they might turn up.'

'And don't forget Tim's pen.'

'Oh yeah, that fancy thing.'

Libby nodded. 'And a very angry man lives next to us. We never see him, don't you think it's strange?'

'I do.' She grabbed some pop and swigged it straight out of the large bottle.

'And then Tim gets that article. Someone hand delivered it. They came here, right up to this door in the hope that they wouldn't be seen. If it was Mr Bull, he could just pop it in the postbox as soon as he heard that there was no one outside. He's messing with us. It's more than obvious. Then there's his flat. There's nothing in it except beaten up furniture. No one lives like that. It's a second home if ever I've seen one and it's a home where someone lives to get up to no good.'

Kirsty giggled. 'It's not a shag pad then?'

'Yuck, definitely not unless whoever goes in there has no

standards. A back alley would be more luxurious.' Her mind was spinning with the idea that Gary might have rented it but even he had better standards. Maybe there was more to him. Her thoughts bounced to Trevor. She could see Trevor living in a place like that, wine bottles and dead things strewn all over the floor. 'Then there's the writing on the wall. Bettina claimed she was being watched. Who was watching her? I wonder if it's the same person who has taken all our things.'

Kirsty shivered. 'I'm trying not to think about that writing. You did say that she might have been taking drugs. Sleeping in a cupboard and paranoid ramblings. It's adding up to drugs.'

'You're probably right.' It was no good, her semi-drunken brain was too addled to work everything out. 'I best go, I have to get up at seven.' Libby yawned.

'I'm glad you came. That was fun. Hope the head's not too bad in the morning.' Kirsty opened up the kebab and began tucking in with her fingers. 'See you tomorrow.'

Libby crept out of their lounge, carefully closed the door behind her and hoped that their noisy return hadn't disturbed Tim. Libby listened in silence for a moment, the building was quiet. A distant bang came from Mr Bull's flat, then another, then a scrape. Only slight noises, but distinguishable. Maybe Mr Bull had been disturbed. She crept up one step at a time until she reached her door. The last thing she needed was a noise complaint against her.

On entering her flat she turned the hall light on and threw her shoes into the corner of the lounge. It was no longer a home. She stared at the hair clip, still where it had been placed by the intruder, then she glanced at the table where the chocolates had been left. She pulled her phone from her pocket and called Olly one more time. The answerphone kicked in. 'Give me a call when you get a moment, sis.'

Heart banging, she rushed to the bedroom to see if the window was still shut and it was. Her cat hadn't been around earlier. She opened the window and leaned out. 'Einstein,' she called. Listening, she hoped she'd hear his paws hitting the flat roof but there was nothing. It pained her to keep the window closed but it wouldn't be for long. Soon the cat door would be fitted and he wouldn't feel as though she'd shut him out. She wondered if he'd come back. He was going to leave her, she could tell. He was being fed and he wasn't as warm towards her as he used to be. Maybe he is now Mr Bull's cat.

She wandered to the bathroom and grabbed her make-up remover. Studying her reflection in the mirror, she saw a sad woman who was now looking slightly older than her thirty-one years. She also saw a horrible woman, one who had neglected her cat by shutting him out. All she wanted right now was his warmth and unconditional companionship. She wanted to hug someone, anyone. Coming back to the empty flat had hit her. It wasn't a place of comfort any more. It was tarnished by an intruder and all she wanted to do was talk to Olly and Olly wasn't there. In fact, Olly was hiding something from her and Libby knew it wasn't just about her and Scott. She'd seemed cagey when they'd spoken last.

Then she thought of Gary and remembered the time he'd surprised her with a weekend away to Bath. She refused to go as it was Saturday until Monday, even accusing him of being inconsiderate as he knew she had an important meeting first thing on the Monday. Then there was Valentine's night the previous year when he'd made her dinner, and she just had to say Olly's pasta was better. It wasn't a premeditated put-down but still, it happened. Then she stared hard into the eyes of the person she really was and momentarily she saw. Work could never demand too much or do no wrong even though the management treated her awfully. Had she pushed Gary to all this? The affair, the horrible messages.

Tears fell as she thought back to Olly's torment as a child, about the abuse. She deserved half of her sister's pain. She tried to forget and sometimes she did forget that Olly had taken the abuse to protect her for the sake of their togetherness. But, when she was feeling low, these memories would flood her mind. What she knew was patchy, but she'd filled in the gaps over the years. Maybe she had a warped view of what she thought she knew, but if she did, it was firmly fixed in her mind; eating away at her soul, not allowing her to love herself or be loved. She cried long and hard. The real her stared back and the real her was vacant, hollow and lacked meaning. Was life all worth it? She'd had a great night but that was all. One great night, but now, she had to go back to work tomorrow. She had to face the Trevors of this world and avoid the Garys too. She had to tread carefully around this shell of a home just in case some weirdo had got in.

She walked into the bathroom and opened the glass cabinet. In it were two full boxes of paracetamol tablets. She pushed all of them out of the blister packing onto the window ledge and poured a glass of water. She could end it all now and all the pain would be over. She grabbed the tablets and threw them at the wall. Most of them dropped into the bath. She knew she'd be too gutless like last time. The last thing she felt like doing was spending the night forcing herself to vomit by swigging salt water. She slammed her blistered foot into the wall tiles next to the sink. Blood trickled onto the white tiles. A hot pain shot up her foot and she flinched.

Her pounding heart began to slow down. As she rubbed the tears from her eyes she saw smeared mascara across her face. Her eyes were red and puffy. She could see why Gary went off with that woman. She peeled the back off a plaster, bent down and dressed the bloody nail.

She dragged her aching body back into the bedroom. Getting into bed fully clothed, she turned off the lamp and curled up like a little ball and cried hard as she tried to call Olly again. She thought she could cope, but she couldn't. The past few weeks were getting her down and the man underneath her was creeping her out.

As she lay weeping on her pillow, she heard a window opening. She jumped out of bed, wiped her eyes and stared out into the darkness. Coils of smoke danced up from Mr Bull's window, swirling as they dispersed into the early morning air. He was out there now. Was he listening to her cries of sadness? Was he disappointed that she'd left her window closed? She called Olly again and left another message. 'Please, Olly, I'm scared. Call me back.'

His window slammed shut and the smoke was gone.

THIRTY-FOUR

LIBBY

Libby called again and again; Olly didn't answer. Something wasn't right. She paced up and down the rug in her lounge, occasionally bumping into the coffee table. She stared out of the window. What for? She didn't know. That wasn't going to make Olly call her. A sister knows when there's something wrong and Libby could sense it. Her stomach turned and her whole body jittered, as if she'd been over caffeinated.

As she stared at her phone, it began ringing in her hand.

'Hi, lovely. Management are asking if you're coming in today. I tried to cover for you as long as I could but you know what they're like.'

She could picture the two emotionless men who ran the company probing Chrissie as to why she wasn't at her desk canvassing more companies. She'd also left Chrissie to check in her workforce and to search for any replacements for the no-shows. She hated to dump that on her lovely colleague, especially as she worked reception.

'Sorry to put this on you, Chrissie. I can't get hold of my sister. Something isn't right. I'm worried about her. I'll be in as soon as I can.' Libby felt tears trickling down her cheek. 'Sorry.

I'll be back tomorrow for definite. I need a few hours to pull myself together.' The grips of depression were dragging her down and there was no way she could sit at her desk, do her job and pretend that everything was okay. 'Bye, I'll call later to see how my contracts are doing.'

She hung up, hoping that Chrissie would forgive her abruptness. She went to the bathroom and picked up the pills that she'd thrown in the bath, then carefully placed them back into the box.

Again, she opened the window and called her cat and again, there was no response. She'd asked Michaela and Kirsty if they'd seen him but neither had. She'd knocked on Mr Bull's door continuously for several minutes, but he didn't answer. She shook her head and bit her lip. He didn't answer because she knew him. That's the conclusion she was going with.

Exhaustion was taking over. She grabbed a blanket from the back of the sofa, wrapped herself in it and rested her head on the sofa's arm, then drifted off to sleep.

Bang. A door slammed below her and the keys on the table rattled. She heard shouting, but she couldn't work out what words were being shouted. Rubbing her eyes, she sat up. She'd only been sleeping for an hour. She stood and bent her legs to shake off the stiffness that had set in. Taking a deep breath, she tried to think. Olly must still be in bed after a busy shift and she would phone Libby back as soon as she saw all her missed calls. Work was already peeved at her but her head wasn't in the right place to go in now.

She turned her computer on, hoping to distract herself until she managed to speak to Olly. Logging on to Facebook, she spotted a personal message sent from Ian Linden.

Hi Libby, Glad I've managed to find you after all these years.
You look as beautiful as ever, not much different from when we

were at school. So what do you get up to now, maybe we could go out one night? I'd love to catch up. Ian.

Great. She hated receiving messages where people from the past cracked on to her and she didn't need more complications. Closing the message, she chose not to reply. She'd never been that close to Ian at school anyway.

She hesitated and stared at the computer before opening the message again. The last thing she wanted was to come across as rude and he would see that she'd read the message.

Hi Ian, It's lovely to hear from you again. I'm so busy at the moment with work so I'll have to decline your lovely invitation. I'm glad you're okay and it's nice to be in touch again. Libby.

She read it back. It was nothing more than a pleasant rejection. She hoped he'd get the hint. A reply pinged back before she'd even taken her fingers off the keyboard.

Too busy to meet up for a drink with an old friend?

'You idiot,' she whispered. Why did she have to reply? Why didn't she ignore him? Now she'd made herself real by replying. She was here at the other end of Facebook and he knew.

Sorry Ian, now's not a good time.

Tactful, she thought. States clearly that he needs to back off.

I think you're playing hard to get. You know you want to. I can show you things you've never seen before, give you feelings you've never experienced. Meet me today, you know you're curious.

Libby stared at the message, not quite believing what she'd read. Although Ian didn't know where she lived, she felt his presence in the room with her, oppressively forcing her into a corner.

Reply to me Libby, I feel so hurt now.

Another message. Ian was relentless. She placed her fingers on the keys. How could she tactfully word what she wanted to say? What would she do if he wouldn't take no for an answer? She knew what Olly would say, *delete the freak.* Olly, where was Olly now? She also knew that it was good advice but she couldn't delete him. She wasn't like Olly in that respect. She couldn't delete and ignore what she knew in her heart had happened. Maybe she should meet Ian. Maybe if she did, she'd be able to punish Gary once and for all. She could just drink with him, have sex with him and leave it at that.

She trembled as her fingers hovered over the keypad.

I'm still waiting. It's rude to keep someone waiting!

She swallowed and stared at the screen.

You can't fool me, you're still there, aren't you? :-)

Her fingers trembled. She knew he was guessing but he was freaking her out now. She logged out of Facebook and navigated back to the Google homepage. She paced to the window. Her gaze darted from the road, to the houses, then to the apartments opposite. There was no one there. Locks and chains on her doors suddenly didn't feel protective. They could come straight to her through her phone, through her computer, through her window if she left it open. Right there in front of her, they played games with her mind. She grabbed the curtains and pulled them together.

Sitting in darkness, she pulled out her phone and selected Ricardo. The call went straight to voicemail. 'Hi, it's Libby again. Can you call me back when you get this message? Just wondering how you are. Bye.' That was the third message she'd left.

Grabbing her jacket and bag off the back of the chair, she left the flat. The Cropton Hotel was her next stop. Something in her gut told her she needed to find him. However much she'd tried to tell herself that he'd found Bettina and all was now fine, she couldn't believe that he would intentionally ignore her like this.

Maybe he'd got too close to the truth. She swallowed the lump in her throat. Every move she made felt dangerous. Whoever sent those messages wasn't Ian Linden. Everything is connected somehow. Ricardo, Gary, Mr Bull.

As she ran down the path, she almost bumped into Tim. 'Morning, Libby.'

'Can't stop,' she called back as she turned the corner past the chip shop. If she stopped, her mind would take her to dark places and she didn't want to enter that dark void. If she did, she might never return.

THIRTY-FIVE

LIBBY

As Libby entered The Cropton she was greeted by the receptionist. 'Can I help you?' The woman held her head high and smiled.

'Yes, a friend of mine is staying here, Ricardo Falco. Can you please check to see if he's in?'

'Sure. Bear with me a moment. I'll phone his room for you.' After a few seconds she returned the receiver to the phone. 'I'm afraid he's not answering at the moment. Would you like to leave him a message?'

Libby nodded. The receptionist handed Libby a piece of paper and a pen. 'Thank you.'

Hello Ricardo, Please call me. I was wondering if you're alright. You've probably found Bettina by now and maybe you forgot that we were meant to meet yesterday but I got a little worried about you. Hopefully I'll hear from you later and all is fine. Libby.

Libby folded the piece of paper and handed it to the woman.

'I'll make sure he gets it for you.' She held out her hand and took the note.

'Thank you.' Libby hurried out of the hotel and headed down the side streets, making her way to the Sun's Rays. Maybe he'd been back to the pub. It wasn't quite twelve so she gazed through the window. There was a young man setting up and an older man perched on a stool at the end of the bar, reading a paper. Libby knocked on the window.

'We're not open,' the young man mouthed back.

'Please.' Libby watched as he walked to the front door and opened it.

'You can come in and wait. I'm not set up yet though.' He held a cloth in his hand.

'Are you Liam?' Libby tilted her head.

'Yes, how do you know my name? You were in last night, weren't you, with your friends. Let me guess, you left an umbrella, lost your phone, purse or coat.'

'No, I was in but it's not that.' If only it was as simple as losing an umbrella. She'd lost Ricardo and that was more important. 'Can I just have a quick chat? Have you spoken to a man called Ricardo, an Italian man asking about his daughter?'

'Come in.' She followed him to the bar. The man with the newspaper looked up at her then continued to read.

'He came in the other day. He was looking for Bettina. I knew Bettina. We had a long chat about her.'

'Me too. I mean I didn't know Bettina but I've been chatting to him about her. I live in the flat where she used to live. He was meant to meet me yesterday but didn't turn up. Have you seen him since?'

'Not since the other night. He said he'd keep me updated. Bettina was a good friend of mine and she just left one day. You can't tame a bird.'

'What do you mean?' Libby scrunched her brows as she leaned on the bar.

'She lived and worked from place to place, not planning much. She just embraced her freedom, that's what I meant.' He smiled. The older man stood from his stool and opened the front door to the public. Three men entered, then waited at the bar. 'I hope you catch up with him anyway, seemed like a nice bloke. Billy, what can I get you?'

He turned away to serve the customers. Libby picked up the pen next to the newspaper and scribbled her number on the corner of a beer mat.

'If you see him, can you call me? I'm seriously worried about him. I just want to know that he's okay.' Liam nodded as he served. 'Thanks.' With that, Libby hurried back out onto the street feeling even more confused and walked back to her flat.

As she placed her key in the door, her mobile started ringing. As she rushed to open the door, she grabbed her phone. 'Hello.'

'Libby,' the caller went silent. Could she hear someone crying?

'Hello. Who is this?'

'It's Scott.'

'Scott, are you alright, is everything okay?' There was something in his tone that caused alarm. She kneeled on the floor as she gripped the phone. 'Scott, what's wrong, has something happened?'

'I've just had a visit from the police.' He broke down. Libby listened to him sobbing.

'Scott, what is it? Is Olly okay?'

'She's...' He cried. Libby began to cry too. Whatever had happened had to be bad. She'd never heard Scott cry. Even though Olly wasn't happy with him, she knew that he still loved her. 'She's on...' the man sobbed, 'she's on life support. It's not looking good.'

'No, she can't be. There must be some mistake. There has to be a mistake. It's not Olly. It's someone else.'

'There is no mistake, Libby. I'm with her now.'

'No, tell me it's not true.' Tear after tear slid down Libby's cheeks. 'Please, not Olly. How, why?' There was no reply. 'Scott, what happened to her?'

'It looks like she was attacked last night on the beach. I should've met her. I should've been there. I always used to walk her home after work but she didn't want me to be there, she didn't want me any more, Libby. I love her so much, I really do,' he cried. 'I can't believe it myself.' Libby heard what sounded like a doctor talk in the background. 'I have to go, the police are here and they want to ask me some questions about Olly. I'll text you the name of the hospital and I'll ring you in a bit.' He ended the call.

Libby threw the phone to the floor and held her knees to her chest. Olly, her precious sister, the only person in the world who really knew her, on life support. She couldn't lose her sister. More than anything else she longed to feel Olly's warmth, to hear Olly's voice – both of which she feared she'd never experience again.

There was a knock at her door. Ignoring it, Libby carried on crying. The last thing she wanted was visitors. Again, there was a knock. She stomped across the lounge and out to the hall. 'What the hell is it?' she wailed, with reddened eyes and a face drenched with tears.

'I was coming up the stairs and I heard you crying. I just wanted to know that you weren't hurt.' Tim stepped back from the door.

'I'm sorry.'

'There's no need to apologise. Are you alright? I didn't know if you were hurt.'

'No.' Libby broke down once more. Tim crept closer to her and put his arm over her shoulder, pulling her closer to him. She nestled into his broad chest and held onto him tightly. 'I've just been told my sister's in a coma and on life support.'

'That's terrible. No wonder you're so upset. What happened?'

'Someone attacked her.' She stepped aside. 'Come in.' She led Tim into the lounge. 'I just got the call. She was attacked on her way home from work last night.'

'I'm so sorry, Libby. That's awful news. Poor Olly.'

She allowed him to lead her to the sofa. Sitting beside her, he held her close and placed his arms around her as she cried. Libby buried her head into Tim and continued to tremble and cry, grateful that she had someone to share her grief with. She held him and embraced his warmth, which filled the hole that was her loneliness. He didn't move. He dutifully provided her with the comfort she needed.

'Have they arrested any one?'

'I don't think so. Scott, her partner, is talking to the police.'

Tim stood and walked into the kitchen, leaving Libby hugging a cushion. She stared out of the window wondering when Scott would text her. She needed to know which hospital Olly was in and then she needed to get over to Tenby and be with her.

Tim came back in with a hot cup of tea. 'Here you go.' He placed it on the coffee table before stroking her hair and holding her again. She couldn't hold back the second wave of sobs. 'Which hospital is she in?'

'I'm waiting for Scott to message me. I knew something was wrong. I've been trying to call her all night. I can't believe someone did this to my sister. She'd never hurt anyone.'

'Come here.' Tim stroked her hair and she liked it. She didn't try to stop him, she didn't want to stop him. That kiss, it wasn't an accident. It was the wrong time. Now wasn't the right time, but he was here for her when no one else was.

'Thank you for being here.' She leaned forward and kissed him on the cheek. It was at that moment, she knew, she did have someone who cared and she could tell that Tim would be there for her while she got through these awful times. She sniffed and grabbed a tissue to blow her nose into. Sitting here crying wasn't helping Olly. She needed to be with her. 'I'm going to head to Tenby, will you look out for my cat and bring him in if you see him. I'm worried about him as he hasn't come home. I don't want to lose him.' Again, she burst into tears. The thought of losing her sister and Einstein was all too much.

'I will find him, I promise, and I'll look after him. He can stay with me until you get back. I can drive you there, if you want. You shouldn't go on the train like this.'

'No, honestly, I'm fine. I'm not going to put you out like that. Looking after the cat is enough and I'm grateful.'

'Okay, if you change your mind, you only have to say. You shouldn't go through this alone.'

'I'm okay. Olly and I have always been alone.'

'It doesn't always have to be like this, Libby. I'm here for you, you know that.' He brushed her cheek with his hand and looked into her eyes.

She nodded. 'Thank you. Do you mind leaving me to it? I need to be alone. I have a few phone calls to make and things to sort.'

He stood. 'Of course not. Just knock if you need me. You have my number too and if you change your mind, I'm more than happy to drive you.'

She pressed her lips together and walked him to the door. As soon as he was gone, she'd pack a bag with a few bits and head over there.

When she heard his door close, she muffled her sobs so that Tim wouldn't hear. Silently she screamed and wailed, and hit the cushions. The loss of Olly would be the biggest loss she would ever experience in her life. Staring at the walls and rerunning memories of Olly was all she could manage. Her phone beeped again.

How's grandad? Is he keeping it up?

She'd had it with Gary. Her phone rang, it was Chrissie. 'Hello,' she said through her hiccupping sobs.

'Love, what's happened?'

She relayed everything to her friend.

'I finish work at two today. You need someone to take you and I'm not letting you go alone on the train so pack up your stuff, I'll be there with the car.'

'Thank you.' For once in her life, Libby was going to accept help from someone other than Olly. She swallowed. There was no way she could lose Olly. Her sister was her life. The one person she could depend on.

THIRTY-SIX

LIBBY

Libby paced outside the hospital as she regained her breath. All those tubes and the rising and falling of Olly's chest had floored her. She'd immediately crumpled into Scott's arms. Her beautiful sister, lying on that machine fighting for her life was a sight she wanted to erase. She wanted to walk right back in there and see Olly sitting up in bed, eating and laughing.

She kicked a bench and grasped her hair between her fingers. The greasy strands tangled and pulled until she held a clump in her hand. That's what comes of messing with it for hours. First during the journey, then during the many waits to see a doctor. She had yet to see the doctor. Everyone was busy, everything was an emergency. Her phone rang.

Grabbing it, she answered to Chrissie.

'Hi, love. I'm on hands-free so if it sounds bad you know why. Have you got any news?'

'She's really bad, Chrissie.' As Libby paced, she bumped into a man dragging a drip in one arm with a cigarette dangling from his mouth. She held her hand up and mouthed an apology. 'I don't know if she's going to make it.' Tears dripped down her cheeks and off her chin.

'From what you've told me, your sister is the strongest person ever. You have to keep hope alive. She will make it, Libby.'

'Someone left her there to die. She was hit over the head many times. She was trying to call me and I missed her call. I didn't answer. I could have helped her. It's all my fault.'

'Libby, love. You're upset and that's simply not true. The only person to blame is the horrible person who did this to your sister. Have you spoken to the police yet?'

She bit her lip and wiped her eyes. 'No.'

'For now, all you need to do is to be there for her. Be strong. You know I'm here for you too. If you need anything or you want to talk, just pick up that phone, okay?'

She nodded, knowing that Chrissie couldn't see her. Scott hurried out of the door and caught her attention. 'I've got to go.' She thanked Chrissie and ended the call. 'Scott, is everything okay?'

'No, I don't know what to do with myself. I sit, I hold her hand and I watch that machine make her chest rise and fall.' He pulled a cigarette from his pocket.

'I didn't know you smoked.'

'I do when I'm stressed. I messed up.' He kept shaking his head as he lit the cigarette. 'She didn't want to be with me any more.'

Libby didn't know what to say. That much was true. From what Olly said, they were both going in different directions.

'I still love her, even if we're not together. I will be here for her if she needs me or needs any help and when I find out who did this to her, I'm going to kill the bastard. I swear it.' He dropped the half-smoked cigarette to the ground and stubbed it out. 'I can't sit there alone. If I do, I think I'm going to go mad. Will you sit with me?'

Libby nodded. 'I'll be there in a minute.'

'Thanks, Lib.' She hugged him and he turned to go back.

She'd always liked Scott and even with their situation, she was grateful that he was around for Olly. She placed a hand over her mouth and closed her eyes as she held a sob in. Rain flecked her nose and a slight gust began to pick up. She checked her phone again and spotted a message from the messenger claiming to be Ian Linden. Shivering, she read it.

I guess you had to leave in a hurry. I'm missing you not being around. Maybe I'll call you again soon. I like to hear you breathe, to know that you're close to me, to hear your voice. You want me as much as I want you. You know we are meant to be together. You don't need those other men in your life. You only need me. X

The one person she needed to speak to right now was in a coma. She tried to breathe in but she couldn't. She was almost choking on air. Leaning on the brick wall next to the entrance, she fought to get air into her lungs, the car park ahead swayed and leaned as she battled her dizzy head. Stumbling through the hospital, she needed to be with Olly. She was safe in intensive care. No one could hurt her there. As she hurried down the long clinical corridors, the smell of disinfectant nauseating her, she soon reached the right ward. The nurse buzzed her in. As she reached Olly's bed, she saw Scott tapping away on his phone. She went to sit on a chair next to Olly but Scott came over and hugged her. It was weird. Too weird. He wouldn't let go and his warm breath that tickled her neck made her tremble. This didn't feel right.

As she went to pull away, two uniformed police officers came through the door. His hands dropped as he stared at them open-mouthed. The taller officer moved in closer. 'Scott Fisher. I'm arresting you on suspicion of attempted murder. You do not have to say anything. But, it may harm your defence if you do not mention when questioned something which you later rely on in court. Anything you do say will be given in evidence.'

Libby stepped back, unable to speak in what felt like such a surreal moment. 'Scott.'

As they took him, he turned back. 'I didn't do it, Libby. I love her. Tell her I didn't do it.'

Libby fell into the chair and stared as they went through the double doors. Visitors sitting next to other beds looked on. The machine continued to beep and Olly lay there, unaware of all that was happening. Her black hair brushed off her face, tube in nose and the larger tube in her mouth – it was as if Olly was a shell.

Scott – the police must have something to be able to charge him. She placed her hand over Olly's and laid her head on the edge of the bed. 'Please wake up, Olly. I need you. I can't do any of this without you. You're my rock, sis. Please don't leave me.' She sobbed onto the sheet, unable to peel her face away. Not wanting to be parted from the sister she might never speak to again.

THIRTY-SEVEN

LIBBY

Thursday, 17 March

Libby parted the curtains and stared at the Tenby beach from the bed and breakfast room, the same beach that Olly had suffered a brutal attack on. She thought of Scott, his face and the way he seemed just before the police took him. That was the last she heard from him but she had heard from the police. They were holding him for now as a man was seen at the scene. He was Scott's height and Scott didn't have an alibi and the argumentative messages on their phones had been inflammatory.

She pressed Tim's number and waited for him to answer.

'Hi, Libby. How's Olly?'

She exhaled and closed the curtains. She'd had enough of replaying Olly's attack in her mind. 'Not good. She could be like this for days, even weeks, that's if she even...' She couldn't contemplate that Olly would die.

'Don't even think that, Libby. She's going to be fine, okay?'

'They've arrested her partner, Scott.'

'Really?'

'Yes, she'd just told him it was over. I'm going to come back home tomorrow.' Truth was, Libby didn't really have the money to stay there and the last thing she wanted to do was to call Gary and ask for her savings money, not yet.

'Okay, do you want me to pick you up?'

She bit her thumbnail. 'No, I'm getting the train. Did Einstein come back?'

'No, sorry. I went out last night looking for him but I couldn't find him.'

She wrapped her arms around herself, not wanting to go back to her empty flat without him.

'I'll go out again tonight and I'll ask around. Someone must have seen him.'

'I've seen him. He goes into Mr Bull's flat. He's in there, I know he is.' She didn't know Einstein was there now. She hit the bed frame.

'Libby.'

Sniffing, she held back the tears that were threatening to spill. 'I saw him in there a couple of times. That man lets him in. Einstein knows him. Mr Bull knows me.'

'Do you know him? I didn't know you'd met.'

'We haven't.' She balled her fists up. It had to be Gary. It had to be Trevor. It had to be... How the hell did she know? All she knew is that since she moved into Canal House, above that man, her life had descended into darkness. Ricardo had gone, her sister had been attacked and left for dead and she didn't know what the hell was going on.

'Libby, I'm worried about you.'

He was sweet, so sweet. Libby was ruining everything she touched. She had to back away from him. She had to keep away from Kirsty and Michaela. All the bad that was happening was telling her that she was the common denominator. Why?

'He's Ian Linden.' Ridiculous, maybe. That's the name he was going by.

'Who?'

She shook her head. 'No one. Sorry. I'm talking nonsense. I just don't know anything any more.' What she did know was that as soon as she got back, she was going to have to get into Mr Bull's flat. She had to see him for herself. It was the only way.

'Libby, you've had a huge shock. Don't be sorry. I'll keep you posted on Einstein, okay?'

'Thank you. See you tomorrow.' She ended the call and sat on the edge of the creaky bed. Less than a minute later, her phone rang and it was a withheld number, again. The sound of purring followed heavy breathing. 'Einstein.'

The caller hung up. 'No.' She lay back on the bed and cried as she pressed Gary's number.

'I knew you'd call.'

'Give him back to me.'

'What the hell are you on, Libby?'

'Why did you take him? I have nothing left. You took everything from me. I loved you and you were horrible to me. First Olly and now Einstein. How could you do this to me?'

'You're losing it, Libby. I do not have the cat.'

'And I'm meant to believe you after all the messages? You follow me, you're abusive. You're a real piece of work but this is low, even for you. Do you like parading around as Mr Bull? Do you?'

He paused. 'Libby, I should explain. I've been going through some things, drinking too much. Those messages I sent and the way I was with you, it's not me. I'll send the money to your account next week. I'll sort it then. You'll never hear from me after that. I have been the biggest dick and I should never drink again. I don't deserve your forgiveness so I won't ask for it. Really, I hate myself. Is that what you want to hear?'

It was a start. 'Why are you pretending to be other people? Mr Bull. Ian Linden. Stop trying to drive me mad, Gary.'

'I'm not. I don't know who the hell Mr Bull or Ian Linden are. I haven't hidden who I am in any message. When I've messaged or called, it's been from my phone.' He paused.

'I don't believe you.' All he'd ever done was lie to her and right now, she didn't believe him. He'd say all this and later he'd send another horrible message.

'Whatever. Believe me, don't believe me. You sound crazy and I haven't got the cat. I never wanted the cat anyway, why would I come back for him? He doesn't even like me.'

She slammed the phone down. He came back for the cat to punish her and he was playing total ignorance when it came to denying he knew Mr Bull. Lying there, all she could see behind her closed eyes as she stared at the ceiling in the dark was Olly. Her happy face, her ambition and her strength. Where would Libby be without the strength of her sister. She thought of Scott... how could he do what he did?

She would expose what a great big liar Gary was as soon as she got home.

THIRTY-EIGHT

LIBBY

Monday, 21 March

The train journey home had seemed the longest ever.

Scott had called her. They'd let him go due to lack of evidence. She'd ignored him several times, but eventually she'd picked up yesterday. One of his neighbour's had provided him with an alibi. She'd seriously doubted him but now he was back by Olly's side. A twinge of guilt flashed through her. She had him pegged as a potential murderer. Scott, of all people. She called Chrissie.

'Hi, how's things?'

'I need some compassionate leave. I'm home but I need to be by the phone. There's no way I could concentrate if I came into work.'

'No worries. No one expected you to come in after news like that.'

She cleared her throat. 'How are my contracts doing?'

'They are ticking along nicely.'

'Has Trevor been back in?' This time was hers now. It was more than compassionate leave, it was investigative leave – but that secret was hers alone. She was going to work out who was behind everything that was happening. She would do it for herself and for Olly.

'He's been lurking outside, staring up at the offices but he's not here now.'

She knew that much. He was after her, no one else but her. She was to blame for everything that went wrong in his eyes and losing that welding contract – that had been the big trigger.

'I laid it down with management, told them everything you've gone through with him. I said that Shelly was scared of him too. They've agreed that we should turn him away in future and call the police if he causes any more trouble. Finally, they listened.'

It might be too late. That's what she wanted to say. 'That's great. I best go, thank you for everything.' Libby ended the call and grabbed her full bin bag to take down to the bin.

When she got downstairs, she listened at Mr Bull's door. Not a sound came from his flat. She'd also knocked at Tim's earlier, but then she remembered he said something about having to go and see his mother.

She threw her rubbish bag in the bin and leaned against the wall. She thought of Olly attached to the ventilator having test after test. Her head injuries were so severe that her body had almost given up. There was hope. The odds were low but hope was something she could still cling to. Olly was a fighter, if anyone could pull through an ordeal as bad as she'd suffered, she could. Libby felt a wetness spreading across her back and shoulders. It had started to rain. Her tears discreetly mixed with the raindrops that fell. She smiled as she cried, she had to be strong for Olly's sake. If her sister was lucky enough to fight death, Libby would need all her strength to help her during her recovery.

She listened to the rain tapping on the bin lids. All around her it fell to the ground and trickled down the road, searching for a drain. Darkness enveloped the skies above, it was morning but it looked more like a winter's evening. She stared at her closed curtains knowing full well that her flat would be as gloomy as the weather. The wind howled. A plastic carrier bag shot past her face before getting trapped behind the wall. Libby leaned down to grab the bag.

A banging noise came from the side of the building. Libby walked round to see that Mr Bull's small bathroom window was open and off the catch. As the wind howled, the window banged in time with it and produced a disturbing symphony. Mr Bull's bin had blown over. She picked it up before placing the bag into the bin, then she leaned the bin tidily against the side wall.

The little window continued to bang. Libby pressed on it to stop the noise before climbing onto the bin. It was now or never. Time to find out who this man was and to get her cat back.

She peered through the tiny window. His bathroom was very much like hers, except a syringe lay on the toilet seat. How odd. Here lived a man, a so-called businessman, and all he had in his bathroom was bleach. Where were the bottles of shampoo, the razors, toothpaste, things people used every day? Her hand slipped on the wet bin. Setting her foot back on the ground, she carefully lowered the other one. Hair dripping, she wiped the rain from her face with the arm of her coat. Libby walked over to the back gate. She'd never been in the back garden before. There was a slide lock on the inside but it wasn't locked. Creeping over to his front window, she noticed his curtains were closed, except for a thin gap

Libby crept to the communal window, then around the other side of the building to look through Kirsty and Michaela's side window. They weren't in. She remembered that they'd gone on a day trip to London. Hurrying to the mystery man's back window, she then realised that she was covered from Tim's line of sight by a small canopy that hung over. Feeling confident that she wouldn't be seen, she leaned against Mr Bull's window and peered through.

The rain bounced off the canopy above her. Adjusting her focus to the gloomy kitchen, she could see that it was similarly laid out to hers. Again, it was strangely bare, no pictures, no bread bin, no toaster, not even a cooker. It was as if no one really lived there. Focusing harder, she could see that there were items on the worktop. A box of cereal, some long-life milk, tablets of some description, empty tins of tuna and some cat food. She thought of Einstein's weight gain and his lack of interest in anything she had to offer him. Her life had become unexpectedly complicated when it should've been simplified once she'd moved into Canal House. There were the phone calls, the mystery of Bettina, Ricardo never making contact again, not to mention the noises coming from beneath her.

Fear ran through her mind, she thought back to the uncomfortable messages from Ian Linden, the unpleasantness she'd gone through with Trevor and Gary, Olly's attack, Einstein's disappearance. It all felt wrong. Mr Bull was all wrong.

A loud scrape came from behind the walls. The kitchen door flew open. Libby's heart thumped as she ducked out of view. Rain pelted on her as she squatted beneath the window and hoped that he hadn't seen her. She estimated him to be slightly taller than her, but she'd seen no more. Her legs began to shake. She knew they'd soon give way. Her dolly shoes were soaked through and were beginning to slip along the pavement. Giving in, she fell onto the slabs and soon felt the water soaking through her jeans and underwear. She shivered as the dampness spread. Thunder crashed loudly above, a flash of lightning filled the sky like a broad sheet of light.

Not knowing how long he'd be in the kitchen for, she remained still. If he was as dangerous as she suspected, she wouldn't want him to catch her snooping. The gate swung and creaked as the wind caught it.

She had to get out of the garden, there was a possibility that he'd come out to close it. If he did, he'd fall over her. She crawled on her knees along the wet slabs towards the gate and opened it as gently as she could. Looking up, she saw that his back was turned and he was holding a mobile phone to his ear. As she stood, she ran out of the garden and back to the side of the building. Immediately her phone rang. She pulled it out of her pocket, it was a withheld number. Her hands began to shake. Was it him? Was Mr Bull calling her right at this very moment? It all seemed too much of a coincidence. The phone stopped ringing. She ran to the front door, unlocked it and then stumbled up the stairs into her flat, locking the door behind her. The phone rang again. She answered. 'Hello.' The other end was silent. 'I know who you are,' she whispered in a broken voice. Still shaking, she forced herself to listen.

'Do you really know me?' the voice said, putting the emphasis on the me. It was a muffled voice she had no recognition of, as if the person was speaking through a piece of material. The call ended.

Soaking wet, Libby slid her back down the front door and listened. Not a sound came from below. Shaking violently, heart pounding, she placed the phone on the floor and wiped her dripping brow. Out of the silence she heard the scraping of a door and then a slam. Moments later she heard him come back through the door, it seemed odd that the sound of him trailed off for a few moments but then came back. She heard him drag a chair from under the table and scrape it across the floor. *Do you really know me?* Those words ran through her head. She had to prove it, she had to get evidence and go to the police. Whoever was behind her misery could have hurt Olly.

She'd sit and wait for as long as it took, until he went out, then she was going in. If she called the police now with nothing but her thoughts, she could look stupid. The man has cat food in his kitchen and a syringe. He may be diabetic and, yes, he may feed cats. It might not make him a serial harasser or an attacker of any description. Every thought she had might be wrong but it didn't feel that way.

Loud bangs came from below. It sounded like a chair had been flung against the wall before being kicked around the room. Glass smashed and the thuds from the room vibrated through Libby's body. A door slammed so hard the cups on her cup tree rattled, then it went silent. Trembling, Libby dialled the hospital. She had to get an update on Olly.

'Hello, it's Olly's sister, Libby. I wondered if there was any change.'

The nurse paused for a moment and flicked through a few sheets of paper. 'Not since you called a moment ago. She's still critical as I said, but her stats are improving slightly.'

'That's brilliant news. But I didn't call a moment ago,' Libby replied.

'I thought—' the nurse paused. 'I'm sorry, I thought it was you, I must be mistaken.'

'Did someone call and pretend to be me?' Libby cried.

'As I say, I must be mistaken. I thought it was you. Maybe it was your mother or another family member?' Libby hadn't even told her mother what had happened. Their parents had never cared before, she couldn't see them dropping their lives and coming back to help, so she hadn't called them.

'Thanks.' Libby cut the call. Someone pretending to be her and calling the hospital... it could only be Olly's attacker. Bangs and crashes came from below. Were they the frustrations of someone who hadn't managed to finish off his victim? The rage of someone who could be identified maybe. Gary hated Olly.

She walked to the bedroom, removed her wet clothes and threw them into a pile on the floor. She changed into her leggings, a long-sleeved T-shirt and soft pumps, then she waited and listened. A door slammed again, then the back door slammed. She ran to the kitchen window and looked out. There was no sign of Mr Bull. He must've left quickly and gone down the side of the building. Running to the living room window she glanced out. There were several people walking up the path, no one she recognised. One of them could be him she thought as she peered through the netting. The crowd cleared. She knew if she was going to act, she had to act now before he returned.

She opened her front door and peered through the gap. A rustling sound filled the stairway and she waited. The postbox slammed shut, it must be Tim. She heard the man walk up the stairs. Closing her door, she waited for his door to close. Tim would definitely not approve of what she was about to do.

She crept out of her flat and down the stairs. The last thing she needed was Tim coming out and talking to her for ages, or trying to invite himself in for a coffee. She opened the main door, which creaked as it closed and ran to the side of the building. The rain had stopped. Darting to the bin, she wiped away the rain that had gathered in a little pool on the lid before climbing on top of it.

The walkway alongside the house was fairly narrow and she couldn't hear anyone about. Standing tall on the bin, she stepped onto the window ledge. She peered through the window, there was no one around and the place was silent. It was going to be tough to squeeze through but she knew she could do it. She lifted her leg through the window, and after a moment of wrestling with the half-drawn curtain, she placed her foot on the inside ledge. Slowly but surely she managed to ease her body in stages through the tiny hole, fearing all the time that she might get stuck. She followed her body through with her last leg, knocking the bottle of bleach over as she lost her balance and almost fell. Her phone dropped out of her pocket and smashed into several pieces as it hit the ground. 'Damn!' Libby picked up the pieces and put them in her pocket.

She massaged her temples and contemplated heading straight out the front door and back upstairs to her flat, then she decided that she might never get the opportunity again and she had to go ahead as planned. She listened intently, the building was silent. She was in the mysterious Mr Bull's bathroom. She had to go and explore before he came back and who knew when that would be. What the hell was she letting herself in for?

THIRTY-NINE

LIBBY

Libby's hand trembled as she brought the door handle down and pushed. She peered through the gap at the empty room before closing the door again. Leaning against it, she pressed her hand on her heart. The thumping of her heart pounding filled her head. If the mystery man came home, she doubted whether she would hear him. Taking a few deep breaths, she gazed around the small bathroom.

The syringe that was present earlier was nowhere to be seen. She opened the bathroom cabinet. There was nothing there. Where had it gone? There wasn't even a waste bin in the bathroom to dispose of any rubbish. She pressed the bath panel in the hope of dislodging it but it remained in place. She could tell that nothing was hidden behind it as the sealant was intact.

Her passing thought that whoever lived in this flat might be diabetic had gone out of the window. Why would anyone who cared about themselves place a syringe they were going to use on something as dirty as a toilet? Especially that one. She gazed at the cruddy yellow grime at the base of the loo and scrunched her nose. Maybe he was a drug addict. That might be a better reason for him having a syringe, especially as he didn't seem to spend his money on comfortable home furnishings and suffers from terrible mood swings. Her mind bounced back to Trevor and his mood swings when he was drunk. Was there more at play? Maybe he was taking drugs. Then there was Gary's confession, that his drinking had caused him to send her all those abusive messages. Her mind was awhirl with possibilities, none that made any sense, and then there was Olly and her cat. What was going on? She wanted to hold her head in her hands and scream.

With trembling hands, she gripped the door handle and opened it again. As she crept into the living room, she noticed that it was exactly as it was on the day she wandered in. The computer was on the table and a couple of kitchen chairs had been thrown on the floor. Beside it, a leather executive chair faced the computer. Hearing footsteps treading up the path outside, she retreated back into the bathroom. The footsteps stopped outside the main door. She slid the lock. If she had to, she'd force her body back through the window and she'd run as fast as she could. She couldn't get caught breaking in. Her heart beat so fast she could barely hear what was going on outside. The loud bang sent her stumbling back against the bath. After listening for a moment, it was obvious that whoever had come up to the door had gone away. She peered out of the window and saw a man in a Royal Mail uniform hurrying past. Exhaling with relief, Libby slid the lock on the bathroom door and went back into the lounge. That had felt like too much of a close thing. She had to hurry, gather the information she needed and get out as fast as possible.

She listened to the noises that the building made, making sure that he wasn't there. The creaks in the old walls, the pipes that growled when the hot water was running, the sound of the whirring washing machine when the laundry room was being used – there was nothing.

The flashing standby light on the computer caught her

attention. She hurried to the table. As she pushed the mouse, the screen lit up. That's when she saw her living room, the perfect bird's eye view of her settee, her table and the entrance to the kitchen. That day when she'd found the pile of dust under the coffee table, it must have been because he'd broken in and fitted a camera. That's how Gary had known everything. That's why Bettina had written that he was always watching her. She knew about the cameras. Suddenly, she couldn't breathe. The pressure in her head felt as though it might explode. All she wanted to do was kick it to pieces. All this time, he'd watched her every move. He'd followed her, saw her with Ricardo and saw her with Tim. He'd heard her breakdowns, her personal conversations. He was Ian Linden. He couldn't get into her online world any other way. Gary knew her well enough to know how delicate she was and how easily she could slip into destructive mode, and he had played her. A banging sound came from the yard. As she stumbled back her heart hammered against her ribcage and she began to sweat.

She stepped away from the computer and hoped it would go back into standby mode. One thing was certain, this wasn't the Gary she knew and she had no idea what he was capable of. She heard a muffled meow. 'Einstein,' she whispered. She couldn't work out where it was coming from. He meowed again. He was in the kitchen.

She crept one step at a time, knowing that her stalker was outside the back but she wasn't leaving Einstein behind. Heart pounding. She needed to grab him and run, then lock herself in her flat and call the police.

There was another bang coming from the yard.

He was home.

FORTY

LIBBY

She hurried along the small hall, past the cupboard under the stairs, then past the bedroom door and into the kitchen. The items that were on the worktop when she'd looked through the window earlier had been put away.

Running into the kitchen, she called out. 'Einstein,' but he wasn't there. That's when she saw what was banging. As the wind picked up, the back gate creaked and slammed against the post. She was still alone. Transfixed by all that was in front of her, she couldn't help but snoop. She needed answers and she wasn't prepared to wait for them. She'd come too far.

Opening the bin, she saw the empty syringe. There were also more empty syringes, a few chocolate bar wrappers and an empty wine bottle. There were several red tissues, not blood red, more of a purplish red. She bent down to smell the contents and inhaled a sour wine smell.

The kitchen cupboards were similar to her own except there were less of them. There were two under the sink topped by a small worktop, it really was a crummy flat. The cupboard contained more cereal, long-life milk, a couple of clear liquid vials. Why was Gary doing this and how long had he been here?

A flutter sent her legs jelly like. This ran deeper than she could have imagined. Did Gary have something to do with Bettina going missing?

She looked at her watch. The house had been empty for about half an hour and she knew he could be back at any time.

She nudged the bedroom door open. The creak echoed through the room as she entered. There was no carpet, no bed, no furniture, not even a light bulb and the curtains were drawn. She breathed in the musty, old wooden floor smell; that same smell that she'd picked up on Einstein's fur. The corners of the room were thick with spiders' webbing and dust balls. No one lived in this flat, it was a haven for bad things. He was rarely around. It was nothing more than a stalker's base.

Libby kicked the door frame, it seemed so obvious now. What she would do with her theory was the big question. She could call the police, tell them about Olly, Bettina and Ricardo and explain her suspicions. Then they'd ask, on what grounds? For them to enter and search they needed more and she would give them more. He wasn't going to get away with this. She couldn't tell them she'd climbed through his bathroom window and snooped around his flat while he was out. She pictured herself being arrested for breaking and entering. She would probably get the sack from work. Her life as she knew it would be over.

Libby leaned against the cupboard door outside the bedroom and hit the frame. She wiped the frustrated tears from her eyes. After a few seconds, she realised that she had something sticking in her back. A key to the cupboard door. Her airing cupboard had a keyhole, but she'd never been given a key. As she rubbed her back, she turned the key and opened the door.

Not what she expected. Her cupboard was full of washing; this cupboard was dark and empty. At the back there was another door. Her hands trembled. Normal people don't have doors that lead to somewhere else in their airing cupboards. She had to open it. It was possible that the answers to all her questions, problems, whatever she called them, would be behind that door.

She pulled the outside door to, just leaving a small gap, which allowed a little bit of natural light to shine through. Einstein meowed again and her heart started to bang. Shaking, she turned the handle. The door opened. The first thing she noticed was the musty, damp smell. Faced with pitch-blackness, she couldn't see ahead. The light from the gap lit up the top four steps of a staircase but where it led, she had no idea. She took the first step, then the second. She felt along the rough wall for a light switch.

Her breathing deepened as she began to panic in the suffocating darkness. Not being able to find a light, she ran back to the top of the stairs and opened the outer door farther. She could now see that there were about twelve uneven, stony steps that led to another door at the bottom of them.

Her eyes began to adjust so that she could see the collection of framed pictures on the walls. She crept down the steps to have a closer look. There were pictures of someone she recognised, Bettina. The woman's words rang through her head. *Scared, so scared.* Bettina had every right to be terrified. Libby had all the proof she needed now. She should have ran at that point and escaped, but something was drawing her further. She couldn't leave her cat. She had to continue and find out the truth. There were framed articles about the Sun's Rays and Bettina taking part in a charity fundraiser.

Walking down a couple more steps, Libby passed a crevice in the wall, which was approximately three feet deep, three feet wide and several feet high. Stacked up in the crevices were several small boxes marked as diaries.

She continued down, staring at the wall as she passed. Her knees trembled with every step, her hair dampened with sweat and her heart pounded. A framed class photo sat above her eye level, she recognised it. It was Olly's class photo. How had this person got hold of Olly's photo? She looked closer. Olly was standing in the row behind. She had a beaming smile. Libby's eyes darted to the person sitting next to her sister. It was Louise, the girl who was found murdered in the well all those years ago. She glanced at the names underneath but none of them were familiar except Jayne's. Olly had never mentioned the others.

Libby took another step down. She tried to breathe quietly and control her emotions but tears began to fall again. With a shaking arm, she wiped the dust off the frame with her sleeve. It contained another article about the well incident in Beoley all those years ago. Libby was taken back to the long summers where Olly would drag her to meet her friends, where they'd smoke and laugh until they had to go home. She shivered as she saw the letter that was pinned underneath the article.

Hi Lou,

I don't know whether you've heard but I've had to go home sick. I felt awful this morning and I don't think all that running in PE helped. Anyway, I really need to talk to you. You know I've been sick a lot lately and well you know I've been seeing Aaron, I'm in a bit of a mess. I really need someone to talk to and you're my best friend in the whole world. I'm so scared, Lou, I'm scared I might be pregnant.

Promise me you won't tell anyone that I've sent you this note, and whatever you do, please don't show it to any of our friends because if my dad finds out, he'll kill me and I mean kill!

Say nothing at all, just please, please, meet me tonight and come alone. I have family around this evening and they won't be leaving until about nine. I can sneak out, can you sneak out and meet me by the old well? The one where we hung out a lot last summer. It's the only place I feel as though I can get some privacy and you live close to it. I'll be there at nine thirty tonight. Don't call me at home, my dad has banned me from phone calls because I let Aaron in when he was out, he came back early and caught him in the house.

Don't leave me alone in the dark tonight. I know I can depend on you.

See you later.

Your best friend, Jayne.

PS: Bring the note. I can't risk your mum seeing it and telling my dad.

Love you X

She touched the letter and stifled a sob. *Say nothing, bring the note; come alone.* That's what got Louise to turn up to her death. What the hell was Libby doing? She had to get out, now.

As she backed away from the wall, she slipped back on the step and fell onto her bottom, catching her tailbone. As she rubbed it hard to ease the sickening pain, she stood. Another photo caught her eye. A picture of her. She recognised the pose and the clothing, it was one of her Facebook photos. She breathed hard, gasping for breath, hyperventilating. Every part of her body shook with terror, her suspicions were right. A mass of information went through her head. She bounced from Trevor, then to Gary and Ian. Maybe Gary wasn't Ian. She scanned the photo for clues. There were no clues. She thought of all the candidates she'd interviewed at work, all the boys she knew at school. Then she caught sight of what was behind her, a wall filled with her face, and Olly's. They had mostly been downloaded from Facebook. Some pictures were stuck onto different backgrounds, others looked like they'd been snapped from a camera above her. There was a photo of her undressed in her lounge. She couldn't see any farther down. The light from the door had reached its limit. There were more, many more. Stumbling up the steps, she turned to run. She had to get out and call the police. They could rescue her cat.

She ran up the steps then stopped. A bang came from above. His front door slammed. She fell onto the steps. He was back. Libby grappled with the wall and steps, then managed to get back into a standing position. Silent tears fell down her cheeks as she heard him walking around the lounge. She heard him walk over to the bathroom door and close it. Had she left it open or was it already open? She couldn't remember. She crept up the stairs to the entrance of the cupboard. He was pacing around and then she heard his voice.

'Hello, could you tell me how Olly is please?' There was a pause. 'Yes, I'm a relative.'

Libby's breathing overwhelmed her, she needed to cry, she needed to scream, and she needed to throw some furniture. The voice was too muffled to identify, just like it had been when she'd received the creepy calls. She heard footsteps again, they were coming her way and the door was open. She crept down to the crevice and wedged herself into a crouching position behind the diary boxes.

Along the spine of one, she saw the name Louise written on the spine. Sliding it out, she placed it away from the others. With her knees wedged in her chin, she held her breath then heard the footsteps stop at the door.

The door was pushed open. Libby bent her head down to her knees, hoping she'd be shielded from view if he came down. The second door opened wide and exposed the elongated shadow of her stalker standing at the top of the steps.

Libby badly needed to exhale but if she did, he'd find her and she feared he'd kill her. Already, she knew too much. He killed Louise. The door slammed and the footsteps became more distant. In total darkness, Libby exhaled and then inhaled urgently. Crying silently, tears fell all over her face, her hands and her top. Her nose dripped, she wiped it on her sleeve. If only she hadn't broken her phone? She then heard another door slam, it was the cupboard door. The key turned in the lock. She was now stuck. She'd wait for him to go out then she'd make her escape, even if it meant bashing the door down. For now, though, she would sit still, be quiet and wait until the time was right. With what had happened to Louise and whatever may have happened to Bettina, Libby knew that alerting him to her whereabouts would be a costly move. Maybe Chrissie would call and worry about her. She thought of Michaela and Kirsty. They'd be home a bit later. Someone had to miss her. Maybe they would wonder where she was. In the darkness, she curled up behind the boxes, weeping and waiting for him to leave.

FORTY-ONE

LIBBY

As her legs stiffened, Libby tried to stretch them out. Hours had passed and she could still hear him walking around above her. She was beginning to think he was never going out, then she tensed up as he unlocked the cupboard door. Curling her body up into a little ball, she aimed to stay hidden behind the boxes. The outer door opened, followed by the inner door. A dull flickering light came on and made a low humming noise that stopped after a few seconds. He took another step. Libby's heart beat loud and fast as her captor stood the other side of the boxes. She closed her eyes and held her breath, hoping that he would soon pass.

Forcing herself to open her eyes, she peered through the small gap between the boxes and the wall. She spotted a hand holding a syringe, followed by an arm, then the waist of someone wearing jeans. Tears welled up in Libby's eyes. They rolled down her cheek, wetting the previously dried on tears from earlier that day.

Her skin felt tight and gritty from the dank environment where she'd been trapped for hours but that was the least of her worries. Allowing herself to breathe as he passed, she remained still, hoping not to be heard. Was the injection meant for her? Did he know she was hidden behind the boxes? She couldn't remember if the computer had gone back into sleep mode or whether she'd closed the bedroom door or left the bin lid up. She inwardly cursed herself for not erasing her presence as she went along. And if she didn't find a way to solve her predicament, he was going to finish Olly off. She'd heard him impersonating a relative. Why? All because of a girl called Louise. That's where it started, but what did that have to do with her sister? She and Olly weren't friends. Why Olly? She needed to gasp and cry so badly and she needed to be out of this prison so that she could protect Olly. Stiff with fear, she remained in her position. She listened as he unlocked the door at the bottom of the steps.

Someone murmured and it wasn't him. She heard a bang that sounded like the floor had been stamped on. Her only option was to run for it. With hands that refused to do anything, she tried to push one of the boxes aside but it was too late. The man was coming back out of the basement. Beads of perspiration slipped down her forehead as she clenched her teeth together to stop them from chattering.

The figure hurried past her as she flinched behind the boxes. He switched off the light and slammed the inner door closed before turning the key. Standing, she bent and flexed her stiff arms and legs. Her back throbbed from her earlier stumble onto the concrete steps. Squeezing from behind the boxes, she felt her way around. The front door slammed. He'd gone out. She turned and faced the darkness. There was shuffling in the distance. Someone else was in the cellar – could it be Bettina? Libby felt her way along the wall and walked down the steps, one by one. She brushed her fingertips over the picture frames, trying not to knock any of them from the wall. As she reached the bottom she fumbled around until she had her hands around the door handle. It wasn't locked. More murmuring came from behind it.

Blood pumped around her body and through her head. She had to be brave, enter the unknown and help her. Then she heard Einstein meowing.

With a hand placed on the handle, she hesitated. What if the person in the cellar was part of a plan? Maybe it was a trap, a lure. Nothing more than a game to send her crazy just like the silent calls, the chocolates, and things being taken and moved in her flat. She had no choice but to find out. Opening the door could be extremely stupid or it could be her only way out. With trembling hands, she turned the handle.

Libby gasped and placed her hand over her mouth. Shaking and breathless, she fell back onto the floor and stared at the horror before her. One dull blue light lit up the scene, the corners of the room were in darkness. She gazed around, making sure nobody else was there.

The man lay in a bed, blankets pulled over him as he looked to be dreaming. She bent over and checked under the bed, just to make sure. 'Ricardo.'

She wiped her tears with her dirty hand. Was he dead? Holding her arm towards the man, she touched his crepe like hand. His eyes half opened but he didn't move.

To his left stood a couple of metal wardrobes. Libby tried to open them but both were locked. She flinched at the tinny noise they made as she pulled at them and then Einstein cried again. 'It's okay. Mummy's here,' she whispered, having no idea how she was going to release him.

She had to find something, anything that could help her lever the door open. She opened the drawer next to Ricardo's bed but it was full of nothing but tissues and baby wipes. Glancing up, she spotted a camera housed on a bracket attached to the wall. They were being watched.

Shaking, she closed the drawer and steadied herself. She

listened to the footsteps above, scurrying back and forth. Then they were coming from the kitchen. Maybe he hadn't seen her through the camera if he was away from his computer. The image of her living room on his screen turned her stomach. Sitting out of view underneath it, she waved at Ricardo.

Ricardo's eyes flickered. 'Have you come for me? Is it Bettina?'

'It's me, Libby, and please whisper. He'll hear us. I'm going to try and help you.'

'The angels are beautiful, why don't you come with me and see. They fly into the sky and they call me. I want to go with them. It's so beautiful.' He smiled, oblivious as to where he was. 'Bettina is an angel now.'

'Ricardo, it's me, Libby. We're trapped and we have to find a way out.'

'I don't want to leave Bettina.'

'Ricardo, please wake up.' There's no way she could carry him up the stairs even if the door was open. She needed him to come around and help her to fight their captor if needed. Slumping back against the wall, she slid to the floor and slammed her closed fist onto the floor. They were stuck with no way out. She held her head in her hands and rubbed her throbbing head.

'Libby?' Ricardo held an arm up and pointed to something she couldn't see.

She bolted upright. 'Yes, it's Libby. I'm here. You remember me.'

'The girl who lives with Bettina—'

'In Bettina's old flat,' Libby interrupted. There was hope. Some of his memories were coming back. The man licked his cracked lips and closed his eyes. 'Ricardo, stay with me. Don't go to sleep.'

She heard the outer door unlock. 'Stay quiet. Don't tell him I'm here.' He was coming. She bolted up and slipped between the cold metal of the wardrobe and the wall. If the figure came too close to the wardrobes, he'd see her but the light, for what it was worth, was pointed towards the middle of the room. She needed to fade right into that darkness and remain hidden. She squeezed as close to the corner of the wall as she could. Right back until her spine was pressed into the wardrobe and her arm was squashed against the wall.

A woodlouse crawled over her ankle sending a chill along her neck. The urge to kick it out of the way was strong as it tickled her foot but she remained still, allowing it to walk over her bare skin as it passed by. Closing her eyes, she tensed up.

'This should tide you over for a short while.' The voice was barely a whisper. His footsteps reached the wooden cabinet. She leaned forward and peered across the room. Ricardo looked at her. She shook her head and placed a finger over her lips, not wanting him to shout out her name or point. He pulled a syringe out of Ricardo's skin. She listened as their captor turned a key in one of the wardrobe doors. Libby retreated to the corner, back firm against the icy metal as she held her breath.

Einstein ran out of the cupboard and began sniffing around. His tail wavered in anger as he spotted her and began to preen himself. Silent tears slipped down her cheeks as she hoped he would move out of the way, maybe even cause a distraction by running up the stairs, but he didn't. Instead, he jumped onto Ricardo's bed. The man was already drifting off again.

Libby gently exhaled; that's when she heard Ricardo let out a loud snore. She flinched as his captor passed the gap and felt for the keys in his pocket. All Libby could see was the back of the dark hooded sports top he was wearing.

The trembling began from her core and quickly spread to her hands. She was never the target, it had to be Olly all along. Olly had forwarded her the details about this rental. They were meant for her or Jayne or maybe some other person in those school photos. Bettina merely got in the way, just like Libby had. Unintended victims.

He leaned against the wall, his face close to Ricardo's and he spoke again in a muffled whisper. 'She knew too much. I couldn't let her leave. I know you can't forgive me but I'm sorry.' The man shook his head and looked at his feet.

Libby feared that her trembling fingers would start tapping against the metal wardrobe. He had to be talking about Bettina. What had he done with her? Bettina was right. The man below was watching her and he'd been watching Libby. Always watching. Scared, so scared. She clasped her hands together between her legs. Her face itched with wetness and her eyes were so sore and gritty, the urge to rub them was unbearable. Her throat tickled with the dust she'd inhaled and she hoped that she wouldn't sneeze. With her head leaning back, she closed her eyes, hoping that he would hurry up and go.

She thought of the good times she'd had with Olly when they were kids playing in the woods. Then she thought of Louise and Bettina. However hard she tried, she couldn't rid her thoughts of the two dead girls and the fact that their killer was in the same room as she was.

Her thoughts were broken. There was a knock at the front door. Libby peered out.

As he went to turn, she ducked back. Their captor began to run up the stairs, taking two at a time.

Libby pushed herself out from the small gap, then accidentally banged the side of the wardrobe.

She retreated.

He stopped. There was a shuffling then he cleared his throat.

Heart banging, she didn't know whether to run back into the corner and hide or whether to stand still and hope that she hadn't been heard.

'I know you're there.' The voice sent a shiver through her

and her legs almost gave way as he walked back towards the wardrobes. 'Libby?' The quietness in the voice made it impossible to recognise.

There was another knock at the door.

Libby knew she had to make a run for it. She bolted from behind the wardrobe and ran towards the door as the man switched off the light and ran back down the stairs. The cellar darkness took her breath away. He knew it better than she did. Libby knew that she had no option but to fight, but the silence had caught her off guard. He was in the room somewhere, but where? She whimpered as she held out her hands, trying to feel for anything tangible, then she tripped over the cabinet and fell straight into the strong arms of her captor. There was no way he'd let her walk out of this, not if he killed Bettina. She tried to push her way through as she poked her fingers at his face but he was too strong. Her nail caught what she thought was his cheek. He grabbed her and with little effort, threw her to the stone floor, taking her breath away. She reached out and grabbed what felt like the leg of his jeans and pulled at them with all she had. If he locked her in the basement, it was game over. She heard a chink as something dropped out of his pocket and landed by her ear. It was a piece of wire and it was thin. As her fingers touched the cold metal, she recognised it as bra underwiring with its curved shape.

There was another knock. It was louder this time.

Libby couldn't breathe let alone call for help.

'Why are you making me do this, Libby? I never wanted to hurt you.' That sinister whisper sent shivers through her as she gasped for breath. With one hard kick to the chest, she was winded. 'Sorry, sorry – you made me do that.' He turned and ran. As he reached the top, the light flickered on again. She heard the door to the cellar close. The inner door was locked, followed by the outer door at the top of the stairs. Pain seared through her back and head. Everything she looked at seemed a little fuzzy as she fought the light-headedness.

Feeling around by her ear for the wire, she eventually grabbed it. A wave of dizziness made the room spin. Closing her eyes, she waited until it passed. The fight in her was nearly all used up but if she died, then so did Olly. She gripped the wire as she drifted in and out of a dazed state. She knew she had to put it somewhere for later, if there would be a later.

Tears drizzled down her cheeks. Unable to move properly, she used her last bit of strength to push the wire inside her pump. As she did it jabbed the flesh on her foot, cutting sharply next to the ball. She let out a little scream as she pulled it out, then she slid it alongside her foot. She tried hard to shout for help but her croaky voice was refusing to comply. Einstein jumped off the bed and laid beside her as he licked his paws. She reached out and stroked his warm fur as her eyes closed and she passed out.

FORTY-TWO

LIBBY

Stirring, Libby tried to stretch. Pain shot through her back and foot. She forced her sticky eyes open and everything looked fuzzy in the dull blue light. Her hands were bound behind her and she lay face down on the cellar floor. She tried to lift her face off the cold concrete and winced as a sharp pain bolted down her back. It was no good, she was too trussed up. She lifted her feet up and bent her legs, so that they touched her bottom. At least she could move.

Wriggling her ankle, she tried to feel for the wire. There was numbness to her legs, but eventually she felt it stabbing her flesh. She wanted to cry, scream and run, but the tape over her mouth kept it sealed shut.

Someone unlocked the door and took slow steps down and a few seconds later, she was faced with a foot.

'I thought I heard you stirring.' Tim's kind gaze met hers as he bent over and stroked her hair. He'd heard what was going on. As promised, he'd kept an eye out for her. She let out muffled cries for help, relief flooding through her body. Kneeling down, he rolled her onto her side. She wanted to shout, *Mr Bull, he's coming back and he's dangerous. Hurry up,*

They caught me once. One of the gang forced me to smoke a cigarette before pushing my choking body to the floor and leaving me in the woods. Louise had been the one to kick me when I fell. I didn't intend for her to die, all I wanted to do was to scare her but it all went wrong so I hid behind a tree, hoping that she'd hurry up and go but she didn't. She sat on the wall of the well and called Jayne's name a couple of times and I didn't know what to do. My heart has never raced so much.' Tim paused.

'What happened next? Please, Tim. I want to know.' She made sure her voice was quiet, calm and gentle.

He stopped and furrowed his brows. 'I ran out from the trees and I pushed her as hard as I could, just like she'd pushed me so many times and I heard a sickening thud as her body bounced off the wall before she fell into the well. I heard her flapping around and gasping but it was too dark for me to see. Picking up her torch, I flashed the light downwards. She'd disappeared into the black abyss below. There was nothing I could do. I didn't mean to kill her, all I wanted to do was scare her so that she'd never come near me again. I was petrified so I ran all the way home. As I did rain began to bucket down and my parents were out that night. No one knew I'd left the house and no one was out in the bad weather. It took the police ages to find her and all that time, I toiled with telling my mother what had happened, that it was an accident but everyone started suspecting her dad and I guess I was a coward.' He exhaled and pressed his lips together.

However much she tried to feel sympathy with him, she couldn't forget about Olly and how he'd hurt her. The man beside her was dangerous and she knew just how much. She didn't want to become his next accident. She knew what she had to say but it felt like an outright betrayal. There was no other option. She had to live through this to save Olly. If he kept her imprisoned in the cellar, he'd be able to do exactly what he wanted to her lovely sister. 'What did Olly do to you? I need to know.'

'And I want to tell you. I don't want there to be any secrets. I've carried this burden for so long, I just want it to be over. I want someone who loves me for me, someone who can accept my past and who loves me too. Being loved is not too much to ask for, is it?' He smiled and sighed. 'Olly could have stopped them but she stood by and did nothing. She could have stuck up for me but no, she was always on their side. She forced me to smoke that cigarette. They egged her on and she did it. That's the person your sister really is.'

Libby bit her lip. 'Tim, Olly was scared of them too. They used to bully every one.'

'You're so gullible, Libby. How can you believe anything she says? She called me that name first. The twitcher. It stuck. I was nothing back then, a weedy little boy with a high voice who looked so young compared to everyone else. That twitch, I spent so long trying to banish it and it still appears when I'm really nervous. Short, pale, sickly looking – that was me. Nothing like I am now. God have I worked for this body.' He sighed. 'I begged my mother not to send me to that school, to enrol me somewhere else but she said no. Apparently I had to learn to stick up for myself. It was character building.'

'I'm sorry, Tim. I'm sorry for what you went through and I'm sorry that Olly upset you like that. I know she would have been just trying to survive like the rest of us. We were kids. Stupid kids. Please find it in your heart to forgive her.'

He jerked up and moved away from her, his twitch becoming more apparent. 'No, I don't care that we were all just kids. I was terrified, but not any more. When I met Louise that night and watched her drown in that well, the tables were turned and you know what? At first I didn't want her to die but after the incident, the bullying at school stopped. I took her out and that was the end of it. She was evil. I promised myself that no one would make my life hell ever again.' He came back to the bed and laid down next to her, staring into her eyes. 'I bet you had it easy at school, I bet people have always been nice to you.'

'Had it easy,' she said with a laugh. 'You think it was easy being me?'

'Yes, look at you. Perfect figure, perfect hair, eyes. Everyone knows you're special. That's why Gary can't let you go. He knows he lost the best thing in his life.'

She bit her lip, trying not to say something she'd regret. 'I'm not perfect. My life hasn't been perfect. Neither has Olly's. We were abused as young children. Our parents abandoned us. Maybe she didn't help you or maybe she made things worse for you, but we were hurt; we were broken. We had nothing. I'm so sorry, Tim. I struggle to cope with everything. I cut my own damn arms to relieve the pain but it comes back, day after day. I can't let it go that Olly suffered to save me and I spend hours thinking about her cowering in a cupboard and being shouted at. Please don't hurt her. If you knew about all the things she went through for me, you'd understand why she tried so hard to be accepted, even if that meant being accepted by a bad crowd.'

'It was only a matter of time before she recognised me. I can't turn away from her and hide behind glasses that I don't need forever. If you were in my life, she'd eventually click. I didn't want to hurt her, not like that, but she left me no choice. All I wanted to do was upset her life somehow, mess with her mind a bit, let her know what it was like to be a target. You changed that, Libby. She would have ruined it for us.'

'She's on life support. That wasn't a bit of light revenge.' Libby couldn't look at him, the pain inside her too raw.

'I had no choice.'

'There's always a choice.'

'I would have given you everything. You kissed me, you enjoyed being with me. You wanted me, too, and I felt it when we were together. We can still be together but it has to be this way. Olly can't be here and neither can Ricardo.'

'But I love Olly and I need her. It's not too late to do the right thing.'

He shuffled and sat up. 'This is the right thing. You'll come to see that eventually. There is no other way. Besides, you have me now.' Sweat dripped down his forehead. 'I share your pain, Libby.' He pulled her leggings up from the ankles and traced one of her scars with his fingertips. 'Soon, your pain will be over and I'll never let you get hurt again.'

Libby turned her head away unable to process what was happening. He leaned over and kissed her cheek.

'It was you calling me, wasn't it? The silent calls.' She needed to know.

'I had to hear your voice. When you were out, I kept imagining you going back to him, your horrible ex, and I admit it, I wanted to check up on you. Sometimes, all I wanted was to feel like we were close.'

'And Ian Linden.'

'A test of your loyalty. You can't blame a man for wanting to know if he got it right.' A sick feeling whirled in her stomach.

She closed her eyes and tried to clench her dead hands back to life but they were still numb. Gary had never used his other phone to scare her, he had been openly abusive in every way.

'The stone thrown at my window and all the lurking in the back garden.'

'Not me, Libby. That was probably your imagination. I left you the chocolates though. They were meant to be a nice surprise and I was going to tell you but you were flapping around, all concerned that someone had got in and left them. You can't blame me for not wanting to say it was me. It was a romantic gesture but that backfired.'

'It was romantic, Tim. I see that now and I'm sorry for not appreciating it. Please, let me go and we can work through this.'

All she wanted to do was get away from him. All this talking was getting her nowhere.

'No.' He wasn't going to let her go. He had too much to lose.

Tears began to well up. She couldn't help Ricardo or Olly. She'd end up wherever Bettina was. If anyone came looking for her, he'd observed her enough to know who to point the finger at. Gary could be blamed, or maybe Trevor.

As she fidgeted, the wire stabbed her foot. In the past, cuts and jabs would represent self-hatred, the need to self-destruct, the release, the guilt caused by the pleasure received, but the pain in her foot represented hope. It wasn't much of a weapon but it was all she had.

A short, sharp cough made her jump, it was Ricardo. She looked over. He stirred and let out a long snort. It was the first noise she'd heard him make since she'd come around. Ricardo needed her and she had to help him.

Tim stood and he opened the other wardrobe. Libby bent her head back to see. Everything was visible to her. One wardrobe was shelved and full of oddments. The large shelf contained various items including her bra and various bits of fashion jewellery. She spotted the necklace that Kirsty had described, a chain with a twist pendant. Several scarves hung on a rack. He grabbed the cigarette lighter and popped it in his pocket. 'That was Louise's.'

'You never lost your pen, did you?'

He shook his head. 'My mother never bought anything that special. She was the most frugal woman I've ever known. You've seen my flat. That's how my mother lived.' He gazed around the room. 'I need to get rid of all this, all of it. I'll burn the diaries, burn everything. Start afresh. Maybe then I'll find someone to truly love who loves me back. It won't be you, though.'

She began to sob. 'Please don't leave me here to burn, Tim.' A flash of fear went through her like a bolt of lightning. He was going to set everything alight. She pictured flames licking the bed, the drawers, filling the cellar with toxic death fumes. 'No, I don't want to die. Don't leave me here.' Her shouting was stirring Ricardo.

He lifted her under the arms and dragged her across the floor, over to the wardrobe. 'I need to think and I can't do that with you making all this noise.'

'Don't put me in there. Please, I can't be shut in.'

'I need to think.'

'No, I'll be quiet. I'll do anything,' Libby cried. She hyperventilated as she thought back to the times that Olly had been locked in a cupboard. She remembered the scary stories that her sister had told her once she'd been let out. Those were the things Olly couldn't bear to talk about any more; the abuse that she shielded Libby from.

Maybe this was her karma. Maybe she'd evaded all those punishments at Olly's expense and now it was her turn. She'd asked Olly what it was like and she'd replied, *you have to be brave. Bide your time and don't let the monsters take over, they're all in your head. Send them away when they start to appear.* She could hear Olly's voice as if she was in the room. *Don't let the cupboard beat you and you'll survive.* Advice of a child, a brave child, one she still looked up to even now that child was an adult. Olly was her hero. She only hoped that she'd survive to tell her, and then she remembered, she had to survive as Olly's life depended on her survival. Olly wasn't perfect. She'd obviously hurt Tim but Libby loved her. Life wasn't easy for any of them back then. No one deserved to die. No one was beyond forgiveness. Olly did all that she could so that she didn't become Louise's victim, too.

'In you go.' He threw her into the wardrobe. 'I'm really sorry it's come to this.'

'Please don't leave me. I'm scared.' Her eyes widened as he looked down on her.

'You'll be safe here.' He leaned over and kissed her on the

cheek. Libby flinched. There was a knock at the door. 'What the hell do they want?' Tim roared as he dropped Libby into the wardrobe. The knocking became continuous. He grabbed the tape off the cabinet and placed a fresh piece across Libby's mouth. She shook her head but it was no good. The knocking was accompanied by someone shouting hello. Libby recognised Chrissie's voice.

There was another knock. Tim stormed off, leaving the wardrobe open. As he left, he locked the bottom door but left the inner door at the top of the stairs open. Libby kicked the wardrobe but then she stopped. She didn't want Chrissie to get hurt. Libby remained still.

She heard Chrissie running upstairs and knocking on her door and Tim was right behind her. The tape came loose. She rubbed her face on the side of the wardrobe, catching it on the edge. 'Chrissie, run.' She shouted as loud as she could but no one could hear her screams from the bowels of the house.

FORTY-FOUR

LIBBY

Libby could just about hear Chrissie's voice as she called her but those calls soon faded to silence. Had she gone? 'Chrissie.' She kept calling her friend, but it was no good.

It was now or never. If Tim was going to burn the place down, she didn't want to be in it. She wriggled around in the base of the wardrobe, banging and hoping that Ricardo would come round.

She had to get hold of the wire, it was her only chance. Maybe she could poke it into the tape and sever it. Hands behind her back, she pushed herself up until she could turn herself into a scrunched up bridge. As she pushed up, her feet wedged against the side of the wardrobe poking the wire into her wound, sending a sharp pain up her ankle. The hot flash of pain made her wince as she tried again. Flopping back down into a scrunched up ball at the bottom of the wardrobe, she sobbed.

Don't stop. If you stop, you will die. She held her breath, pushed her body up and finally, she did it. She managed to get her bound hands below her bottom. Adrenaline pumped through her veins, thrumming through her head with every heartbeat. She shuffled her arms down to her feet. After a moment of wriggling, her bound hands had reached the shoe. Fumbling, she pushed her index finger and thumb into the side of her pump. She reached, straining every muscle in her body but getting that wire would make it all worth it. She yelped as her shoulder clicked and a pain shot down her arm. Tugging at the wire, she managed to get it to the top of her shoe, and then she flinched as a bang came from above. As she lost her grip on the wire she cursed under her breath. He was coming back. She remained still and listened.

Tim was locking the top door. He didn't need to be there to check on them, he had cameras. He'd know exactly what was going on in the basement at all times. With every last bit of strength, Libby bashed her shoulder into the door. It creaked under the pressure. She did it again and again until she almost fell through it as it popped open. Her bra fell from above onto her head. She shook it away.

Ricardo murmured. With closed eyes, his facial expressions flashed from tortured to happy within a few seconds. He opened his eyes a little and gazed at things that weren't there. Occasionally, he smiled and murmured to the Bettina he was hallucinating. Libby knew she had to hurry. Ricardo was waking. He could help them to escape. She needed him. They needed each other.

Again, she pushed her finger and thumb down the side of her shoe and gripped the wire. She pulled it upwards. With shaking hands, she continued tugging until she finally had it in her hand. She felt the thin strip of metal against her palm before shifting her tangled body onto her side. As she bent her wrist she began to poke at the tape, then she stabbed harder and harder.

There was a scrape against the outer door. Her breathing quickened. He was opening up the lock. Had he sensed or seen what she was doing? The camera wasn't pointing towards the wardrobe, it was focused on Ricardo. She wriggled into a scrunched sitting position, placing the wire under her bottom where she waited. With every footstep, Libby's stomach somersaulted, then he stopped at the bottom door and pushed it open.

'Sorry, but this has to end now. I didn't want it to be like this, Libby.'

Ricardo looked up at Tim with one eye half open. A tear rolled down his face, he'd clearly given up as he lay in that bed.

Shaking his head, Tim hurried over to the wardrobe. Libby felt her shoulder click as he pushed her back in and slammed the door. It bounced back on its hinges but settled on a closed position. Libby could no longer see what was happening. 'Please, Tim. Don't hurt Chrissie.' She knew he was capable. Self-preservation made a person desperate and with Tim's track record, she could only hope that her friend was safe. Libby heard her voice. Chrissie was upstairs, outside her flat, or had she left and gone back to work? Maybe she was imagining Chrissie's voice now it was in her head.

'Why did she come here, Libby? Why? I never wanted to hurt anyone, now it's happening again and I don't know what to do. I don't need the stress. The only way is to start again.'

'Don't leave me here to die.'

She listened as he paced across the stone floor. 'I don't want anyone to die but you've all left me with no choice.'

'You do have a choice. This can all stop now. You can do the right thing. Tell them that Louise and Bettina were accidents. You didn't mean to kill them. That has to count for a lot.'

She listened as he laughed. 'You must think I'm stupid.' He slammed his hand against the other side of the door and Libby's heart banged in her chest.

'I don't. Tim, please. I thought we had something. If you care about me, you won't hurt anyone. Please don't hurt Olly.' Sobbing, she continued to repeat herself.

'This all has to go away. I'm sorry, Libby. I'll make sure your cat gets out and I'll look after him. He loves me, you know. I'm the hand that feeds him now, not you. I won't let you down.'

'I don't want to die,' she yelled. With that he hurried out of the room, slamming the doors behind him.

Heart banging, stomach growling with a nauseating emptiness, Libby felt around for the wire? She couldn't feel it any longer. There was no time, she needed to get out. Sliding her body up and down, she grappled around on the floor aimlessly until her finger brushed over it. Snatching it, she closed her eyes. With her fingers she felt it; in her mind she pictured it. Positioning it the correct way up, she continued poking at the binds that held her wrists together. She pushed and wriggled until the binds loosened and fell from her wrists. Crying out with relief, Libby used both hands to unravel the rest of the tape before dropping it beside her. Bringing her hands up, she tore the rest of the tape that hung off her mouth and laughed. She was unbound, now she had to fight with all she had.

Shuffling her body out of the wardrobe, she landed on the hard stone. Wriggling like a worm, she worked her away along the floor on her belly so that she remained underneath the camera.

'Ricardo,' she whispered. His eyes half opened and he looked her way. She could see a twinkle, almost a smile. She only hoped he was seeing her and not some trippy dream. She needed Ricardo to act quickly if they were to survive this. And she needed to survive this. As soon as she got free, she'd call the hospital and tell them to guard Olly until the police got there. She wiped the small trickles of blood that fell from her wrists onto her T-shirt, where she'd caught her skin with the wire. 'Ricardo. We have to get out of here. It's Libby. We will die if you don't wake up.'

Planting her feet on the floor, she slid up the wall until she was standing under the camera. The blue light behind her cast an elongated shadow that ran all the way to the bed. Movement had to be kept to a minimum. Sweat trickled down her face and neck. She trembled as she held her arm up behind the camera. Standing on her toes, she reached for the base of the camera and she could just about reach it. As she took a deep breath, she placed her hand firmly over the lens, then turned it around to face the wall before removing her hand. All the camera would show now was a close up of a blank wall. Hearing a thud, Libby remained firm against the brick while breathing deeply. He was in the kitchen, which meant she had to move quickly.

Libby limped over to Ricardo and gave him a shake. Pulling the sheet back, she could see that his feet were bound. 'Ricardo, wake up. We have to leave now.' She unpicked the tape until it loosened enough to pull it from his ankles.

'Ricardo, get up.' She pulled his torso until she had him in a sitting position, then she placed an arm under his and pulled. The man's eyes half opened. 'Get up,' she yelled. He looked up at her and smiled. 'You're free, you need to get up.'

Libby gritted her teeth as she tried to hoist him up again. As she got him to a standing position, his legs gave way and he fell to the floor, dragging her down. 'You have to try. Please try for me.' Libby wept as she held his hand

'Libby.'

'Yes, it's me, Libby, we don't have long. You have to try and stand.'

The man used all his strength to move his body. He rolled over onto his back and lay there red faced and gasping. Libby wedged herself in behind him and with all her strength, she lifted him under the arms from behind until he was sitting up again. 'That's it. We have to get you standing.'

Ricardo strained as he moved, his muscles stiff from being in the same position for so long. 'I can't do it. I feel funny, weak.'

The outer door unlocked and Libby heard Tim shout. 'You're just like the rest, Libby.' He kicked the inner door, not once but several times like he was possessed. Kicking and shouting with rage. The inner door opened and she heard glass smashing. He'd smashed one of his pictures that adorned the walls along the stairway. Fearing the worst, she placed the wire in her other shoe and held on to Ricardo, leaning his weak body against hers.

'I'm sorry, Ricardo, I tried.' She laid her head on his shoulder. 'I won't go down without a fight. Please help me.' She wiped her face and stared at the door. She wasn't ready but she wasn't calling the shots.

Tim burst through the door. His face blotchy with rage, he breathed deeply and stared. Like a bull he charged at her, grabbed her by the arm and dragged her away from Ricardo.

'All I wanted was another chance. I met you and I wanted things to be different, but you're all the same. Just like the rest. Louise and me were close once but she turned on me in high school. She made my life hell. Bettina was lovely until the same happened again. I thought you were different. You're all the same.'

'I want to give us a chance, Tim. We can go away together, away from all this. Take me away, right now. Leave Ricardo. Leave Chrissie. Leave everything behind and you can live as someone else. We can live as different people and I am different. I do care and I want to be with you.' If she could get him to take her, maybe, just maybe he'd spare everyone else. She had to try.

'You think I haven't heard that same line before. Bettina said all those things.'

'I'm not Bettina.'

'Bettina.' Ricardo sobbed as he tried to focus without his glasses on.

'Shut up.' Tim stepped back, staring at the chaos he'd caused.

'Please, he needs help. You're a gentle person. Remember

the dinner we had and the times you listened to me when I was upset? This isn't you.'

'How do you know? You don't know me, Libby. It was all about you. Not once did you say you'd listen if I wanted to talk. I was there for you but you weren't there for me. The only person who saw my pain was my sister.'

'We're the same like that, Tim. Olly is there for me in the way your sister is there for you. I'm sorry I didn't listen. I was so wrapped up in what was going on, I wasn't a good friend.'

It didn't help that Tim was sending her all those horrible messages in the guise of Mr Bull. He was the cause of all her pain. She swallowed as she thought of Olly and all she wanted to do was to hurry to Wales and be beside her.

'No, you weren't. None of you were, which is why I need to end this.' He pulled the lighter out of his pocket and lit it. Mesmerised by the flame, he watched as it flickered and danced in front of him. 'This ends today.'

'Don't hurt Olly,' she called out, sobs filling the room. 'Do what you like to me, but don't hurt Olly.' It was game over.

'I'm sick to death of hearing that name. She was with them. Louise, Jayne and the others. No she wasn't at the front with them but she was one of them. I thought I could almost forget when I saw you, so nice, so perfect but then that sister of yours turned up. Seeing her in the flesh again brought everything back so I knew I had to finish what I set out to do.' He checked his watch. 'Enough talking.'

He dragged Libby back towards the wardrobe and he exhaled. 'I had a plan, you know, and you weren't a part of it. I put the letting details in the school Facebook group. Eight people showed an interest in that flat and I ignored them. It was such a good price, you know, it was bound to attract many people, but I didn't want them. When Olivia took the bait and forwarded it to you, I knew I'd struck gold. It took years to get Olivia that close. Years of pretending to be Aaron or Glen just so that I could be a trusted member in that group and years of fake opportunities to try to lure her or Jayne in. Of course Olivia didn't mind sharing a post in the group made by Aaron. If only Olivia had moved in, the right person would be here now. You had to come here and ruin everything.'

'I'm sorry.' Tears of defeat fell down her cheeks.

'You're like them. See the way you look at me, like I'm subhuman?'

'I have never once seen you as subhuman,' Libby replied. 'They were just kids, Tim, kids. Olly was a child. She didn't mean to upset you.'

'Olly is as bad as the rest and she will pay.'

Libby reached down and grabbed the wire out of her shoe. She was done with reasoning. It wasn't working. Tim grabbed her arm and almost brought her to the ground. Off balance, she swung it around and slashed Tim's cheek as he grabbed her free arm. As he slammed her into the base of the wardrobe she fell in a crumpled heap. Weak and dehydrated, her unrewarded act of bravery had cost her dearly in energy.

Ricardo lay on the floor beside her, barely able to move. Tim shook his head before grabbing her hair and arm, and then flung her violently into the wardrobe. He grabbed her kicking legs and forced them into the small space and slammed the door shut. Pain and hopelessness descended upon her as she cried in the dark. She cried in the cupboard like Olly once had. The darkness was filled with ghosts of her past, horrors of the present and dread of the future.

'Please let me out, I'm scared.'

'If you step out of that wardrobe, you both die. That camera will be pointing at you, Libby. I'm always watching. Just remember that. All I have to do is pour the petrol down those steps and set the place alight.' She flinched as he kicked the cabinet. Shaking she wondered what was next. Burn the place down or would he keep her and Ricardo in the cellar for good?

What would Gary, the police and everyone she knew think had happened to her? Would they suspect Gary or Trevor? Would Olly ever come around and tell her story before Tim got to her?

Questions whirled around in Libby's thoughts, fast and furious, repeating themselves and mixing themselves up, but no answers came. No answers gave any way out of her predicament. Helpless acceptance was all that was left. Mouth dry and muscles worn, Libby began to shut down. Lying still, she conserved the little bit of energy she had left.

Tim ran up the steps, pulling the cellar door closed as he left. The lock turned on the outer door.

'Ricardo?' Libby called. He didn't answer. 'Ricardo?' Again, there was no answer. She burst into uncontrollable sobs. Wanting so much to kick, scream and hit the doors. Fear stopped her. She didn't want to die. All those times she'd played with the idea of death, she wanted so much to be here and see Olly again.

FORTY-FIVE

TIM

All I wanted was Libby. I wanted her to love me and I wanted to be her everything. I wanted the fairy tale ending like you see in films. Why do I have to be such a hopeless romantic?

Standing, I pace up and down. Thirsty, I'm thirsty. I dash to the kitchen and pour a glass of wine. Anything to stop the shaking. Then I turn around and catch my reflection in the mirror. I run my fingers over the scratch on my face. Libby hurt me. I need to change my clothes, clean myself up back in my apartment upstairs. I listen at the door, there's no one around. It's safe for me to leave so I lock the door. Sneaking up the stairs, I reach my apartment. Running to the bathroom, I examine the cut to my face. It's not too deep but it looks a bit sore. I flinch as I dab the wound, then I rub some antiseptic cream in to avoid infection.

Someone slams the main door and laughter follows. Michaela and Kirsty are back – damn it. That's all I need, those two snooping around while I have pressing business to attend to. I gaze at my reflection. All the stress has made my twitch come back and I've worked so hard to get rid of it. I can hear their taunts in my head and I can't forgive Olivia, she came up with the name. She started it. Yes, she may have hidden behind the rest of them after that one day but she is where it all began. That first day in high school when Louise abandoned me for Jayne. The start of my personal hell. When Bettina called me that name, I flipped. I damn well lost it.

The names go through my head. *Twitcher Boy. Twitch Freak.* I punch the wall. My hand crunches and throbs hot. Vengeance is all I have. Nothing can stop me. They deserve all they get for what they did to me. In the mirror, I see what I am. I'm a monster – they've all turned me into a monster. If I deal with them, I'll no longer have to be this... this person. I can be me, the real me, Toby. What I need to do is leave Tim behind. I can block up the cellar, and sell up. I have power of attorney over Mother's finances and the insurance money for this place would help. House fire caused by a cigarette or a faulty cooker. I can go, leave the country, start my quest to find real love, after all, doesn't everyone simply want to be loved and accepted? That's all I ever wanted.

I stare into my own reflected eyes, reading my own mind. Libby wasn't the one, and she'll be history soon. I weep when I think of her beauty and how infatuated I was with her. Why did she turn out to be like all the rest? I was kind, I listened, and I treated her with respect. I'd never cheat on her like that pathetic excuse for a boyfriend, Gary, did. Why is it that good people never get love? They have to fight for it. Then they give it their all only for their hearts to be trampled on. She's trampled on mine and crushed it.

Composing myself, I leave the bathroom for the bedroom and I change my clothes. Inhaling the cleanliness of my clean jumper and jeans, I smile and check my appearance one last time. Now, I look like normal, everyday Tim, except for the cut on my face. This is what Kirsty and Michaela will expect to see.

I have to sneak back down and sort out the mess I've made. Grabbing the keys, I leave and close the door. As I walk down the stairs I hear Michaela and Kirsty chattering. Their door opens and Chrissie walks out. I thought I'd got rid of her when she came knocking.

'If we see her, we'll let you know.' Kirsty stands at the main door.

'Thanks.' Chrissie looks at me and watches as I walk down the stairs.

'Hey.' I didn't hear her come back into the building. She must have sensed that something wasn't right when I answered the door to her earlier. The girls must have let her in while I was in the bathroom. Maybe I had the tap running at the time.

'Have you seen Libby?' she asks as she runs up to me.

'No, not for a while. I haven't even heard her come or go today.'

'I've been trying to call her all day. I'm worried about her.'

'I'm sure she's fine.' I force a slight smile. 'Maybe you should go home. If I see her I'll get her to call you.'

'No. Something's not right.' She presses her lips together and a strand of hair falls from her French pleat. I can see her eyeing up the place as she stares along the hallway into the communal lounge ahead. Her boots clip on the tiled floor as she snoops.

'Are you okay? Has something happened?' I'm nervous now. It's as if this woman has a sixth sense and the way she's staring at me is making me twitch. She hurries up to the top of the stairs and I follow her. She stops outside my apartment.

'What's happened to your face?' she asks, staring at me.

I open my apartment door and take a step back, crossing the threshold but keeping her out.

'I cut myself shaving.'

'You shaved since I last saw you?'

'Of course.'

She pushes past me and runs into my flat. I remember the dirty clothes I'd dropped on the bedroom floor, but they're just dirty clothes. They mean nothing. She glances around the lounge, then the kitchen.

'You need to get out of my flat, seriously before I call the police.'

'Call them.'

I can't. The police can't come here. 'Look, what's going on? You come around barging into my home.'

'Sorry about that. I had to make sure she wasn't in here. I'm Chrissie, I work with Libby and I need to speak to her. I have reason to believe she's in the flat underneath. I need to know that she's okay.'

'Really? Why would she be in the flat downstairs?'

'I can't say. We need to get into her flat.'

'Are you insane?' I need her to go, now.

'Don't call me insane. Can you open her door, do you have a key?'

'No,' I lie. 'I don't have a spare key to her apartment. Libby has the only key.'

I've always been able to get into Libby's apartment. She always thought someone was coming in through her window but only the cat ever did. I still don't know who the man was though, the one who was lurking around. It's irrelevant. I don't need to know any more. This place will be history by the end of the day.

'I guess I'll have to call the police, then.' Chrissie goes to press the digits on her phone. I can't let her do that but I don't want to hurt her. She's done nothing wrong. I need her to go.

'Wait, if you're that worried, I'll get the key. I do have one but I really don't like breaching the trust of my tenants. It's unethical but I'm sure she'll understand when we explain how worried you were.'

'Thank you.' She hurries out of my flat and onto the landing. I grab the key. The best thing I can do is show her around and then she'll leave.

As soon as I unlock the door, Chrissie runs in. 'Libby...
Libby.' She hurries between each room. I hear a faint bang
coming from below. The commotion is stirring Libby and
Ricardo up. Deflated, Chrissie sits at the kitchen table frowning
and checking her phone. I watch as she tries to call Libby again
but the call goes straight to voicemail.

'Maybe she's gone out for the day.'

'What a pathetic suggestion. She sounded like shit when I
spoke to her. She's waiting for news on her sister in hospital,
there's no way she'd go out or not answer her phone.' As
Chrissie leaned on the kitchen table, she nudged Libby's mouse.
On the screen appeared an article titled, 'The girl in the well –
twenty years on.' She clicked onto another tab.

I take a deep breath as she skim reads the article in the *Mail*
showing Bettina raising funds for charity with the Sun's Rays
patrons. Another tab. Facebook – Chrissie scrolls down her
page to see nothing out of the ordinary.

I need her to go now. 'Look, Chrissie, we shouldn't be here.
Libby wouldn't like you snooping on her computer and she'll be
angry at me for letting you in. Maybe, I should call the police.
You're intruding.'

'Call them.' The woman leaned back in the chair as she
stared me out.

'She's only been gone half a day. I don't think they'll do
much.' Beads of sweat start forming along my brow line. I need
to sort this situation out quickly. Why did I say that I would call
the police?

She clicked the mouse and brought up Libby's messages.

'You can't do that. They're private.'

'So sue me.' In front of me were the messages I'd sent as Ian
Linden. Chrissie read them in silence, barely noticing that I was
still in the doorway.

I hear another bang coming from below. Chrissie furrows
her brow and stops reading. 'What was that?'

As if on cue, Einstein walks in, his tail swishing in the air as he runs to me. 'I guess this little guy is hungry. I'll leave you to it, I have to feed him. Libby asked me to look out for him as he's been missing for a few days.'

She nods and turns back to the messages. As I leave, I lock the door and leave the key in it from the outside. She can't leave.

I hurry into my flat and put some music on, turning it up to its fullest. Best of the eighties, not my usual type of music but it was distracting and I knew the bass would boom through the building.

I stare at Einstein who is meowing like mad and I pick him up. He wriggles to get free but I can't hurt him. He's never judged me, called me names, hurt me. He is all I've got and when this is over, I'm taking him to start afresh somewhere. I throw him out of my kitchen window and he lands on the shed roof.

None of this was a part of my plan but it's my only way out. I have to burn this building and all its secrets to the ground. No one can ever know. They wouldn't explain that everything I did was out of pain. Any bodies found in the basement would be Mr Bull's problem. I can blame it all on him, the elusive man who was never there. I could allude to the fact that I thought he might be up to something illegal and if I have to describe him, he'll look like Gary.

I'm staring out of the window when there is knocking at my door.

'Pull yourself together, Tim,' I say as I pour some of the petrol over the worktop and up my cupboards. Then I take Louise's lighter and watch it go up. It all has to go, every last bit of it. I pass my desk and hold the photo of my sister and me. That has to go too. There can't be anything left. A new start means just that.

There is another knock at the door. While approaching it, I take a deep breath and smile as I open the door. All I can now do is keep my fingers crossed that the flames take a while to spread. I've disabled the smoke alarms and the one in Libby's flat is a camera anyway.

'Tim, there's something strange going on in Mr Bull's flat. I can hear an awful lot of banging. We thought it was just the music but when I get close up, I can hear shouting as well,' yells Kirsty, as she's trying to make herself heard over my music.

'Okay, I'll have a look.' I lock my door, knowing that the fire will now be spreading. 'I'm sure it's nothing, probably his telly or something.' I stop in my tracks. Erasure's 'A Little Respect' begins to play. 'Don't you just love this music?' I smile. Nothing can dampen my mood at the moment. If only everyone I'd ever met had just shown me a little respect then I wouldn't be in this situation.

'Are you alright?' Kirsty stares at me with her thick brown furrowed brows. I realise that I've remained standing still on the top step, staring ahead and oblivious to her presence.

'Yes, don't you just love this music?' I'm sure I said that a moment ago but I can't quite remember. Michaela appears outside their front door at the bottom of the stairs. She grimaces at me and holds her hands up as if to say, *what the hell's going on.*

'Bloody racket.' Kirsty isn't in a good mood and neither am I.

'I'm sorry. I'll turn it down when I get back up if it's upsetting you.' I stare at Kirsty. Turn my music down! It's my flaming property. I'll do what the hell I like. I smile and place my ear against Mr Bull's door as I knock.

'Can you hear it? The banging and shouting.' Kirsty steps closer to me and all I want her to do is go away and stop asking me questions. How can I deal with all this when she's hovering over me?

'Yes. It does sound noisy in there. I think it's the telly,

though.' We're both shouting over the banging and each other. She can tell something isn't right.

'That is not the telly. There are people in there and he's not answering. Maybe he's hurt.'

'Yes.' I pause and look at Kirsty. Her annoyance is so clear in her expressions. 'There's a lot of shouting, it sounds quite nasty. I think you two girls should go into your flat for a few minutes and let me deal with it,' I say as I usher them in.

Michaela places her hand on Kirsty's arm and leads her into the flat. 'We don't want to get hurt.' Kirsty shuffles a little way into the living room.

'It's a Sin' by the Pet Shop Boys fills the room, the beat fills the building. Once again, so apt. My life the musical.

'I can smell smoke.' Kirsty hurries back to the door but I can't let her leave. Micky screams as I grab their vase and smash it over Kirsty's head.

'Why did you do that? What have you done, Tim?' Micky flicks her long hair away from her face. I'm literally shaking and sweating. How did I get into such a mess?

FORTY-SIX

RICARDO

Ricardo banged his shaky fist as hard as he could on the wardrobe. It had taken every ounce of strength he had to drag his body along the floor as he'd panted and cried in pain. He squinted as he stared at the blue light. Although dim, the glare was too much for his splitting headache. Bettina was gone. What he'd seen hadn't been real. It broke his heart to know that there was no more that he could do for his darling daughter but he could help Libby; after all, he had got her into this situation. She came looking for clues, for him, and she ended up in this hellhole.

Libby screamed from the metal wardrobe as she banged. 'Don't let me die in here.'

He tried to call her, to reassure her, but the words stuck in his throat. 'Libby.' His voice was no more than a croak but Libby stopped banging. 'Ricardo, don't open the door. He's watching on the camera. If I get out, he's going to set us alight. We will burn to death in here.'

The music coming from above rang through his ears. Straining his neck, he looked up. The camera was pointing at the wall. He lay there panting as he gazed around his prison cell. The door to the cellar was pulled to but there was a gap, the door was open. Grabbing hold of a chair, he grunted as he pulled himself up. The chair slid across and fell on its side sending him tumbling back onto the floor. As he lay there in agony, he made a promise to himself and Libby, he would not give up. He had to try again. Libby was someone's daughter and he wouldn't let her down. He placed his hands under his chin and pushed. His neck cricked as he woke up his stiff joints and muscles. Straining with clenched teeth, he stretched the pain out. The drugs were wearing off and everything hurt like hell itself.

Sweat dripped from his nose and blood pumped through his head. He pushed again and after a struggle, he got himself into a kneeling position beside the chair. Panting, he stopped for breath before grabbing the chair again. As he leaned his upper body weight on his biceps, he used the chair to pull himself up and this time it didn't slip. His legs trembled and almost gave way, his bones clicked with every movement but he was upright. He felt in his top pocket for his glasses, they were gone. That's why everything was a blur.

He remembered flying, seeing his beloved wife and Bettina. The alternative drug induced reality he'd surrendered to had been better than the real one. He could have easily surrendered to it; in fact he had done for what seemed like days. Within the basement, there had been no day or night; no concept of time and no routine. He'd tripped along in oblivion. The reality of the situation was dark, gloomy and filthy. Yes, the odour was coming from him.

'Ricardo, we're going to die.' Crying came from the wardrobe. As he let go of the chair, he flung himself towards it, crashing hard.

Libby let out a terrifying scream that stopped him cold.

'Ricardo?' she called.

'Yes, Libby?' He paused. Confused, he listened for her reply.

'Ricardo, I'm scared.'

The man fiddled with the door and wrenched it open.

Libby's eyes were glazed with tears. 'He said, if I came out, he'd kill us. He'd set the cellar on fire.'

Ricardo shook his head. 'We will die if we don't. Get out.' He held his hand out to help her hoping that she didn't grab him too hard. If she did, he knew he'd fall. Shaking all over, she stood and stared over his shoulder as she stepped out. 'The camera is still pointing away, it was all a lie. He isn't watching us.'

'He's left the door open.' Ricardo pointed. 'I'm not going to be able to make it out. You have to escape and get help. Go, I'm right behind you. Don't look back, Libby.' He would follow her at the only pace he could manage but there was no fight left in him.

She leaned in and hugged him. Even with how gentle she was, he almost toppled. 'I'm going to get help and we're both getting out of here. I won't leave you.' She ran through the door and up the stairs. The music filled the house and he couldn't hear himself think.

He had to do his best to follow Libby. It wouldn't be long before the monster returned. During lucid periods he'd tried hard to move his feet and joints. He'd shuffled his feet and clenched his muscles, all in the hope that he'd get a chance to escape.

He hobbled towards the blur that was the wide open door. Every step carried his frame closer. His legs were shaking and his hands trembled. As he grabbed the door to steady himself, he paused for a moment. He watched as Libby slammed into the heavy door at the top of the stairs, over and over again.

The steep stone staircase was broken up by a shadowy

recess halfway up. His eyes adjusted to the darkness. The only light came from the cellar.

As he pulled himself up the steps, his knees cracked. One step achieved, still about twenty to go. As he stopped to get his breath back, he glanced up and saw a shadow in the darkness. His mind filled the recess with images that weren't there. A distorted face appeared on the wall. He looked away as his heart hammered against his ribcage. Those drugs were powerful. The palpitations sped up. He took a deep breath and leaned against the wall. Opening his eyes he stared, the face looked back. Through blurry eyes he recognised his captor in what he could now tell was a picture. That monster had a collage style photo, showing his Bettina standing next to him. 'No.' He stumbled up a few steps and grabbed the picture with contempt. He flung it into the cellar, shattering the glass on the floor. His gaze was diverted to a similar picture. This time, Libby was the subject. How many were there? How many? All the suffering, the pain.

'I'm sorry, Bettina, I should've come earlier. I should have made you come home.' He took another step, then another, his muscles were beginning to warm. Although he was shaky, he was making progress.

He took a step past the recess and finally reached the top. Coughing violently, he couldn't breathe. Palpitations took over, his hands trembled and sweat covered his body. He closed his eyes and willed himself to take control of the symptoms, then he breathed regularly and deeply; in and out. He thought of Bettina, then Libby, then he opened his eyes. He needed to get Libby out.

'Help me, Ricardo.' As he joined her at the top of the steps, he slammed his body into the door, then Libby did the same and they kept going.

Music boomed so loudly, it felt like the walls were pulsating. The door frames vibrated in time with the bass. He heard a woman call and then a door slam. He couldn't even begin to guess what danger lurked behind the door but getting through it was their only chance to survive this ordeal. If what Libby said about him setting them on fire was true, he had to at least get to a room with a window.

He placed his ear against the door and listened but the music was too much. Maybe their captor was sitting there, waiting to attack. Maybe there were others. Who was the woman behind the voice he heard? Maybe they're all in on it. 'Let me out. Let me out, you bastard.'

'Ricardo.' Libby stared into his eyes. 'Keep focused. We have to keep bashing down this door.'

Ricardo stepped back and with Libby they slammed against the door. It shook but remained in place. His body ached as he drew back and poised himself to slam into the door again. With every slam he thought of Bettina, then he went at it harder. He had to escape this hellhole. If there was a hell, this was it. Maybe he was already in hell. If this wasn't hell he decided he was no longer going to fear hell. Nothing could ever be as bad as what he and his beautiful daughter had been through.

Maria's dying wish was for him to find Bettina and he had, but he'd been too late to save her. His lucid moments in the cell, when the monster told him about her so-called accidental death, would haunt his dreams and his waking days alike until he died.

He slammed into the wooden door, expelling an agonising groan as he hit it again. He would do it for them.

FORTY-SEVEN

LIBBY

As Libby and Ricardo bashed into the wood and burst through the heavy door, Libby found herself trembling as she crawled out of the cupboard and into the living room.

Micky and Tim stood by the table, his hands positioned on her shoulders as he shook her hard. Her red hair had fallen from her ponytail. She wiped a smear of blood from her cheek as she stepped back, shaking. Ricardo rolled around, screaming out in agony on the wooden floor.

'Micky, get out now. Get help. He killed Bettina.'

Tim shook his head and grinned. 'Micky, don't you dare move.' He snatched the petrol can from against the wall and swished the liquid around as he dragged Michaela over towards her and Ricardo.

'Tim.' Michaela stared open-mouthed. 'Please, don't do this.'

'Libby knows. She knows everything. I'm sorry but we have no choice.'

Libby watched on as Micky slapped Tim across the face, tears sliding down her cheeks. 'What have you done?'

Holding his hands to his face, he sobbed. 'I need your help,

Micky. You're my sister, the only person I can depend on in the whole world. Please? I'd do the same for you.'

The little girl in the family photo had been Michaela. She was Tim's sister. They were both in this together, they had to be. As Libby went to dart past him, Tim grabbed her and threw her to the floor so hard, she couldn't breathe. Ricardo dragged himself along, wincing with pain every time he moved.

'I can't help you out of this. You hurt Kirsty. I need to help her.' Smoke began to billow into the room.

As Michaela went to run, Tim grabbed her arm, wrenching her back. 'I'm your brother.'

'You're no brother of mine. It suited me to pretend you were nothing more than someone who managed the flats. I can't bear to be in the same room as you. I'm only here because Mum pitied you and begged me to stay close when she still knew what she was saying. I don't even know you.'

'Micky, you don't mean that.'

'Don't I?'

'If she comes around and tells the police what happened, I'm doing life. I didn't ask for any of this. All I wanted was to get back at them.'

Libby flinched as she heard a startling crashing noise coming from above. 'Micky?'

All this time Michaela had pretended to only know Tim as their landlord. They'd become good friends and what did she mean about Kirsty? Tim must have hurt her. They were all going to die. The sound of smashing glass, followed by a loud thud came from Libby's flat. She took the opportunity to stand and try to dash past them a second time but Tim's fist came out and caught the side of her face. Dizziness sent her hurtling to the floor again.

'Who's upstairs?' Michaela cried. 'Why are you doing this?'

Libby knew it was Chrissie. She'd heard her arrive now her friend was trapped in her flat and a fire was ripping through the building. She trembled at the thought of her friend choking for breath but every time she lifted her head, the room spun.

Tim stared at Michaela. 'If I go down, you go down. You have to help me. Everyone in this building has to burn. It's the only way, Micky. Either you help me or I tell the whole truth.'

Every cell in Libby's body came alive. If she didn't buck up, she, Chrissie, Kirsty and Ricardo were going to die in the soon to be inferno that was spreading through Canal House. She coughed hard as a plume of smoke filled her lungs.

'Micky, don't let us die.' She gasped for breath and tried to stand but her wavering vision kept her rooted to the spot. If she took a step, she'd fall. She reached for a chair and tried to shake the feeling away. As Ricardo tried to stand, Tim kicked him in the shins. He crashed into the table, sending the computer tumbling. Michaela seethed at Tim as she pushed him against the wall. 'I hate you.'

'Don't say that. You're all I have.'

'You should burn in this house. This will only end when you do. How did I not know what was right under my nose?' Michaela shook her head and paced up and down. 'I thought we told each other everything.'

While they bickered, Libby reached down and offered Ricardo a hand, helping him to his feet. One tiny step at a time, they cleared the dining table.

The fire alarm coming from the flat next door sent Libby's heart racing as it started up. The fire was getting closer. She had to get Ricardo out.

'I do. Look, we either work together or one of us dies today and it won't be me. Blood is everything. That's what we said.'

Ricardo's weight now fell on her shoulder. His eyes half-rolled as he dragged Libby to the ground with a thud. With one final reach over, Ricardo grabbed Tim's ankle and yanked him with all he had.

'Ricardo,' Libby yelled, as the petrol can crashed and some

of the flammable liquid sloshed across the wooden flooring. Michaela quickly stepped out of the way just before it reached her trainers. She grabbed the can and placed it upright to stop it spreading even further.

The fire alarm rang out and the music became distorted before finally stopping, that's when Libby heard the roaring flames. As soon as they reached the petrol, the room would turn into an inferno.

'Libby, get out. I've got him.' Ricardo refused to let go of Tim's leg, however many times Tim kicked him in the face and shoulder.

She stumbled towards Michaela. 'Micky, help me get Ricardo out.' She couldn't leave him to burn to death. Tears ran down Michaela's face as she left the petrol can on the floor.

'I can't. I have to save Kirsty.' She hurried out of the room, leaving her and Ricardo with Tim.

'Call emergency services.' She could only hope that Micky would do the right thing.

It was down to her and her alone. Ricardo couldn't get up, Michaela had left them. Tim began to kick out and try to stand. They had to take him down or he would kill them. With gritted teeth, she stood and kicked Tim as hard as she could. Ricardo pulled at the younger man's leg. Between them, they kept him down. That was the only time she saw real fear in Tim's eyes.

'Are things not going to plan?' She couldn't resist saying that to him. He thought he had it all sewn up, that they wouldn't fight back, but they did.

The blurry room swayed from side to side as Libby stepped forward and hit him again for Olly. Blinded by the evening sunlight beaming through the window, she covered her eyes with one arm. The idea of escape seemed impossible a few hours ago. Shiny beads of sweat dripped off her nose. It was getting hotter, too hot.

Tim went to pull the lighter out of his pocket to ignite the fuel.

'No you don't.' Libby kicked it across the floor and it stopped in the middle of the living room. 'It's over, Tim.'

Tim let out a roar as he stood. He elbowed Libby in the ribs and grabbed Ricardo with a renewed sense of strength, dragging the weak man back towards the basement. 'This is far from over.'

Ricardo screamed out as his back hit the cupboard wall.

Libby had to do something, anything. She placed a hand over her throbbing chest. If she and Ricardo ended up in that cellar again it was game over. Death was the only outcome. This house was on fire and it wasn't about to stop. As Libby ran across the room, the diary marked Louise fell to the floor. That too would be burnt to a crisp and the entire truth of Louise's death would never come out.

As Tim went to push Ricardo over the edge of the steps, the older man dodged to the side and with a teeth-clenching yell, he hooked his arm around the back of Tim's neck, sending him flying down the cellar steps. The cries as he fell would haunt Libby forever. They had Tim exactly where he'd had them. Ricardo grabbed what was left of the petrol and poured it down the steps. 'Pass me the lighter.'

'No, we need to wait for the police. Micky is calling them and the fire brigade.'

'He needs to die for what he's done.'

'No, we need to get justice.'

Micky ran in. 'Where is he?'

'We managed to get him in the cellar.'

Ricardo grabbed the door handle for balance. Clothes hung off him like rags as he limped out of the understairs cupboard. Micky stepped in his way. 'I can't let you leave.'

Libby scrunched her brows and stared at the young woman who was blocking Ricardo's exit. Michaela pushed the weakened man to the ground. He had nothing left to give. Libby could see that.

'Micky, what are you doing. We have to get out or we'll all die.' Heat filled the room and smoke began to billow.

She shook her head. 'No, you're not going anywhere.'

'Micky, help me.' Tim reached out as if pleading with her to go down the steps and help him. Michaela stared down at him, then back at Libby. 'Micky, we can start afresh, go somewhere new. I have it all planned. Don't let me die, Micky.'

Tears rolled down Michaela's cheeks as she barged into Libby. 'Sorry.' She grabbed Libby's arm and dragged her closer to the stairs.

'I can't see him suffer. You people hurt him enough.'

'Micky, please. He hurt those people. He killed Bettina and Louise. Don't let him take you down with him. You have to do the right thing. Help us all get out of this and we can all start again. What he did isn't your fault.'

Tears slipped down Michaela's cheeks. 'I didn't ask for any of this.'

'Micky, you have to get me out of here before it's too late. Finish them off, they mean nothing. It's you and me.' Tim's pleading eyes stared up at her.

'It's me and you,' Michaela shouted.

As Micky went to push Libby, Libby bashed into her, knocking her off balance and hitting her head hard on the wall. 'You would have killed me,' she shouted at her.

Tears flooded the young woman's face. Libby could see that she was torn.

Libby dragged Ricardo across the room. 'Get up. Get up now or you die.'

The man had no strength as he murmured away. That's when Libby's hero smashed the window. 'Chrissie.' Her colleague and friend looked like she'd been through the wars. Torn tights, no shoes.

'I had to jump out of a friggin' window.' She threw her coat over the glass. 'The fire is right at the bottom of the stairs. You have to hurry. I've called the authorities.'

Libby helped a mumbling Ricardo to stand as she pushed him through the window.

'I've got him. Get out.'

Libby glanced back as smoke wafted through the room and the fire began to lick the door frame. 'I need to do something.'

'No, Libby. Just get out, now. The place is going up.'

'I'll just be a minute.' The crackling flames began to catch the walls. Very soon, they would reach the spilled petrol. She wiped the glistening sweat beads from her arms and ran towards the cellar. She had to get the diary. She couldn't see any more. She pulled her T-shirt up, holding it over her mouth but her chest felt raw. She bent down and picked the diary up.

As she stumbled to the top of the cellar steps, she stared down and saw Michaela trying to help Tim up the stairs. She held the lighter up and grabbed the petrol can. She could finish them both, right now.

'Libby, please put those down.' Michaela's wide-eyed stare unnerved her.

'You were going to kill me.'

'I wasn't, I was confused.'

'Libby, don't.' Chrissie coughed and grabbed her arm. 'Let's go. They're not worth it.'

Chrissie was right. Libby dropped the lighter and put the petrol can down. They had to get out. As they reached the window, the petrol can caught light and a whoosh filled the living room. Clambering out of the window, she stumbled over to where Kirsty sat on the wall, holding her head. She hurried over to the other side of the road where Ricardo lay.

Sirens filled the air as the fire engine pulled into the road. It was soon followed by two ambulances.

Without hesitation, a paramedic ran over and pushed her away from Ricardo. 'Where are you taking him?'

'The Queen Elizabeth.'

Libby stepped back, allowing them to do their job. He was breathing and he was murmuring. He was going to be okay. She hurried over to Kirsty and sat next to her, finally relieved the worst was over. All her worldly possessions were going up in flames but it didn't matter. Nothing mattered any more apart from living.

Chrissie sat next to them and Einstein meowed as he darted towards them. Libby pulled him onto her lap and kissed his head.

A police car pulled up and Chrissie ran over to the police officer.

'Was it you who called?'

Chrissie nodded. 'Yes, I work at Top Staff Recruitment, the same as Libby over there.' Libby nodded as the uniformed man glanced over. 'One of our temps came in and told me that Libby was climbing through the bottom window and that he was worried.'

The police officer said something that Libby couldn't hear.

'Yes, Trevor Stevens.'

'I'll come over and take a full statement in a moment.'

Chrissie nodded and hurried back over to Libby and Kirsty.

'Chrissie, how did Trevor know?'

'It's a long story, love. He was quite agitated, a little drunk. He admitted to watching you, said at first he was angry when he started, that he wanted to scare you and make you pay for messing him around. But today, he said he wanted to knock on your door and say sorry but, in his words, he bottled out. As he was leaving, he saw you climbing in through the window and he stood and watched. When you didn't come out, he got worried and thought it was all a bit weird. He said he'd never tell all that to the police because he knew he shouldn't have been watching you, but he said that I should check to see if you were okay.'

Libby laughed and placed a hand on her sweaty head. 'My stalker saved my life. It sounds like a tabloid headline.'

Chrissie shrugged. 'I guess.'

'He must have been the one lurking in the garden and throwing stones at my window. Can I borrow your phone?'

'It's dead.'

'Kirsty?'

The sore-looking woman handed over her mobile.

Libby did a search for the hospital's phone number and called it. 'Hello, it's Olivia Worthington's sister. Could I have an update, please?'

She watched the firefighters at work as she heard the nurse tap away on a few keys. 'We're bringing her around tomorrow. She's showed real signs of progress and her stats are constantly improving.'

Libby smiled as she ended the call. 'Olly's going to be okay.'

Chrissie hugged her and kissed her head, and Libby nestled into her shoulder.

'Thank you for saving me.'

'Aww, come here.' Chrissie gave her the motherly squeeze that she so badly craved. 'You can stay at mine while you sort yourself out.'

'Thank you.' She stroked her cat.

'And Einstein. He can come too.'

'I don't know what I'd do without you.'

The police officer called Chrissie over and Kirsty got taken to an ambulance. Libby pulled the diary open and began to flick through it. She knew she'd be turning it in to the police at any minute, but first, she was going to have a quick flick through. She wanted to know everything.

FORTY-EIGHT

LIBBY

It had felt strange sleeping in Chrissie's spare room in the same bed as Kirsty but she'd been made welcome. Chrissie had got her set up with a spare phone so that the police could contact her. Gary didn't have that number. Changing it should have been something she'd done a long time ago. It felt good not having her stomach drop every time it went.

She checked her emails and swallowed. There was one from Gary.

Money's in your account. I guess it's goodbye.

Finally, it had ended. There wasn't much money but she needed every penny at the moment. After giving a statement to the police with all that had happened, she had gone to the hospital to see Ricardo. He looked so much better after a clean up. His fractured ribs would heal and there was no lasting damage, just dehydration, cuts, bruises and exhaustion. They had survived what had seemed to be the unsurvivable.

Kirsty knocked and entered the bedroom. 'Car's packed up.'

They were going to see Olly and be there for when she came around. With Kirsty and Chrissie by her side, Libby finally felt like she had some good friends. 'I'll be out in a minute, Kirsty.' As Kirsty went to leave, Libby said, 'I'm sorry about Micky.'

'I still can't believe it all. All that time and she never said anything. She left me for dead in that burning house. If it wasn't for Chrissie...' Kirsty wiped a tear from her pale cheek. It was the first time Libby had seen her without her trademark red lipstick.

'It's going to take a lot of getting over.' Libby stood and embraced her friend.

'I'll never get over it. I'm going back to Wales, to live with Mum.'

Libby pulled away. 'Will I be able to visit?'

Kirsty wiped her tears away. 'If you don't, I'll be well angry. You have to visit. My hometown local is the best and my mum makes the scrummiest lava bread.'

'How could I refuse? The lava bread is selling it.'

'Right, car in five. Don't want to miss seeing Olly's eyes open.'

'I'm on my way.'

Kirsty ran down the stairs leaving Libby to pack up the toiletries and clothes that Chrissie had given to her. The leisure suit was an ill fit and so was the blouse and trousers but she had clothes and for that she was grateful. She'd called Scott and for the foreseeable she'd be staying at Olly's and caring for her. Work had given her all the leave she needed but, in all honesty, she wasn't sure if she wanted to go back. The compassionate pay would help for now. Maybe management did have a heart after all.

She gave one last thought to the diary, to Bettina and to Louise. Right now, only she, the police, Ricardo and Kirsty knew what was in that diary. She thought back to the others. So much information lost to fire. Tim dead – he would never get his day in court. Micky – dead. She'd never get to tell her full story. Soon the whole truth would come out and when it did, it would shock everyone.

FORTY-NINE

LIBBY

Libby stared out of the hospital window as she held Olly's hand. The breathing tube had now gone but the feeding tube was still inserted into her nose. She'd stirred a couple of times but had not yet opened her eyes. Instead, she'd tugged at her sheets, almost twisted her catheter tube and mumbled a few incoherent sounds.

'It won't be long now,' the nurse said as he pressed a button on the monitor.

Libby smiled.

Kirsty stood and walked to the end of the bed. Chrissie leaned over and placed a hand on Libby's shoulder. 'We're going to get a cuppa. I think it might be a bit much if she comes around and sees us all here. I'll give Ricardo a call now. He seems a lot chattier. They're discharging him tomorrow and one of his sons has come over to be with him.'

'Thank you. I can't wait to see him again.' Libby smiled as they headed out of the ward. Her stomach fluttered with excitement at seeing Olly wake up. She looked like she'd been through hell and she'd feel like it but Libby would be by her side. She'd help with every part of her recovery and with the setup of her new restaurant.

Scott remained at the other side of her bed. Libby knew that even though their relationship was coming to an end, Scott would never abandon Olly as a friend. She glanced at him as he ran his hands through his messed-up hair. She couldn't believe that at one point she thought he might be capable of attacking Olly. He didn't have a bad bone in his body. 'I... err...' He played with his hands. 'I paid the deposit on the new restaurant. I didn't want Olly to lose it. I know we lost our way but she shouldn't lose out because of this.'

'That's so kind of you, Scott. She's going to make such a go of it, I know she is. She will get that Michelin star and it'll be the best place to eat in Tenby.'

'I know she will. I'll always love her but she was right. We both want different things.' He bit his lip. 'I'm going to get a bit of air, leave you to it for a while.'

She nodded just as Olly gripped her hand.

As he left, Libby stood and stroked her sister's forehead. 'Olly, it's Libby. Hurry up and wake up. I can't wait to see you. We have so much to talk about.'

Her sister flinched and then frowned.

'Olly.'

Slowly, Olly prised an eye open and frowned. Confusion spread across her face and Libby kissed her head.

'It's over, Olly. It's all over. You're safe. I'll tell you all about it when you've had a chance to come around properly.'

Olly grabbed her hand and Libby stroked her long black hair that had splayed out across the white pillow.

'Love you, sis.'

A tear drizzled down Olly's face as she tried to mouth the word love. It was going to be a long recovery time but things were looking up. She'd soon be able to fill Olly in on Tim and Michaela, the basement, Ricardo and the fire. She could then tell her about the diary and Louise. That was a mystery solved and Libby was sure that Louise's father, the original accused, would be grateful that the truth was out. He must have lived in his own personal hell. While mourning the loss of his daughter, he became a suspect.

The diary.

Libby now knew that Tim wasn't the only one at the well that night. What he'd told her wasn't exactly how it happened. He'd roped Michaela into helping him. He was going to bottle out but Michaela ran out from behind the tree and pushed Louise into that well and once that had happened, there was no going back so they left her to die.

She tilted her head and smiled again. Nothing was going to ruin this moment. Olly would get the whole story as soon as she was feeling better.

All in good time.

EPILOGUE

Six Weeks Later

Ricardo hobbled out of the taxi using a walking stick for balance, before opening the back door for Libby. Kirsty and Olly got out of the other side. Visiting Louise's grave in the village of Beoley had been a joint decision. Whatever she'd done wrong, however she'd hurt people in the past, it didn't matter in the end. She'd paid the ultimate price with her life. That didn't mean she shouldn't be remembered. For the group of friends, it had been where it all started and the visit would allow them to begin healing.

Olly snivelled as she took a few cautious steps. It was harder for her, knowing she was the reason too. She'd spoken to Libby extensively about what had happened at school. She had joined in with the mean girls and she too had to come to terms with her part in everything.

The warm spring day shone golden over the gravestones

and a few daffodils grew around the graves, dotting a little bit of sunshine on the grass.

'Libby,' Kirsty wheezed as she struggled to catch up. The smoke that she'd inhaled had been bothering her a little but her recovery was still going well. 'I can't believe it, it still doesn't feel real. All that time, Micky wasn't who I thought she was and I lived with her. I didn't see it.'

'It'll never feel real. Come on.'

Ricardo had walked ahead. They ambled over the moist, grassy earth, until they reached him. Standing, he winced. He turned to hug Libby. 'I wanted to thank you before I went home.' He flinched and rubbed his cricked neck.

'Thank me. For all that you've been through. You got us out of that cellar, I should thank you.'

'I was a stranger here. You helped me find out the truth. It wasn't what I wanted it to be but, well thank you for being you.'

Libby smiled back at him before they all took a minute's silence to process what had happened.

Olly squeezed her hand. Her sister was her rock and she always would be. Scott was back on the scene, she hoped that he and Olly could work their relationship issues out, but whatever the future held she'd always be there for her lovely sister. One thing was certain, Scott wouldn't be working at *Chez Olly's* with her.

A tear rolled down Libby's cheek, followed by another, then another. Unable to contain her sorrow, she allowed herself to sob as she thought back to all that had happened to them. She thought of the justice that would never be served to Tim, then she wanted to kick herself for still calling him that. His real name was Toby. Everything about him was a dangerous lie.

That surviving diary would make the news one day and their lives would be upturned every time his crimes were mentioned. There would be documentaries, interviews, articles. Reporters were already circling like vultures. She cried harder which started Olly off too. They all huddled together and enjoyed the solidarity that only forms through mutual suffering of extreme tragedy. She knew they'd all remain close for the rest of their lives.

As they walked back to the road, Ricardo and Kirsty hurried ahead to call the taxi now that they'd finished. It was brief but it had to be done. They'd come back to where it all started, now they could really feel their way to the end.

'Sis, do you mean what you said?'

Libby nodded. There was no going back now.

'I can't wait. We're going to be the best-known sisters in the town. You as maître d', me, the famous one obviously as I'll be the chef.'

Libby nudged Olly and laughed. 'But they'll see me first. You'll be hiding in the kitchen.'

'No way. My food will be that good, I'll be out at the end of every service in my chef's whites, ready to take that bow as they all clap.'

'Okay, you win. You have the talent. First customers, Chrissie, Ricardo and Kirsty.'

'Without a doubt. Dinner on the house for them.'

They glanced at Ricardo and Libby's momentary happiness faded. The police had reported that a body had been unearthed under the cellar floor. A DNA test had confirmed that it was Bettina. Her body would return home to Naples for burial very soon. Her heart broke for the man who had lost his daughter. Her heart broke for the father that had never bothered with her or Olly. She hoped that they'd keep in touch.

'Let's go and have that drink for Bettina.' Olly blew her nose. They'd arranged a wake of sorts at the Sun's Rays where some of Bettina's friends were coming together.

Slowly and without speaking, they all got into the taxi to embrace their unknown future.

A LETTER FROM CARLA

Dear Reader,

Thank you for choosing to read *The Houseshare*. I was thrilled to bits to have the opportunity of rewriting the book that I self-published quite a few years ago under a different title.

If you enjoyed *The Houseshare* and would like to keep up-to-date with all my latest releases, just sign up using the following link. Your email address will never be shared and you can unsubscribe at any time.

www.bookouture.com/carla-kovach

Whether you are a reader, tweeter, blogger, Facebooker, TikTok user or reviewer, I really am grateful of all that you do and as a writer, this is where I hope you'll leave me a review or say a few words about my book.

I enjoyed exploring Libby's character and her vulnerabilities. Libby's job in recruitment is a job I've actually done myself during my early working years.

I can laugh at this now, but I remember being in the office with one of my colleagues back then when someone threatened to smash the office windows because of a slight wage mix up. I have memories of locking the main doors and closing the blinds while waiting to see if this person would actually turn up. He never did. Of course, my situation wasn't as scary as Libby's but it got me thinking about the *what ifs* and that drove the writing of this book.

Again, thank you so much. I'm active on social media so please do contact me on Twitter, Instagram or through my Facebook page.

Thank you, Carla Kovach

facebook.com/CarlaKovachAuthor

twitter.com/CKovachAuthor

instagram.com/carla_kovach

ACKNOWLEDGEMENTS

So many people helped to make this book happen and I need to say a mega thank you to them. I feel like the luckiest person in the world having them in my life.

Helen Jenner, my editor, gave me so much help with this book and for that I'm hugely grateful. I'd like to say a mahoosive thank you to her. She always brings more out of the story than I can see and I'm thrilled to be working with her.

Bookouture is amazing. I'm grateful to all who work incredibly hard to make all this happen, from the rights team to the fantastic people who work in accounts. They are all amazing and the pleasure is all mine.

The cover is the first thing that people see and it's incredibly important. Jo Thomson has done a brilliant job and I absolutely love this eye-catching stunner.

I have to express my gratitude to the publicity team. Noelle Holten, Kim Nash, Jess Readett and Sarah Hardy are all fabulous people who exude energy and positivity. They make publication day special with all their shares and shout-outs.

The bloggers and readers who share reviews and book love are wonderful and I'm always super appreciative of their enthusiasm and selflessness. I'm grateful that they chose my work to read and review.

My ongoing gratitude goes to The Fiction Café Facebook group and the Bookouture author community. I'm always made to feel welcome and the support I've received from them is heart-warming. I need to extend a special thanks to fellow Bookouture author, Angela Petch, who helped me with the Italian translation.

Beta readers, Derek Coleman, Su Biela, Brooke Venables, Anna Wallace and Vanessa Morgan all read one of my earlier drafts. Their feedback and comments are always welcome so thank you. I also need to thank Sharon Manley and Caroline Bayliss, my previous work colleagues, who also read and commented on an old draft.

I need to express special thanks to Brooke Venables who writes under the name Jamie-Lee Brooke, and Phil Price, my fellow author buddies. We have a motivational support bubble and it helps me immensely.

Last but not least, I need to say a big fat thank you to my husband, Nigel Buckley, for all his support and help. He's definitely my rock.

8-23-22 √+++

Made in United States
North Haven, CT
12 August 2022

22625182R00178